Moe's Villa
& Other Stories

Moe's Villa
& Other Stories

James Purdy

CARROLL & GRAF PUBLISHERS
NEW YORK

MOE'S VILLA AND OTHER STORIES

Carroll & Graf Publishers
An Imprint of Avalon Publishing Group Inc.
245 West 17th Street
New York, NY 10011

AVALON
publishing group incorporated

Library of Congress Cataloging-in-Publication Data is available.

ISBN: 0-7867-1417-4

Interior design by Maria Elias
Printed in the United States of America
Distributed by Publishers Group West

*I would like to pay tribute to John Uecker,
whose creative editorial support over many
years has made this collection possible.*

Moe's Villa
& Other Stories

Contents

Kitty Blue

Many years ago in a far distant country there was a famous opera singer who was very fond of cats. She found her greatest inspiration in talking with her cats both before and after she sang in grand opera houses. Without the encouragement and love of these gifted beasts she felt she would never understand the various roles she interpreted on the opera stage. Her only sorrow was that very often a favorite cat would die or disappear or sometimes even be stolen by a person who was envious of her.

Madame Lenore, the opera singer, was admired by the Crown Prince who at the time of this story was only fifteen years old. He never missed a single one of Madame Lenore's performances and showered her with costly gifts, and after one of her appearances he saw to it that the stage was piled high with the most expensive and exotic flowers.

One day the Crown Prince learned that Madame Lenore had lost the last of her favorite cats. The Prince immediately decided to send her a new one, but he knew this one should be not only the most beautiful cat in his kingdom but the brightest and most gifted.

The Prince scoured his realm looking for a cat worthy of so eminent a singer. He went to over a hundred shops in his search. At long last he found the cat he was looking for in an out-of-the-way bazaar run by a young Abyssinian youth named Abdullah. Abdullah pointed out to his majesty that although the cat he presented to the Prince was only a few months old it already displayed extraordinary mental powers and under his careful tutelage could speak fluently in human language.

The Prince was carried away with enthusiasm for his find and immediately struck a bargain to purchase so splendid a puss.

"There is only one thing I must warn you of, your majesty," Abdullah said as the Prince was about to leave with his purchase. "This cat must not be allowed to keep company with other ordinary cats, but he must remain always close to his human owner and guardian. For in my opinion he is only a cat in his exterior, his soul is that of a higher being."

The Prince was even more delighted with this new information from Abdullah, and he promised he would obey the instructions to the letter, and with that he set out with the gifted cat.

On their way to the palace the Prince was suddenly dumbfounded to hear the cat speaking to him in a soft but clear and unaffected voice.

"My Prince, my name is Kitty Blue," the cat began, "and I am honored that you should wish to adopt me into your royal household. You may depend, your majesty, on my always being a faithful subject who will never disappoint you or leave your royal company."

"Thank you, Kitty Blue. I am most touched by what you say," the young Prince replied. "But unfortunately," he stammered, "unfortunately. . . ."

"Unfortunately what?" the cat inquired, for he saw his royal owner was upset. "Please tell me what is worrying you."

"Dear Kitty Blue, the fact is I have promised you to another."

"To another!" Kitty Blue raised his voice. "How can that be?"

"I promised you, dear friend, to the most beautiful and most talented opera singer of our day, Madame Lenore."

The cat said nothing, and the Prince saw that the gifted creature was deeply hurt that the Prince had promised him to someone else.

"I cannot very well go back on my promise, can I?" the Prince spoke in anguished tones.

"I suppose not, your highness," the cat said hesitantly. "But it will be hard to leave your royal presence even for so gifted and beautiful a person as Madame Lenore."

"But I will always be near you, Kitty Blue, and you can always call on me at any hour. Remember that."

The Prince noticed a few tears falling from the cat's wonderfully blue eyes, and he remembered that Kitty Blue had the name he was known by because of the beautiful blue color of his eyes.

Hugging the cat to him, the Prince tried to comfort his unusual pet with many sweet words, but he saw, alas, that nothing he said could console the cat for having to leave his royal protection and company.

The next day the Prince summoned Madame Lenore to the palace to receive the gift he had promised her.

It was a beautiful June evening. The odor of jasmine was in the air, and the sky was a cloudless blue over which songbirds flew in countless numbers, and the many trees surrounding the palace stirred in a faint breeze.

Madame Lenore came accompanied by a young attendant

who was extremely devoted to the famous singer and who almost never left her side.

The Prince forbade Madame Lenore to bow to him.

"You are the sovereign here this evening," the Prince said and took her hand in his, "and I shall bow to you."

When they had all taken their seats, the Prince slowly began speaking.

"I have a gift for you, dear singer," the Prince informed her. "A gift such as I myself would be thrilled to accept for my own."

He clapped his hands, and an attendant brought in a great silver box with tiny windows, the top and sides of which sparkled with precious gems.

"Kitty Blue," the Prince said, rising. "Will you now come forth, and meet your new mistress."

"I will, my Prince," a small but clear voice resounded. And Kitty Blue, attired in a handsome suit with small diamond buttons, emerged from the box and immediately after bowing to the Crown Prince advanced toward Madame Lenore and said in perfectly articulated tones, "Good evening, esteemed Madame Lenore."

Madame Lenore was so overcome with surprise and joy at hearing so beautiful a cat address her she came close to fainting. Immediately a servant brought her a glittering glass of refreshment which she quaffed quickly and so regained her composure.

Kitty Blue then leaped into her lap and looking up into her eyes, exclaimed: "You're just as beautiful and charming as the whole world says you are."

"How can I ever thank you, my lord," Madame Lenore cried, turning to the Prince. "You have given me the one gift I have longed for day and night."

There was all at once a clarion call of brass instruments summoning the Prince to leave so that he rose hurriedly and kissed the singer's hand by way of leave-taking.

He then turned to Kitty Blue. "Be good and considerate, Kitty Blue, to your new mistress, for no one except for myself will love you so devotedly. But should you ever need anything, remember I too am your loving friend."

Having said this the Prince bowed low to the wonderful cat and his new mistress and then surrounded all at once by his guards left the room.

Just before he got into his horse-drawn carriage the Prince remembered the warning of Abdullah, and he wrote out a note which he asked one of his attendants to hurry back and give to the singer.

The note read:

> *Under no circumstances, dear Madame Lenore, are you to permit Kitty Blue to associate with common cats. He must speak only to persons such as ourselves.*
> *The Crown Prince*

Madame Lenore read the Prince's note carefully several times and afterwards put it away in one of her voluminous pockets. But she was still so captivated by the gift of the wonderful cat the Prince's message of warning soon slipped her mind.

Madame Lenore had never known such a devoted companion as she found in Kitty Blue. Because of his fluency in speaking, there was no subject on which she could not converse with him. He asked a thousand questions about her life and her career as a singer. They often spoke far into the night and fell asleep together in the singer's sumptuous four-poster bed. If Madame Lenore awoke during the night and did not find Kitty Blue by her side, she would call out to him, and then to her relief and joy she would find him at only an arm's length away from her.

Madame Lenore began taking Kitty Blue with her to the opera house. He would wait patiently in her dressing room during the performance of the music drama, and during the intermission the two of them would confer lengthily.

The public and the singer's countless admirers had never remembered her to sing so beautifully or look so stunning as she interpreted her various operatic roles.

It was indeed a new Madame Lenore who appeared before the operatic stage.

The singer gave full credit to Kitty Blue for her resurgence, and she was not ashamed to tell her manager and the conductor of the orchestra that it was Kitty Blue who often coached her in her interpretation of her roles.

She was at the acme of her happiness.

One day an invitation came from the ruling monarch of Constantinople, requesting the favor of her appearing in a series of private performances at the royal court. She was about to accept so important an invitation when she learned from an official of the court that she could not bring any pets or animals.

"But Kitty Blue is not a pet or an animal," she spoke to the delegate of the King.

But the delegate was adamant.

At first Madame Lenore declined the invitation, but Kitty Blue then spoke up to her. "Madame Lenore, your career is your life, and you must go to Constantinople without me. I will be waiting for you here, and you will be gone in any case only a few days or a week or so at the most."

But Madame Lenore could not be consoled. She wept and sobbed, and kept repeating that she could not stand to be without her tried and true companion Kitty Blue.

Finally, at the insistence of her manager and the representative of the royal court of Constantinople, she made the hard decision and agreed to go.

She entrusted Kitty Blue to her faithful attendant, beseeching him to look after her prized and beloved cat.

Their parting was heartbreaking for both the singer and the marvelous cat, and Madame Lenore had almost to be carried out to the ship waiting in the harbor.

Kitty Blue was if possible even more unhappy without the companionship and love of Madame Lenore than the great singer was without her wonderful cat. The young man who was to keep him company, Jack Morfey, treated Kitty Blue kindly but only as he would any cat, seldom spoke to him and never sang to him as did Madame Lenore. True, Jack fed him excellent meals, brushed his fur and changed his suits, often three times a day, but otherwise ignored him.

One day in his lonesomeness, Kitty Blue observed that off the large drawing room was a great window overlooking a spacious garden. From then on the cat took his position always in front of the window to gaze longingly out at all the trees and flowering plants and the butterflies and birds flying endlessly across the sky. He was almost happy then.

Because of his sitting in front of the window so many hours, he attracted the attention of a great monarch of a cat who considered himself in fact the king of the garden.

One day Great Cat strode up to the big window and addressed Kitty Blue: "What are you doing here so close to my garden?" he inquired, and he flashed his coal black eyes with indignation.

Now Kitty Blue had never spoken with a cat before, for he had learned only human language, so for a moment he was not sure what Great Cat was saying, but being so bright he soon deduced what his visitor had said.

"I am Kitty Blue, sir, friend and companion to Madame Lenore, the famous diva."

Great Cat was nearly as bright as Kitty Blue, and he soon had figured out what Kitty Blue was saying in human language.

"I see," Great Cat spoke in a slightly sneering tone. "Well, you certainly have on pretty clothes, don't you, and ribbons besides, and is that by chance a jewel in your left ear?"

Kitty Blue nodded and looked wistfully out at all the trees, flowers, butterflies and dragonflies.

"Would you care to take a stroll in my garden?" Great Cat spoke coaxingly.

"I am forbidden to leave this room, Great Cat."

"By whom are you forbidden, may I ask?" his visitor wondered contemptuously.

"By the Crown Prince."

Great Cat showed utter indifference for this explanation.

"Kitty Blue, think what you are missing. Look out way over there," Great Cat said, pointing with his paw to a wildflower garden in the rear of the garden proper. "Have you ever seen anything so beautiful. And you want to stay cooped up in this stuffy room because some Prince says you must! When we cats all know royalty

don't give a hoot about us, and in the first place the
Prince has given you away to Madame Lenore, and
Madame Lenore herself can't care too much about you
since she has gone gallivanting off to Constantinople
leaving you behind."

Kitty Blue was so pained by this last remark that two fat
tears dropped from his very blue eyes.

"See here, Blue," Great Cat said, "supposing I come by
here tomorrow at ten o'clock and by then maybe you will
have made up your mind to visit my garden. Toodle-oo."

And Great Cat having given this speech rose loftily and
without another word departed.

Kitty Blue could not think of anything but the words of
Great Cat, and though he tried to speak with Jack Morfey,
Jack paid little or no attention to what Kitty Blue said. Jack
confined his attentions to serving Kitty his meals punctually and changing his costumes every few hours. (He had
a morning costume, an afternoon costume and finally a
sumptuous evening wear suit.)

The forlorn cat kept looking out at the beautiful garden
all that day and all evening too, and when night came
instead of going to his bedchamber he lay in front of the
window and watched the stars come out in the eastern sky
as a lazy, red moon rose over the sycamore trees.

He made up his mind then and there he would accept
Great Cat's invitation and go for a stroll with him in the
garden.

True to Great Cat's promise, he arrived the next day
punctually at ten o'clock.

"Well, what is your decision?" Great Cat said in an off-
hand and curt manner. "Are you coming with me to the
garden or aren't you?"

"I would like very much to, but isn't the window tightly bolted?" Kitty Blue said anxiously.

"What's bolted can always be unbolted," Great Cat responded, and putting all his considerable weight against the window pane, he pushed it wide open.

"Coming?" Great Cat spoke in a scolding tone.

Kitty Blue cast one look behind him at his room and the different velvet cushions on which he reclined, and then with a sigh followed Great Cat out into the immense outdoors.

Kitty Blue could not help exclaiming about the marvelous variety of things the garden had to offer. He had never seen such an abundance of trees, shrubs, and climbing vines, or so many birds, chipmunks, and bluejays and crows.

"And beyond the garden, Kitty Blue, are even more wonderful things waiting for you! Why you want to live in that old house crowded with antique furniture, bric-a-brac and thick dusty carpets I will never know."

Great Cat then proceeded to give the younger cat a complete and comprehensive tour, pointing out all the different varieties of trees, bushes, creeping vines and flowers, and drawing attention to the many gray squirrels and last of all to a number of huge crows who watched the two cats with extreme suspicion. And all around them there was a constant moving circle of butterflies, dragonflies and small twittering wrens.

"Excuse me a moment, Kitty Blue," Great Cat said suddenly. "I see a friend over there near the tulip tree who I am sure would like to meet you. Stay here until I speak with him."

Great Cat rushed over to the edge of the garden where

a gray tomcat with only one eye and massive jaws and paws had been observing them.

Kitty Blue watched with considerable uneasiness as the two large cats spoke together. From time to time they would both look over in his direction and grin.

All at once Kitty Blue heard someone call him by name. Looking up toward a rhododendron bush, he caught sight of a very pretty mourning dove who now addressed him: "Kitty Blue, if you know what is good for you, return at once to Madame Lenore's house. You are keeping the worst possible company by coming out here with Great Cat and his friend One Eye. They are both bad actors and will get you into plenty of trouble if you are not careful. Mark my words."

The mourning dove then flew up to the roof of an adjoining church where his mate was waiting for him.

Kitty Blue was so frightened by the dove's warning he hurried back to Madame Lenore's house, but not only was the window now tightly closed but an enormous shutter had been placed over the window preventing entry.

All at once a strong even melodious voice said: "So you are the Kitty Blue we have all been hearing about." A young man, dressed as if for a pageant wearing a high hat and a feathered vest with rings on almost all his fingers, was addressing the unhappy cat.

Kitty Blue had barely enough strength to say yes.

Great Cat and One Eye now approached also and began speaking, but the young man severely warned them to be quiet, and better still, be off.

"You alley cats have served your purpose, now skidoo!" he cried. Both Great Cat and One Eye made a great cat-erwauling until the young mountebank (for this is what he was) threw them several helpings of catnip which the cats greedily seized and then ran off into the bushes.

"Let me introduce myself, Kitty Blue," the young man said, and all at once he took hold of Kitty Blue and sitting down on a bench held him in his lap. "My name is Kirby Jericho," he said, "and I am a long-time friend of your mistress, Madame Lenore. I happened to hear those two alley cats by chance talking about you, for I understand puss language since I am in the pageant and theater business. They brought me straight to you." As he spoke Kirby fondled Kitty Blue gently and then carefully touched him on the ear.

"I don't suppose you noticed, but Great Cat robbed you of your earring and your necklace."

Kitty Blue gave out a short sob when he realized this was true.

"Madame Lenore," Kirby Jericho went on, "has been detained in Constantinople. The young sovereign there has absolutely refused to let her leave for another month or so. Since I am one of her friends of long standing I am proposing you come and stay with me until she returns. Meantime I want to train you for appearing in the theater of Herbert of Old Vienna, who is also a former friend of Madame Lenore."

Kitty Blue was so miserable at having been locked out of Madame Lenore's apartment and of being robbed by Great Cat, he barely heard anything Kirby Jericho said to him, but being in a desperate mood, he reluctantly allowed himself to be persuaded to go with his new protector, for that is what Jericho said he was.

Kitty Blue was considerably surprised to see that a brand new roadster was waiting for them beyond the garden walls.

"Sit in the front, if you please, so we can talk on the way to my studio, if you don't mind," Jericho advised.

Kitty Blue took his place beside Jericho, and in one second or two off they went through the lonely deserted streets on the way to the vaudeville and dance theater, and to what Kitty Blue was later to learn would be a new and entirely different life.

After a while Jericho slowed down and turned to the cat, and after stammering badly, he managed to get out the following: "Kitty Blue, do you realize the danger you were in trespassing in Great Cat's garden?"

Kitty Blue was so miserable and unhappy without Madame Lenore he barely heard what Jericho said. Finally however he managed to say, "I suppose so."

"I see you don't," Jericho sighed. "But let me tell you another thing. Madame Lenore could not have cared very much about you if she up and left you without anybody to watch over you. No, don't interrupt, don't defend her. She is a fickle woman. On the other hand if you will come live with me in the Vaudeville and Paradise Theater, you will find a true home and what's more, a profession. I will teach you to be a dancer and performer, and a guitar player. Doesn't that sound like the real thing now?"

Kitty Blue nodded, but he was so heartbroken to hear that Madame Lenore was fickle and had deserted him that he burst into tears.

"There, there now," Jericho comforted him and handed him a handkerchief to dry his tears with. Jericho started the motor again, and they were soon across the river and into the backstreets of a district given over to acrobats, dancers, jugglers and other entertainers.

They drove up to a theater ablaze with pink and violet

lights, and over the front entrance shimmered a great marquee with the words:

THE VAUDEVILLE AND MUSIC HALL OF HERBERT OF OLD VIENNA

"Don't be upset that my name is not in lights," Jericho said, helping Kitty Blue out of his car, "it will be one day soon, for Herbert is longing to retire. By the way did you know Madame Lenore got her start in this very vaudeville and music hall? Well, she did, and Herbert was her maestro. They quarreled of course, and Madame Lenore went on to be a famous diva."

Kitty Blue dried his tears and with a great sigh allowed himself to be ushered into Herbert of Vienna's Vaudeville and Music Hall Theater.

Madame Lenore's appearance in Constantinople was thought to be a stunning success by everybody except the singer herself and her manager, a young man from Milan who had watched her progress from her early days. "Something was missing," she confided to him one evening as they sat together in their spacious hotel suite. "Don't tell me I was perfect for I was not!"

"Correct me if what I am going to say is wrong," the manager said, "but, Madame Lenore, strange as it may seem, you miss Kitty Blue. Being away from him has taken something out of your voice."

Madame Lenore sadly agreed. "How perceptive you are, my dear friend. Not only do I miss him but I have had terrible dreams and a presentiment something has happened to him while I have been away."

"I am sure everything is all right with him," her manager

replied, "for you left him in the company of your most trusted servant. So don't worry on that score. You are homesick and homesickness is one of our greatest sorrows."

Madame Lenore tried now to look on the bright side, but she noted again the next evening that her voice, despite the rapturous applause greeting her, was lacking in a certain strength and conviction. She knew then how much she loved Kitty Blue and that she could not be happy without him.

After her performance that evening the stage was filled with hundreds of large bouquets and wreaths of flowers of every kind, but their perfume and beauty failed to touch the singer's heart, and her eyes were streaming with tears.

All the way back on the ship she could think of nothing but Kitty Blue and his amazing gift of speaking to her in her own language.

"As soon as I set eyes on him," she told her manager, "my heart will be lifted up and then, you see, my voice will again have all its former resonance and power."

The next day they arrived home, and Madame Lenore flung open the door with fervent expectation and called out the name of the cat.

The young attendant appeared immediately. As she looked at his troubled face, Madame Lenore's worst suspicions stirred in her mind.

"What is your news?" she inquired in a chilled, weak voice.

"Madame Lenore," the attendant began as he helped her off with her coat, "something very upsetting has occurred."

"Is it Kitty Blue?"

He nodded. "Kitty Blue has disappeared," he explained. "We have made every effort to locate him, but he has left without a trace except for the little scarf which he sometimes wore around his neck. This we found in the garden outside." And the attendant produced the scarf which was the same color as the eyes of the cat.

Madame Lenore lay back in her chair, closed her eyes, and shook with choking sobs.

All kinds of dire fears and suspicions tormented Madame Lenore's mind. After realizing Kitty Blue had disappeared without the least clue to where he had gone, the great singer took to her bed, refused food and lived on ice water and an occasional glass of champagne. Within two weeks she had lost so much weight and was so frail she could scarcely rise from her sumptuous four-poster. She canceled all of her appearances to the anger and bitter disappointment of the great Gatti-Casazza, the director of the opera house.

Against the advice of her manager and her friends she summoned many world famous detectives. Only the enormous amount of money the singer promised them prevailed upon the detectives to take a case involving the disappearance of a cat, despite the fact the cat had been the gift of the Crown Prince.

One of the detectives who listened to her story was a more humane and benevolent man than his colleagues who merely had taken huge sums of the singer's money and produced no results.

The detective, named Nello Gambini, listened quietly as Madame Lenore poured out all her sorrow together with the few facts she had gathered about Kitty Blue's last days.

"What you need, my dear lady," Nello Gambini finally said, "is not a detective but a seeress."

"A seeress!" Madame Lenore exclaimed and sat up in her bed for the first time in days. "I think, Signor Gambini, you are absolutely right, but . . ." and her voice quavered, "where on earth can I find a seeress who will not be dishonest and grasping."

"Ah, but there is one, and only one. The difficulty, however," Signor Gambini said, as he accepted a cup of coffee, "the difficulty is Señora Cleandra no longer will see anybody."

"Then why have you given me her name," the anguished singer broke into new weeping.

"Listen to me, dear Madame," Signor Gambini comforted her, "if I call her she will see you, for I once located her lost diamond necklace."

Madame Lenore smiled.

The famous detective handed her a card with the name and address of the seeress.

Rising, the detective wiped his mouth carefully with a linen napkin and said, "Be sure to tell her that I arranged for you to meet one another and under no circumstances is she to refuse to help you."

Madame Lenore was too ill and weak to go to Señora Cleandra's home, and only after emphasizing it was a matter of life and death did the old fortune-teller agree to visit the singer though, as Señora Cleandra remarked on the phone, it was against her considered better judgement to leave her own domicile.

Señora Cleandra's appearance was astounding. She was nearly seven feet tall and her hands were laden with jewels and a strong herbal odor emanated from her person.

Besides this she was so heavily veiled from head to foot one could scarcely see her eyes. She said she would only partake of a raw onion as refreshment, but after chewing thoughtfully on the onion for a while, she changed her mind and said she would take a cup of beef broth.

"And now, dear Madame Lenore, tell me what person so beloved of you is missing, and I will attempt to locate him."

"When you say *person*, dear Señora, you are speaking the truth. Yet I must tell you the loved one, whose absence has brought me to my death bed, is a cat. . . ."

Señora Cleandra hearing who the missing party was stood up in all her seven feet and gave out an ear-splitting shriek followed by a volley of curses.

"Pray be seated, dear Señora," Madame Lenore begged her.

"You have brought me here to locate a *cat* for you," the seeress cried. "Have you no realization of what an insult that is to me, the Señora Cleandra who has hitherto only been a consultant to members of royalty and other crowned heads. A cat! Indeed!"

"Dear Señora, listen to me," Madame Lenore whispered, shaking in a fit of trembling. "Though he has, it is true, a cat's body, he is not a cat but a young Prince I am convinced. He speaks the language of aristocracy and not the mewings of an ordinary feline. And he loves me, and I love him. If he does not come back to me I shall die."

"Have you any spirits in the house?" Señora Cleandra inquired of one of the attendants. "Some eau-de-vie perhaps," she added.

The servant immediately brought the seeress a snifter of the finest brandy, and after sipping the liquor lengthily, Señora Cleandra lowered her veil and, looking closely at Madame Lenore, said, "If he is not a cat but as you claim a Prince, I could extend to you my services. But first I must have an article the disappeared one often touched—I suppose in his case something he held in his paw."

"Bring the Señora Kitty Blue's velvet breeches," Madame Lenore commanded, and for the first time in weeks the singer rose and painfully walked over to the largest chair in the room.

Madame Lenore was about to add some more information to Señora Cleandra about her missing pet when she saw that the seeress had fallen into a deep trance: her head had leaned to one side and the veils about her face had fallen away so that one saw her chin and upper lip were covered with a heavy growth of beard.

The seeress then began speaking in a greatly altered voice: "Your beloved Kitty Blue is a prisoner, dear lady, of the notorious live-animal trainer and pantomimist, Herbert of Old Vienna. Kitty Blue was handed over to Herbert by the notorious rapscallion Kirby Jericho, and your dearly beloved is required to appear nightly as an entertainer and guitarist and is also forced to dance and perform acrobatics."

Señora Cleandra now opened her eyes and adjusted her veils so that her growth of beard was no longer noticeable. She stared balefully then at Madame Lenore.

"You should eat nothing but rare beef for the next two weeks," she advised the opera singer.

"But where, dear Señora, can I find Herbert of Old Vienna?" Madame Lenore entreated the seeress.

"You, a singer, have never heard of Herbert of Old Vienna? Then I pity you."

Señora Cleandra hurriedly wrote out the showman's address and handed it to the bereaved Lenore.

"How much am I indebted to you for, Señora?" Madame Lenore inquired after getting possession of herself and reading again and again the address of Herbert of Old Vienna.

The seeress had moved toward the door. Then turning around she said in a voice as low as that of a bass baritone, "Owe? Are you crazy! Nothing. Do you think I would accept money for locating a cat, whether he is a Prince in disguise or maybe a goblin? Señora Cleandra does not receive pay for locating animals."

She opened the door and rushed out.

Weak as she was, Madame Lenore followed after the seeress and cried, "You must have some recompense, dear lady. Please come back and accept any gift you may desire."

But Madame Lenore was too late. The heavy outer door had slammed behind the visitor and a cold current of air came in from the street, causing Madame Lenore to cough and sneeze.

Madame Lenore was filled with hope on hearing Señora Cleandra's words that Kitty Blue might be found at Herbert of Old Vienna's, but this information also caused her great pain. Madame Lenore now recalled that many years ago she had been a pupil at Herbert of Old Vienna's Ventriloquist and Vaudeville Studio as it was then called. He had been very fond of her and she was his favorite student in that long ago epoch. But they had quarreled violently because Herbert, who was once world-famous in Vienna, had proposed marriage to Madame Lenore. She had refused his suit, and as a result he had become her bitter enemy. She realized that it would be very difficult to return to the Ventriloquist and Vaudeville Studio, especially when her coming was to beg the favor of returning Kitty Blue to her. But Madame Lenore was now only too aware that unless she could find Kitty Blue again she would never recover her health or her operatic career.

Herbert of Old Vienna had already been alerted by Señora Cleandra that Madame Lenore would be coming to his studio and would attempt to abduct Kitty Blue.

Although the singer was heavily disguised the evening she paid her call to the Vaudeville Theater, she knew Herbert who was also clairvoyant would spot her, even if she appeared as a bundle of brooms.

Nonetheless she took her courage in her hand and boldly walked into the small theater and sat in a prominent place near the stage.

A young man dressed in lemon-colored tights was juggling what appeared to be a hundred brightly colored balls, but of course clever use of lights had made one ball appear many. It was easy to believe the young man was throwing countless balls in the air and catching every one with more ease than the best trained seal.

He bowed to Madame Lenore at the end of his act and blew her several kisses.

Next a young girl dressed as a mermaid appeared and again through Herbert's clever use of lights she gave the illusion she was swimming in a beautiful green sea. She too recognized Madame Lenore and bowed low after her act.

Giuseppe Fellorini, the strong man of Herbert's troupe, now came thundering out. He raised one heavy object after another in his brawny arms, including what looked like a grand piano, and a Fat Lady reputed to weigh 500 pounds. He was too proud of his strength however to bow to Madame Lenore and barely would look at her, but instead he blew kisses to the audience which was applauding him fervently.

Then the lights dimmed, and soft if slightly sad music from the cello and the harp sounded. Madame Lenore knew her "prince" was about to appear, and she had to reach for her smelling bottle to keep from fainting.

Kitty Blue dressed in a suit of mother-of-pearl and diamonds came forward with a guitar. He did not seem to recognize Madame Lenore at first, and began strumming his guitar and then sang the famous words:

> *In your sweet-scented garden*
> *I lost my way.*
> *Your window once full of light*
> *Closed forever against my beating heart,*
> *I lost my way because you had gone away.*

But here Kitty Blue's paws trembled and his voice became choked. He had recognized Madame Lenore. He rose from the shining silver chair in which he was seated and cried out: "Madame Lenore, is it after all you? Tell me what I see is true."

Madame Lenore could not contain herself. She rose from her own seat and rushed upon the stage. The cat and the great singer embraced and kissed one another and burst into tears.

"You must come home with me at once, dear Blue," Madame Lenore managed to get these words out.

But at that moment they heard a terrifying voice of such volume that the chandeliers of the small theater vibrated and shook.

"You shall do nothing of the sort, Madame Lenore—for

it is you, isn't it? Take your hands off my star performer, and you, Kitty Blue, go to your dressing room!"

It was of course Herbert of Old Vienna.

"How dare you interrupt a performance here!" he shouted in the most terrible rage Madame Lenore could recall.

But she was no longer the cringing young pupil she had been in Herbert's vaudeville and burlesque house.

Madame Lenore almost spat at the great ventriloquist as she cried, "Kitty Blue is mine, not yours. He was a gift from the Crown Prince, and you have no claim on him."

"If you so much as touch this cat," Herbert shouted in an even louder tone, "I shall have both you and him arrested and sent to the Island. You are in my theater, and furthermore you are still facing charges for having run out on me years ago, owing me thousands of pounds sterling and gold guineas. And once you are jailed you shall stay there till you are turned to dust!"

"Jail me? You shall do nothing of the sort, you low mountebank," Madame Lenore cried.

Because she was living in a dangerous city Madame Lenore always carried a pearl-handled pistol. And so she drew out this pistol from one of the voluminous folds of her gown.

Now Herbert of Old Vienna had an almost demented fear of firearms, possibly because both his third and fourth wives had shot him, seriously wounding him.

When he saw Madame Lenore leveling the gun at him, he fell on his knees and burst into an unmanly series of sobs.

Still holding the gun in his direction, Madame Lenore, walking backwards, reached the stage door and then the dressing room. She found Kitty Blue hiding under a player piano. Kitty Blue, hearing the singer's voice, rushed into her arms.

They hurried into the back part of the theater and went out the stage door where fortuitously one of the horse-drawn carriages was waiting for the Strong Man. They jumped in and, as Madame Lenore was still holding her pearl-handled pistol, the driver was too terrified not to obey her and started in the direction of the singer's palatial residence.

Herbert had recovered partially from his fear and raced out after them, but at this point Madame Lenore fired her pistol in the air, and when the mountebank heard the gun-fire he fell in a dead faint to the pavement thinking he had been shot.

The carriage was soon rushing away and within minutes had reached the residence of the famed opera singer.

Exhausted from his ordeal, Kitty Blue was easily per-suaded to be ensconced in his comfortable place in Madame Lenore's four-poster, but sleep was out of the question. And the singer was avid to hear of the cat's adventures.

But before he could begin, the new servants (Madame Lenore had dismissed all her former help on the grounds they had neglected the safety and person of Kitty Blue) brought his favorite dessert of candied deviled shrimp and strawberries in brandy and anise cream.

He had barely begun to enjoy the repast when all the doors of the chamber were flung open and in strode the Crown Prince who had got wind of the rescue of the cat.

The Prince was nearly as overcome with joy as his friend the opera singer and they all embraced one another in an excess of joyful thanksgiving.

"He was just beginning to tell me how it was he was lost to us," Madame Lenore told the Prince.

"I had forgotten, Your Grace," Kitty Blue turned to his highness, "that I was forbidden to talk with common cats."

"And from what I have heard," the Prince said, "you could hardly have chosen a worse creature to speak to than the notorious Great Cat and his accomplice One Eye, who I am glad to tell you have both been sent to prison for life."

Kitty Blue could not help smiling.

"After Great Cat had robbed me of my earring, I was rescued by a young theater scout sent to locate promising talent by Herbert of Old Vienna."

"And don't I know the theater scout you mention," the Prince was indignant. "Kirby Jericho is his name."

Kitty Blue nodded. "He took me to his training chamber," the cat went on, "and for six weeks I was his prisoner while he coached me and instructed me in the art of guitar playing, elocution and soft-shoe dancing, prior to his turning me over to Herbert of Old Vienna."

The Prince could not help interrupting the narrative here by cries of outrage.

Madame Lenore cringed at the thought of what her beloved cat had suffered in her absence.

Despite his painful adventures and the accompanying pain and suffering they had inflicted on Kitty Blue, both Madame Lenore and the Prince had to admit that the cat's experiences had given him if possible an even more ingratiating and splendid personality, and what is more an almost inexhaustible repertory.

"Before, dear Blue," the Prince expressed it this way, "you were a marvelous companion and a sterling intimate, but having been trained by wicked but brilliant Herbert of

Old Vienna and Kirby Jericho, you are without an equal in the entire world.

The Prince then stood up and folded his arms.

"I want to invite you, Madame Lenore and Kitty Blue, to accompany me on an ocean cruise around the world beginning tomorrow at noon. Will you kindly accept such an invitation?"

As he waited for their reply the Prince added: "I think both of you could stand with a long vacation, and this one is scheduled to last for seventeen months."

Madame Lenore turned to her favorite cat for a response.

Kitty Blue fairly leaped for joy at the thought of a world cruise with a royal protector and the greatest living singer, and nodded acceptance.

And so the three of them became during that long sea voyage inseparable friends and companions. And almost every night, at the Prince's command, Kitty Blue would entertain them with the story of his adventures, interspersed with his guitar playing and singing and soft-shoe routine. The narrative of his adventures changing a little from night to night, new details coming into the story, new additions not imparted before, gave the Prince and Madame Lenore such entertainment they never knew a dull moment on their sea voyage. The three of them became the most famous trio perhaps known then or thereafter.

Easy Street

Mother Green and her faithful friend Viola Daniels, shut away as they were in their old four story brownstone, at the end of the mews, were unprepared for a sudden change in this unfrequented neighborhood. Big trucks with deafening sound equipment had moved in, men with bullhorns were shouting at other men up and down the street, and the whole area was roped off from access to the adjoining neighborhood.

Mother Green had recently celebrated her 96th birthday, and her companion Viola (she looked on her as a daughter more than an attendant) was some thirty years younger.

Their neighbors spoke of them as ladies in retirement who seldom ventured out into the great city beyond. At the unusual noise and tumult today the two friends stood at the windows in wonderment and incipient alarm.

Then all at once (it was July) a summer thunderstorm of unusual violence struck the neighborhood. Hail and blinding downpour and, as the newspaper called it, "dangerous and prolonged lightning" descended. The thunder was so loud no one had ever heard such peals. It reminded the older men of the sounds of battle and bombing.

The rain continued to come down in unpitying volume, interspersed with hailstones the size of duck eggs.

The two retired ladies drew away from the window and

pulled down the blinds, but curiosity tempted them to occasionally peek outside.

What they saw was that all the men and the bullhorns and the trucks and the infernal shouting had ended. The disturbers of the peace could have been swept out to sea, who knows. Except for the unceasing downpour the street was as quiet as an uninhabited island.

It was then they caught sight of somebody seeking shelter from the flood. He was standing under their tiny front porch, drenched to the skin, his clothes so tight pressed against his body he resembled a naked drowned man, and such streams of wetness came over his face he appeared to be weeping in torrents.

Catching sight of Mother Green and Viola, the stranger made frantic gestures in their direction with his dripping hands.

"Open the door for him," Mother Green spoke to Viola.

Viola was taken aback by such a command, for Mother Green seldom if ever admitted anybody inside, and her voice now rang out like that of some woman preacher.

Viola hesitated only a minute. She flung open the door, and the drenched man staggered inside, and whether from being blinded by the torrent or through weakness, slipped and fell on his knees in front of the two ladies.

Streams of water flowed from his sopping vestments.

Meanwhile Mother Green was whispering to Viola that in the little closet off the parlor there was a man's bathrobe left from a roomer who had stayed with them some years ago, and a number of towels.

The stranger was given the bathrobe and towels and was ushered into the "little room" off the parlor. The two ladies waited uneasily for him to come out.

Many things crossed the two women's minds of course. Such as who, in fact, had she admitted to their solitary domain. What if he was dangerous or wanted by the authorities.

When their visitor emerged, Viola let out a short gasp, and Mother Green gave out a sound somewhere between astonishment and relief.

They saw the stranger was, like Mother Green, a very dark African, but he was also very young. His almond-shaped eyes betokened something very like benediction.

He sat down on the carpet and crossed his bare legs. He gave out his name which was Bewick Freeth.

"We were filming out there," he said, and he stretched his right arm in the direction of the downpour.

Neither then nor later did the ladies take in the word "filming." If it was heard at all, it was not understood.

But what made the impression now on the older woman was she heard in the stranger's speech the unmistakable accent of Alabama from where she had come so many decades ago.

Replying to her question if she was right about his speech, Bewick did not smile so much as grin, and all his gleaming white teeth reinforced his good looks.

It slipped out then both Mother Green and Bewick Freeth were from almost the very same section of Alabama, near a small lake, and the name Tallassee was mentioned.

Both ladies could now relax and smile.

Mother Green, at hearing the town named in a peremptory, even a slightly grand manner, urged Viola to go to the kitchen and bring some refreshment.

Bewick smiled at hearing her order and closed his eyes.

Mother Green liked the way he tasted the drink he was given, in small almost delicate sips, nodding his head with each sip as a kind of thank-you.

Yes, she saw she had not been mistaken in him, had not run any risk. And meanwhile the sound of Alabama in his speech brought back to her in a rush her almost forgotten memories of the South she had put behind her.

Looking at him closely, she wondered at times if she was not "seeing things." The terrible storm, his sudden appearance, their reckless admitting of a total stranger— Mother Green did wonder, but she knew she was right. She knew then she must have been meant to know Bewick Freeth.

Viola Daniels listened then as the visitor and Mother Green spoke. Viola Daniels was light-skinned and what Mother Green sometimes joked was that she looked almost more white even than an octoroon, while the more one looked at their visitor his very dark skin stood out deeper in hue.

Mother Green was easy then, not only because of his Alabama speech but the deep darkness of his face, as well as his long eyelashes, and she could sense the sweetness of his breath coming to her in waves.

Later, much later as Mother Green recalled his coming, it was as if they had been expecting him. He had walked in and they had spoken to him like he had been there before. No stranger. Even the glimpse Mother Green got of an earring in his left ear was no surprise to her.

They set aside for him the large front guest room up two flights of stairs. It had not been resided in for some years.

Bewie, as he asked to be called, one day after some time

noticing Mother Green's limp, asked if she was in some discomfort from the way she walked.

Mother Green hesitated and fidgeted.

"She suffers from bunions," Viola informed him, and Mother Green stared reproachfully at her.

Bewie in a strange gesture clasped his hands.

"I know the very thing," he cried in the face of Mother Green's displeasure her affliction had been made known.

The next day Bewie instructed Viola to prepare a small basin of mildly hot water to which he added some herbs he had purchased.

Had he not done another thing, his bathing of Mother Green's painful feet would have insured him a refuge with them.

Only Viola looked a bit uneasy. More and more she had a kind of bewildered air.

"What is it, Viola, dear?" Mother Green wondered while Bewie busied himself with some self-appointed task in the kitchen.

"Nothing, Mother."

"You act a little put out," the older woman spoke almost in a whisper.

Yes, she saw perhaps Viola was hurt or maybe just jealous. And her almost white face between Mother Green and Bewie's fierce complexions may have been a cause. She felt in a way set aside. And she wanted more than anything to be close to them, important to both.

Mother Green patted Viola's hand and kissed her middle finger. "It's *all* all right, Viola," she whispered.

And so it began, their life together, Mother Green and Viola and this perfect stranger from Alabama.

He did not tell them what his work or calling was from outside. He only indicated that he would be out from part of the day and perhaps even some of the night.

"It's my present livelihood," he added, letting them know he would have to be absent every so often.

It all seemed unsurprising at least to Mother Green— as in a dream even the unbelievable will be perfectly believable.

He had come to stay with them and they were to respect his absences and his sparse explanations. "It's his livelihood," Mother Green repeated his words to Viola.

Then, as the stranger stayed on, Viola's uneasiness grew. Often she would go to the big hall mirror and look at her own face. She saw that not only was Mother Green closer to him because he spoke in an Alabama accent, but closer likewise because like her his face was the welcome dark color.

"You will always be dear to me," Mother Green said one afternoon when they were alone and she realized Viola was grieving.

Viola tried to swallow her pride and went about as before, caring for Mother Green. In fact, after the arrival of Bewie she was more attentive and caring than before, if that was possible.

But Viola as if confiding to herself would think, "Bewie is everything to her. More than if he were her own flesh and blood."

One day Mother Green acted a little uneasy. "Where do you suppose Bewie goes? We don't as a matter of fact know much about him now do we," she reflected.

"We don't know nothin', you mean."

"Oh Viola, who is he, yes, who is this Bewie?"

Mother Green then held Viola's hand tight in hers.

One thing of course they could not help noticing. Bewie hardly ever returned without he was carrying a heavy package or two.

At the ladies' look of astonishment, he sat down and said in a joking tone, "My wardrobe. In my profession, you have to look your best. And the film people of course insist on it."

Again the word *film* did not register with the ladies. And they were too shy to ask him outright what required so many clothes.

The clothes, or the *wardrobe* to use his term, intrigued Mother Green and Viola. They spent—yes hours discussing all the clothes he was required to possess because, yes, his *livelihood* made them a necessity.

The curiosity became too strong for Mother Green. One afternoon she told Viola she would like to go upstairs to see how he kept his room.

Viola frowned, "Those stairs are steep and rickety. And dangerous!"

"Oh you can come along then and steady me, Viola dear."

Mother Green was nearly a cripple from her bunions, but she must see how he kept his room.

It was more than a big surprise to her.

She opened the big closet door and stared at some brand-new three-piece suits, fancy cravats, big-brimmed straw hats, and shiny elegant high-shoes.

"All bandbox new!" Mother Green sighed and sat down on the easy chair Viola had brought from downstairs.

"What are you doing?" Mother Green exclaimed, for she saw Viola had brought with her the big thermos bottle.

"I fetched us some hot coffee."

Mother Green sipped the steaming brew.

"What did I ever do, Viola, to deserve a child like you."

A little sob escaped Viola, undetected probably by Mother Green.

So the mystery of Bewie deepened. Yes, who was he after all, and where did the expensive suits and shoes and ties and gold cufflinks come from.

Yet both Mother Green and Viola believed in him. He did not scare them. Even had he had no Alabama accent, he was one of them they were sure. He was not really a stranger in spite of his mysterious ways.

If only Mother Green loved me as much as she does Bewie, Viola would sometimes speak out aloud, knowing of course Mother Green's deafness would not let her hear.

It appeared to Viola Daniels at times that both Mother Green and Bewie had returned to Alabama to take up again their life in the South and converse in their unforgettable Alabama speech.

Viola sometimes thought about running away. But where could she go after all. She was no longer young. Who would want her. And beside all that she would never have the heart to leave Mother Green.

"Let her love Bewie more than me!" Viola would then say out loud.

"What's you talking about over there," Mother Green would say in a joking voice.

"I hardly know myself, Mother Green," Viola would say in a loud voce, and then the two ladies would both laugh.

It became if possible less and less clear both to Mother Green and Viola Daniels how and why Bewie had become part of their lives. It was especially unclear at times how he had appeared at all. Once Viola almost got the word out, "Like a housebreaker!" but she caught herself from saying it at the last moment. But it would have been true maybe to say an apparition.

"We always knew Bewie," Viola said long afterward.

Something had been on Bewie's mind. Perhaps that's why he was so happy always performing so many tasks for Mother Green. He tidied the place up. He even washed the large front windows. And one evening he insisted on preparing a real Southern dinner for them.

But his presence in the house became shorter, less frequent. Sometimes he did not come home at night. Sometimes he barely spoke to them. He became sad, downcast . . . even tearful. Once Mother Green had heard this terrible sobbing in the front parlor. She didn't know what to do. It didn't sound like anybody she had ever heard. It sounded almost like a heartbeat. She opened the door ever so soft and there he sat slumped in the big chair just crying his eyes out. She closed the door as soft as she had opened it, waited a while, and then called out very loud, "Bewie is that you?" When she went in the front parlor his face was as dry as chalk, and he was composed and looked like always. Yes, as Mother Green kept repeating, "Something is on his mind. Something is worrying him."

Something too was on Mother Green's mind. She would start to say something to Viola, and then she would stop all of a sudden, or in Viola's words "clam up." She would clear her throat and relapse into silence.

"Do you remember Ruby Loftus?" the old woman broke her silence.

Viola said yes though she was not sure she did remember Ruby.

Mother Green smiled, lapsed again into a brief silence. Then she began to speak hurriedly, "She was what they call a psychic reader. She had second sight. Well, she often read for me. What she got for me was usually mighty interesting if not exactly calming. But what she told me one time happened years ago. Before your time, Viola. She 'read' me, and lord how she read me. She told me that in my later years there would come into my life a wonderful presence, a shining kind of being who would bring me many of the rewards and fulfill many of the promises I had never thought would be mine. It would be harvest time."

Viola closed her eyes.

"That prophecy has come to pass," Mother Green went on. "My reward, my shining blessing has got to be Bewie Freeth."

Up until then Viola had never known Mother Green to offer her strong drink except in case of illness.

Tonight she asked Viola to go to the little cupboard in the pantry and on the first shelf reach for the whisky and then pour out two glasses.

Viola was even less used to strong drink than Mother Green, but she knew she must not disappoint her old friend after she had told her of the prophecy of the psychic reader.

And Viola was as sure as sure could be Ruby Loftus had

told the undeniable truth. Sad as Viola was that Bewie occupied so deep a place in Mother Green's heart, a place Viola would never hold, nonetheless, Bewie Freeth, beyond the shadow of a doubt, as if foretold by an angel, had come into the old woman's life a late blessing and a special gift.

Mother Green was so happy when Bewie was around, Viola Daniels later remarked often to visitors. She never did seem to reckon it would all come to a close.

The first night he didn't come home, or rather the first dawn, Mother Green was calm.

"Bewie will be home soon, mark my word," she would smile.

But one day was followed by another. Mother Green would hobble up to where he had his room.

"He'll be back if only to wear his outfits," she told Viola.

"Maybe we should notify the police," Viola said one evening after several weeks went by.

It was the only time Viola and Mother Green disagreed.

"Don't never say police ever again in my presence, Viola Daniels. If you have to do somethin' get down on your knees and pray, but don't say we should call the law."

Mother Green relied on Viola Daniels in so many ways, but principally to keep her straight on time and events. Viola knew the old woman's memory had begun to show the effects of time.

Often Mother Green would inquire, "When was it that Bewie came to us?"

"Don't you recall, Mother. He come on that blusterous July night."

"Which July though?"

"Why, July last, dear."

But in a day or so Mother Green would ask the same question over again.

Viola choked up then with the realization her old friend was beginning to fail, and she could not restrain a tear. She knew Mother Green was only holding to life at all because of Bewie.

"He was her all and everything." Viola would tell of it some time later.

Another thing which worried Viola was that Mother Green continued to steal upstairs to Bewie's room despite the fact she had such a problem managing the rickety stairs.

At the foot of the stairs Viola would listen. She could hear Mother Green lifting up his shirts and muttering something like, "Why ain't you come home, Bewie, when you know we miss you so."

Finally though if Mother Green didn't guess at the truth, Viola did. The truth that Bewie Freeth was gone for good.

But yet, if he had gone, his duds and finery was left behind.

Viola herself could not help stealing up the stairs and going to his closet. She took down his silk underwear, his pure cotton shirts, and once while arranging his Palm Beach suit on a handmade hanger, something fell out of one of the pockets onto the floor. The slight sound it gave out falling frightened her almost as if it was a firearm going off.

Slowly she picked the object up. It was a newspaper

clipping. And the clipping was rather recent from a Chicago newspaper. Its heading read: METEORIC RISE OF UNKNOWN YOUTH. Her eyes moved on the article! Bewick Freeth who made hosannas ring nation-wide from his two previous films is now the undisputed charismatic idol of the hour. He has never been greater, his success unanimous.

Viola let the newsprint slip to the floor and sat down heavily on one of Mother Green's upholstered chairs. She felt faint, she felt, yes, betrayed, perhaps even mocked. Here he had been with them and never let on who he was. Yes, he had deceived them.

At the same time she felt he had not really lied to them. She knew he must have cared for them, a little perhaps, but, yes, he had been happy with them. He had often said he never wanted to leave, that she and Mother Green were "home to him." And now the clipping.

Sitting with Mother Green that evening, she was gradually aware the old woman was staring at her.

"Yes?" Viola managed to say.

"You look like you seen a ghost," Mother Green said. When there was no answer from Viola the old woman clicked her tongue.

"You know somethin' I don't know, Viola. You know somethin' and you know you know somethin'."

"Maybe I have found out who Bewie really is, Mother Green. And how come he ain't here anymore I guess."

"If you know something Viola, let's hear it, all of it."

"Bewie Freeth is not like us, Alabama accent or not. He's a famous movie star. What he was doin' here with us, well who knows."

Slowly, unostentatiously, as if handing Mother Green

something she had perhaps asked for, Viola handed her the clipping.

The old woman put on her spectacles. She read and reread the article from the Chicago paper.

To Viola's consternation Mother Green, after putting away her spectacles, handed back the clipping to Viola without a word. Was the old woman beginning to fail, beginning not to take in things. No, not at all, Viola was sure. The truth about Bewie, the truth who he was had shocked her into this silence. After a long pause Mother Green smiled a kind of smile that meant, who knows, the dream was broken.

Doing her evening sewing, Viola stopped working for a moment and said, "Mother Green."

"Yes," the old woman answered.

"I come across upstairs in the little store room along beside the games of checkers that old German OUIJA board, planchette and all."

Mother Green's jaw dropped, and she reached in her side pocket for her handkerchief and wiped her eyes.

"You don't say," she spoke in a far-off voice. When Viola said no more, Mother Green, adjusting the lavaliere she wore about her throat said, "You mean you want to bring Ouija out then."

Viola nodded. After a silence she said, "I thought, Mother Green, Ouija might explain things to us, do you reckon?"

"You mean Bewie?"

"Yes, maybe."

"Explain him how."

"You said yourself the other evening as we lingered over

tea that we can barely remember when or how he came to us."

Mother Green sighed in an odd off-hand way. "And you think Ouija can tell us the why and how of him. And whether we'll ever see him again."

The next day Viola brought the Ouija board out and set it on the card table.

"I declare," Mother Green said.

When they had arranged the board both ladies admitted they hardly dared begin.

"Do you ask Ouija somethin', Viola, now."

They put both their hands on the planchette. It did not move.

"You got to ask it, Mother Green, dear."

Their hands began moving slowly, sleepily after a while.

"No, no, Viola, you ask it."

The board moved jerkily, stopped and then began slowly to move to the letters.

It spelled KEWPIE.

The ladies giggled in spite of themselves.

The planchette moved wildly, then slowed down, then very pokily spelled

LUKY THE DAY HE COME TO YOU
& LUKIER THE EVENIN HE BE GONE
LUKY LUKY LADIES

"Mother Green, whether it's me or Ouija, but Ouija don't know how to spell now, do he?" Viola commented.

"But is he gone forever?" Mother Green asked Ouija. The planchette was still, perfectly still.

Viola began to see then that she should never have let Mother Green know that Bewie was a famous film actor. It was after Mother Green found out that fact that she began going down hill in no small measure. She complained too of what she called the weight of memory.

"After a while," Mother Green spoke in a low voice now to Viola almost as if she was praying, "there is too much to remember. And there is too much of past days to know *when* it happened, and sometimes there is the doubt maybe it did happen or I dreamt it. And the people! All the faces and the talk and the shoutin' from the beginning until now. Why all those years of mine in Alabama alone would take another fifty years to tell you about."

But Viola was sure it was Bewie's absence and his never coming back which pushed her down to what she called the shady side of life. "I'm going down the shady side now" she had once said before Bewie came, and now it had got worse than shady—it bespoke the deep night.

"Where is he?" she would often shout coming out of a dozing spell in her chair.

"Now, now Mother," Viola would respond.

"You don't tell me nothin', do you, Viola."

"Whatever you ask I will tell you if I know," Viola answered.

"I feel I am bein' kept in the dark," Mother Green would mumble.

And so they spent many evenings consulting Ouija, but sort of dispiritedly now. If Ouija had had one fault, that of misspelling words, now he had a worse fault, he was tongue-tied most of the time. When not silent Ouija stammered.

Mother Green spoke more and more of Ouija in fact as if he was a person, a person sort of like Bewie Freeth who was visiting them but wouldn't be permanent, a kind of transient somebody, yes, like Bewie Freeth had been.

Sometimes Viola wondered if she and Mother Green had only dreamed there was a Bewie Freeth. And Viola often thought Mother Green might be having the same thought.

They were both waiting for something, and Bewie had intercepted the wait, but now that he was gone, as Ouija said, they would have no occupation but to wait together.

Viola had taken over the tasks that Bewie had performed, bathing Mother Green's feet and bunions in the medicated water, cleaning sometimes the wax out of her ears (though it didn't cure her deafness) and answering the endless query, "Do you think Bewie is ever comin' back?"

Then one day she up and told Mother Green Bewie had been gone for nearly a year, but she was glad for the first time Mother Green's deafness had prevented her from hearing her words.

Viola's sorrow grew as she often confided to herself when alone.

Mother Green seeing Viola's sorrow spoke up sharply, "Viola, Viola, what ails you you are so weepy. What is going on, dear child."

"I didn't know I was weepy, dear Mother," she said trying to smile.

"You miss Bewie, don't you."

But the mention of Bewie brought back to her how Mother Green's memory was playing tricks on her. For she always wondered where Bewie had gone, and she kept asking when he would return.

As many times as Viola told her that Bewie was gone, and would not come back, she saw that Mother Green either did not hear this explanation or having heard it erased it from her memory. For Mother Green, Bewie was a timeless part of their life, and so if he was gone, no matter, he would be back.

The heavens themselves seemed to give warning of what was happening, Viola Daniels would later tell people who visited.

Mother Green and Viola heard the sound that was like thunder, only probably closer and scarier. The sky seemed to blossom with many flaming colors which then fell like stars.

Difficult as it was now for both of the ladies to trudge up the long stairwell, they felt they had to find out what the commotion was.

It took Mother Green nearly a half hour to reach the top. How she sighed and groaned, and her bunions were killing her. She would rest on some of the steps before going further.

"I should have brought the smelling bottle, dear heart," Viola muttered, but Mother Green only gave her a reproachful look.

The top floor had great high huge windows. They no more got up there than she realized what it was.

"Fireworks," Mother Green exclaimed.

"It means something," Viola shook her head.

"If that's what you feel, we might consult Ouija."

This time Ouija was not evasive. The planchette began to move as soon as they touched it.

Mother Green came up with a start when Viola queried, "Where's Bewie?"

Ouija responded, "IN THE SWEET BY-AND-BY."

"And what do you mean *by-and-by*, Ouija?" Viola asked as Mother Green stared at the board.

Viola stirred uneasily for she knew Mother Green was alert tonight.

"HE GONE," Ouija responded.

At this, Mother Green sat up very straight in her chair but retained her hand on the planchette.

"Gone where?" Viola raised her voice.

Ouija moved at once.

"GONE TO CAMP GROUND."

"Where Camp Ground?"

Ouija did not move. Viola raised her voice, but the planchette was still, and then finally Ouija spelled again:

"CAMP GROUND."

Viola Daniels' own memory was getting almost as bad as Mother Green's, and it wasn't exactly due to her drinking the strong spirits she found in the cupboard. No, Viola's memory was not what it was, say, the day Bewie had arrived.

She tried to remember how she had learned for a proven fact that Bewie had passed over.

Soon after their episode with the Ouija, one day while out shopping, Viola in one of her now common absent-minded spells, found herself more than a few blocks away from Mother Green's, in a kind of promenade where there were expensive shops, saloons, and motion picture theaters. She saw that one of the movie houses was draped in black cloth, and there were wreaths and flowers and signs all everywhere. Her eye caught sight of the marquee. She stopped dead in her tracks. She kept reading over and again the lettering:

"YOU WILL ALWAYS BE WITH US BEWIE. FOREVER AND A DAY"

Viola braced herself and went up to a uniformed man who was in charge of inspecting tickets as you went into the theater.

"Excuse me," she began. The uniformed man looked at her carefully and blinked.

"Tell me if Bewie Freeth. . . ."

He did not let Viola finish but pointed to a large over-size photo from a newspaper. Without her glasses Viola was hardly able to read the print, but finally at least one sentence came clear. Yes, Bewie Freeth was no more, had, in the words of Ouija, gone to Camp Ground.

It was several nights later that the first of the gatherings outside Mother Green's house began. They were mostly of young men, some of whom played every so often on a horn, others on a sax, and still others blew on what looked like a little cornet. When they quit playin' they shouted to passersby, "Bewie lived here for your information!"

Viola crept out on the frail front porch.

A smothered shout went up from the musicians.

There was the strong smell of something smoky, and as if it were their final number, each of the players took out big handkerchiefs and waved them at her in token, one supposed in tribute, to their idol Bewie.

Mother Green slept through it and other "live" perform-ances that would take place as a tribute to their hero.

Looking at Mother Green after one of these performances,

Viola heard her own voice say, "Lucky you, dear heart, you don't know what this is all about on account of I wouldn't know how to tell you, and I don't understand it maybe any better than you do or would."

"So, he in the sweet by-and-by," Viola said later that night to herself after she had had a shot of spirits in the kitchen.

Time got more and more mixed up. After the night of the fireworks there was a long vacant pause in everything.

Viola was the first to say she thought something was about to bring them news.

And this time it was not Ouija who warned them, no it was a ticking sound Viola heard coming from Bewie's closet.

Viola trembled and even sobbed a little. Yet she had to investigate what on earth was making a ticking sound in the clothes closet.

It took her a long time to locate where the sound was coming from. She had no idea Bewie would carry an old-fashioned very heavy, yes, antique pocket watch. Why it seemed to weigh three pounds.

She removed it from his breast pocket. The sparkling gold watch was ticking! After all these—was it months or years?

Later Viola talked with a very venerable watchmaker, oh Mother Green said he must have gone back to the early days after emancipation. Watches and clocks, old Tyrrwhit assured her, like dead people, sometimes would come to life whether by means of a loud noise, or a building shaking, or often because of an earthquake or cyclone, a very old clock or watch, that had not ticked for ages, would all of a sudden begin ticking away. Clocks he assured Viola were imbued with a spirit all their own, and a watchmaker, a good watchmaker, knows the clock has a mind and knowledge superior to the watchmaker.

She took the ticking watch down to Mother Green who stared openmouthed at it and agreed, oh yes it was a sign.

Nehemiah Highstead accompanied by two lawyers arrived in weather even more stormy than the day when Bewick Freeth had entered the lives of the two ladies.

Nehemiah was an elderly black man who wore very thick colored glasses from which there extended a fluttering kind of frayed ribbon. His right hand trembled and he continually wiped his eyes with a large handkerchief from which there came a faint sweetish aroma.

"This is a very strange bequest, ladies," one of the attorneys finally began after looking about from ceiling to floor suspiciously. "Mr. Freeth came to our offices only a few days before his sudden decease."

Viola Daniels' full attention now rested on Mother Green whose face was devoid of expression. Had she heard the word *decease*? And having heard it did she understand it, understand, that is, what Viola had tried to tell her time and again that their Bewie was no more.

"You are the sole inheritors of what is more than a modest fortune. Much more!" the attorney continued.

He waited sleepily peevishly for his statement to take hold of his auditors as a judge will wait before he gives the verdict.

"He also provided for Mr. Highstead to look in on you ladies and be of any assistance as you may wish. Reverend Highstead was an acquaintance of Mr. Freeth from the actor's first days in the city. He is the pastor of the Ebenezer Resurrection Church which is on the other side of town. It would be completely up to you as to how much and to what extent you would request his support."

Viola nudged Mother Green from time to time as the old woman kept closing her eyes and breathing heavily, but the three gentlemen appeared not to notice this.

Finally the second attorney drew out from a Moroccan satchel a sheaf of papers. "If you ladies then will sign here on these dotted lines," he pushed the stiff legal pages to Mother Green.

Grasping tightly the pen he gave her she was able to sign:

Elgiva Green

The attorney repeated the name she had put down, confirming that she was the Mother Green designated in the will. It was, strange to say, the first time Viola Daniels had heard Mother Green's Christian name spoken out loud.

When the ladies had signed, Nehemiah Highstead rose, bowed his head, and asked everyone to join him in prayer.

It went something like this, as Viola recalled it some time later, "We are gathered here today chosen to represent a young man who went under the name of Bewick Freeth, originally from Tallassee, Alabama, who gained brief but almost universal fame as a film actor. We applaud his devotion to Mother Green and Viola Daniels and his generosity in bequeathing these two respectable ladies with his entire fortune. May the Almighty grant us the wisdom that we can administer it with integrity and zeal. We ask thee, eternal Master, to bless us all as we stand here in prayer and supplication."

No one could have foreseen the result of the two ladies coming into what even to wealthy persons would have been a sizable fortune.

Their disbelief they had inherited so much money was followed by a kind distemper and unwillingness to accept their change of fortune.

Ladies from the Ebenezer Resurrection Church called frequently not merely to rejoice with Mother Green and Viola so much as to give them the courage to accept their unbelievable change of circumstance. They also discreetly suggested that some of the money could go to the Church.

Mother Green hardly heard anything anybody said to her. She began to live in many different divisions of time. There were her early years in Alabama, then there were her later years of toil and poverty, followed by her proprietorship of the ramshackle mansion, and then the time when Bewick Freeth came out of the friendless blue and the unknown to stay with her and minister to her needs; then there was the time when Bewick, having left her without a word of goodbye, showered her with wealth.

She sat in the front window of the old mansion she now owned and nodded to passersby. She was the Mother Green then people came to recognize. She would raise her hand in blessing to them in the manner of an old film star herself. Everyone thought she was Bewick's mother. And at certain times of the day she herself may have thought so, for hour by hour her impression of reality changed.

"We missed knowing he was a world-famous movie star," Viola would confide sleepily to the visitors who now dropped in as if Mother Green's house was a sort of gathering place. Mostly young ones came. Crazy about their idol. They wanted to see too where he hung his clothes. But their request to go upstairs was vetoed of course.

The past, the present, the future became all mixed up in Mother Green's mind. Sometimes she thought Bewie was her own flesh and blood. Again he was her hired man. Sometimes he seemed like her grandson. He was hardly ever the famed movie star the world knew him by.

Often out of complete bewilderment and confusion as to what to do, Viola would hold Mother Green's hand and even kiss its worn flesh.

Once after holding her hand in hers for an unusually long spell Viola heard Mother Green say, "He'll be back, don't you believe now otherwise. Bewie will be back here whatever any folk may say he won't."

Viola actually almost believed what Mother Green said. For how could so vital so fresh so overwhelmingly youthful a young man disappear, any more than sunbeams would one day cease to visit this world of sorrow and loss.

In this resplendent light then they went on with their lives, allowing Nehemiah Highstead and the Ebenezer Resurrection Church to tend to whatever arrangements so immense a bequest had visited upon the two retired ladies.

"I think he was sent," Mother Green often confided to Nehemiah on one of his frequent visits. To Viola's relief she saw that Nehemiah acted as if he agreed with Mother Green. Yes, he was not playacting. She believed the old man too felt Bewie's kind of splendor was not extinguished, would in fact make its presence known again.

From then on Mother Green if not Viola always spoke about Bewie as "amongst the living" and not ever amongst the departed. "He was like her very own," Viola often told the ladies of the Ebenezer Resurrection Church and the steady stream of young visitors who were Bewie's followers.

If for no other reason Mother Green's and Viola's daily lives were made more cheerful, more enjoyable, and yes more sociable. Their long years of lonesomeness and solitary grief (save when Bewie had come to them) was set aside for hours of joyfulness and even quiet mirth.

The church ladies brought from their own kitchens sumptuous repasts for supper, and lighter but even perhaps more enjoyable victuals for lunch. They brought daily fresh flowers and made other arrangements for brightening the premises. They hired at times limousines and entertained the two ladies with little excursions. They even undertook to restore the ruined mansion to its original splendor.

There was also singing, for all the ladies were members of the choir.

And like Viola Daniels they would often agree with nearly everything Mother Green remarked, such as, "Bewie ain't gone far," or "Bewie will be here amongst us again, mark my words."

And so, even had the two ladies not inherited great wealth, the presence of the many young visitors and of old Nehemiah and the church choir ladies made Mother Green's last days, if not quite as heavenly as the fortune teller had foretold, nonetheless a peaceable kind of half-light that suggests the growing presence of angels from beyond.

Reaching Rose

Mr. Sendel in his late years spent almost the entire evening in his favorite saloon, seated in an imposing manner on the center barstool from where he could survey very close to Richard, the bartender, all that went on. After a few drinks which he sipped very slowly, Mr. Sendel would gaze absentmindedly at the telephone booth nearest him.

Then giving another taste to his drink, leaving it more than half full, he would make a rather stately progress to the booth, partly closing the door. He would take down the receiver and hesitantly begin speaking into the mouthpiece.

Actually Mr. Sendel was talking only to himself. He would talk for several minutes into the silent phone, explaining how worried he was and how despairing it was at his time of life when all or almost all those dear to one have departed.

Opening the booth door wide, Mr. Sendel would stroll back to the bar and finish his drink. Feeling the eyes of others fastened upon him after a while he would again leave to go back to the phone booth.

He was convinced that nobody suspected he was in the booth talking to himself. Not even the bartender who was smart suspected it, he consoled himself.

Mr. Sendel always went through the motions of dialing

the number, however, to throw anybody off the scent who might be watching, and then he would begin speaking again through the black opening of the phone. As he spoke the cold blackness of the mouthpiece warmed up slightly, throwing back the smell of the liquor he had drunk, the tobacco fumes, even perhaps the smell of the dental work he was always having done.

As he talked into the phone he felt, if not quieter, more of one piece, whereas when he sat at the bar he would often feel like a pane of glass struck by an invisible hammer and so about to crash, not in one piece, but all over, so that the broken glass would fall into shimmering and tiny silver particles to the floor.

Mr. Sendel now talked to prevent himself from collapsing like glass into smithereens.

When Mr. Sendel first began going to the telephone booth he had talked only to himself, but this had never really satisfied him. First of all he no longer had anything more he wanted to say to *himself*. He was an old man, and he did not care about *himself*; he no longer actually wanted to exist as he was now. Often as he sat at the bar he wished that he could become invisible, disembodied, with just his mind at work, observing. He wished the painful husk of ancient flesh which covered him would be no more, that he might live only remembering the past currents of his life. Perhaps, he reflected, that was all immortality was: the release from the painful husk of the flesh with the mind free to wander without the accumulated harvest of suffering.

Later when he would go to the telephone, he would pretend to talk with people whom he once knew, but after a while he tired also of this pretense. The people he really cared for were all dead. They had all been gone for many years. He realized this for the first time when he was in the phone booth. *"They are all gone,"* he had said into the mouthpiece. *"All of them."* He had sat there for a long time after that, thinking, the mouthpiece unspoken into, the receiver lying in the palm of his hand like a wilted bouquet. Finally a man had tapped on the pane of the telephone booth. "Are you finished?" he asked Mr. Sendel somewhat anxiously. He had looked at the man a moment, then nodded slowly, and turning to the mouthpiece he said, "Goodbye then, dear."

He saw that the man in his hurry to get into the telephone booth did not notice anything unusual in his behavior.

He went back to his place at the bar and ordered another brandy.

It was the next evening things came to a head.

"What I like about you, Mr. Sendel, is you are always busy," the bartender greeted him. "You always have something on tap. That's why you look so young."

He looked at the bartender without changing his expression, despite the surprise which he felt at such a remark.

"Isn't that true, sir," the bartender asked him hesitantly.

"You really think I look occupied?" Mr. Sendel wondered in a tone rather unlike himself, perhaps because for the first time in that bar, for the first time perhaps in many years, he had made a comment about himself.

"You look completely . . . well, in business," the bartender finished.

"Thank you, Richard," Mr. Sendel retorted.

Then as Richard looked peculiar at him, he said, "I *am* terribly occupied," and bartender and customer both laughed with relief.

"I admire you, sir," Richard said.

"And you know what my estimation of you is," Mr. Sendel winked.

Richard was one of the few persons whom Mr. Sendel actually *knew* any more. Everyone else, somehow, was somebody you talked generalities with, but occasionally he and Richard managed to say some particularity that made up the little there was of meaning.

Usually after exchanging one of these particularities, Richard would move on to another customer, but today something impelled him to stay, and not only stay, but to question or rather to comment.

"Sir," Richard spoke somewhat awkwardly for him. "About the phone calls."

Mr. Sendel's mouth moved downwards and his pale brown eyes flashed weakly.

Seeing his look, Richard said, "It's so wonderful."

Mr. Sendel was vague and unhelpful.

"What I mean, sir," Richard continued suddenly lost as he had never before been with his old friend, "it's wonderful you have so much to . . . tend to."

Then seeing the old man's look of distant incomprehension, he continued, "For you to be so alive at your age is, to me, wonderful."

"Thank you, Richard," Mr. Sendel managed to say, and his old warmth and vivacity rushed back, so that the bartender was moved almost to tears.

"Richard," the old man began, "have one drink with me, why don't you," and he handed the bartender some bills.

"For you it will be all right," Richard said, grinning awkwardly.

Richard began to pour a drink for himself from one of the nearby bottles, but Mr. Sendel tapped imperiously and pointed to a large, seldom-used flask. "That one, Richard."

The two men drank then to one another.

Outside the sound of a saxophone drifted over to them, and both men exchanged looks. Richard tightened the string of his apron.

Mr. Sendel wanted to look at the phone booth nearest him, the one he always used, but he did not.

"Of all the men who ever come in here," the bartender said sleepily, "you're the finest," and with a special gesture of his hand, he moved off and out of the presence of the old man.

Mr. Sendel stared after him. He was not sure what Richard had meant exactly, as he thought it over, and his pleasure at Richard's friendliness turned suddenly to anguish and fear that perhaps the bartender knew something. He had not liked his mentioning the telephone. And the more he thought about it, the more worried he became. *Richard should not have mentioned the phone*, he repeated to himself.

Then the thought came that perhaps Richard did *know*, that is, that there was nobody on the wire, and that he had *no* business whatsoever, that there was *nobody*, nobody but Richard and him. Bartenders, like Delphic oracles, are naturally defined by their very profession as anonymous. They administer haphazardly and are Great Nobodies by reason of their calling.

"He could *not* know," Mr. Sendel said aloud.

He was surprised as he heard his own voice and, turning

around, was relieved to see that nobody had heard, not even Richard.

He could NOT know, Mr. Sendel spoke almost prayerfully.

He thought how terrible it would be if Richard did know. There would be nothing left of his world at all. His mind had never before dwelt on the exact components of that world before, but now, at a glance, he saw everything just as it was: his world was merely this bar, was Richard, and most important of all the telephone booth; but all of them went together, the booth and the bar and Richard could not be disassociated.

He paused before the thought of all this.

If Richard knew, there would be nothing.

The thought—so simple and so devastating—completely unnerved him.

And now a second disturbing thing occurred to him. Tonight he had not telephoned. He had barely looked at the phone booth, and he knew that Richard was, after their conversation, waiting for him to do so. Richard expected, had to expect, him to phone.

And all at once he feared he could not go to the booth. And quite as suddenly he felt sure that Richard knew. He must know. Why would he have brought it up otherwise. In all the years he had been coming to the bar, Richard had never made so much as a sign that he saw Mr. Sendel go to the telephone booth, but tonight—perhaps Richard was growing old too—he had wanted to show comradeship, show pity, sympathy, what you will, and he had, Mr. Sendel saw with horror, destroyed their world.

The thought that all was destroyed came to him now with complete and awful clarity. Not only had Richard always probably known, but he had always kept the knowledge to himself, had told nobody. Perhaps he had nobody to tell, but then to whom could one tell such a thing, a thing as insubstantial as the mind itself.

"He knows," Mr. Sendel said aloud.

He sat with his brandy whose delicate aroma suddenly resembled the faint perfume of flowers he had smelled many years ago in a room he could barely remember, perhaps forty years had passed since he had even thought of that room. The room was real, but its occupant was lost to him.

"And what does he expect me to do?" he said to himself. He was suddenly a prisoner of decision. He could not act, he did not know what to do next, he did not know what was expected of him.

He managed once or twice to look back at the phone booth, and as he did so he fancied Richard saw him from the far end of the bar where he was talking with a young man who was said to come from Sumatra.

Mr. Sendel could only sit there now with the brandy, hoping that his tired mind would give him at last the plan that he must pursue and the method by which he might extricate himself.

He saw weakly and with growing nausea that the final crisis that is said to come with old age had struck hard, peremptory, unannounced and with full authority. And he had not even the strength to drink.

Then forcing his hand which trembled badly, he gulped down the entire brandy.

With an unaccustomed energy and a tone never before used with him, he clapped his hands and shouted, "If you please, Richard."

Richard stopped talking with the young man from Sumatra and came over to his favorite customer, but as Mr. Sendel stared at him he could see that in the few minutes which had passed Richard had changed just as fundamentally as he himself.

"Is this your best brandy?" Mr. Sendel wondered, and his voice resembled the whining complaint of men in hospitals.

Richard watched him.

"I'll get you the best," Richard spoke vaguely.

"And what would that be?" Mr. Sendel asked, as though he no longer knew what words were being put into his mouth.

Richard pointed to a bottle near them both.

"Of course, of course," the old man said.

"This should make you feel less tired," Richard said.

"Tired?" Mr. Sendel was loud and worried.

Richard poured, not speaking for a moment.

"Aren't you a bit, sir?" he wondered.

Mr. Sendel observed the change in his bartender. Richard was all at once like a stranger. The change was complete, terrifying. And even this stranger whom he would have to go on of course addressing as Richard, this stranger seemed to have already joined the many passed-over voices to whom he spoke on the telephone. He could actually, he felt, now phone Richard.

But he knew that his bartender was waiting for him to say something, and a daring, even foolhardy plan crossed his mind.

"I've lost my most important telephone number." He was intrepid and rash and looked boldly into the face of his bartender.

"A telephone *number*," Richard wondered, and Mr.

Sendel was sure now that the bartender *knew*, had known perhaps from the beginning.

"I've lost it."

"A local number?" Richard was cautious, quieter than he had ever been before.

Mr. Sendel hesitated. "Yes."

"Can't we look it up for you," Richard's voice was nearly inaudible.

"Oh no," Mr. Sendel was calm now, deliberate, as though the offensive had passed to his hand. "It's something that can wait. Only it's irritating, you know."

"But we could look it up," Richard ignored the mentioning of irritation.

"But I can't remember her first name, and her last name is so common," Mr. Sendel told him.

Richard blinked rapidly.

"Maybe," Mr. Sendel began. "Maybe if I just went and sat in the phone booth there," and he turned and motioned toward it, wanting to be sure Richard saw which booth he meant. "Perhaps both the name of the lady and the number will come to me."

He saw that Richard's eyes narrowed under these words, and he was now more sure than ever of Richard's knowing. A fierce anger made Mr. Sendel's temples throb. He felt he hated Richard, that he hated everybody, and that he was ridiculously trapped.

"I think I may recall her number if I sit in the booth," Mr. Sendel confided weakly, looking into his glass.

Wiping the bar dry with a long cloth, Richard spoke softly, "Call on me if you need anything, Mr. Sendel," and he went off like an actor who has finished his lines for the evening.

Mr. Sendel sat on, his rage and despair growing, but a feeling of strength was returning after the frightening weakness he had experienced at his first suspicion of Richard.

Sipping his brandy, he tried to think what he must do next. He could not sit here of course all night, and it was imperative that he go to telephone.

At the same time he was not sure he would be able to reach the booth, a realization which wiped out once and for all the thought that his strength was being restored.

Suddenly, however, a thing happened then as though a message had been written in letters of fire over the bar mirror. The aroma of the brandy and the perfume of flowers in the forgotten room merged, and he could now *remember*—that is, the bridge to the past was visible, and he could, he felt, cross into that room of an obliterated time. He need not stay where he was.

He left the tip on the bar, for he believed he would not be back, not tonight at any rate.

"Not with the bridge ahead," he said to himself.

He waited after he had got off his seat at the bar, then walking stiffly but he thought well he advanced toward the telephone booth under the silent gaze of everybody in the room.

Then miraculously he remembered the number! Effortlessly, clearly, completely!

This time he put in the coin meticulously, loudly.

He dialed slowly and effectively the number which he knew tonight would bring him closer to the forgotten room.

He waited.

He closed his eyes now because he knew that if they watched him, if they had watched him all those years, it did not matter tonight because he had *remembered*.

"Is Rose there?" he said with the quiet and satisfied tone of a man who knows that the answer to his question will be yes. He waited.

"This time, Rose, nothing kept you," he began, and she laughed. He had forgotten what a complete joy her laugh was.

"I have something," he said smiling, "that will amuse you. I found a counterpart of you somewhere. I found part of you, my dear, in a most out-of-the-way place."

She spoke now quite at length, and he realized how tired he was, for he could not hear all of her words, and he found himself almost nodding over what she said.

"This has, my dear, to do with your special perfume."

"Which?" she said in a rich contralto voice, "For I have so many!"

"Which but the one you always wore in the music room, of course," he said.

There was suddenly no answer.

"Rose, Rose!" he called.

Then after a wait he felt she was again on the line.

"I thought that we had been disconnected," he cried, happy to know she was there, was still listening.

"It's been so long since I got even the slightest whiff of your perfume," he went on.

She said something witty and rather cutting which was so typical of her.

"You won't be offended if I tell you your perfume is in French brandy!" He laughed. "Of course it's the best . . . the best Richard has to offer."

His hand involuntarily went up to the door.

"Rose," he almost cried, for there was a discordant hum now on the wires. In dismay his hand pressed against the booth door. It was, he saw, with horror, locked. Someone had locked the door!

He did not want to alarm Rose, but kept his hand tightly pushing the door, struggling against it at every conceivable point to measure the extent of its being sealed and locked against him.

"My dear, is everything all right otherwise," he inquired in his desperation.

He waited for an answer.

"Rose," he cried.

The phone slipped from his hand as though it had turned to a rope of sand.

His head fell heavily against the pane of glass which all at once broke sickeningly into scattered bits and fragments.

He remembered at the same time his old, long-standing fear:

Struck by an invisible hammer.

A blinding crash shook the telephone booth.

He stretched out his hand to grasp something, anything, but his fingers felt nothing, not even air.

"Mr. Sendel!" came Richard's voice from very far off.

"Mr. Sendel! Can you hear what I am saying to you?"

Mr. Sendel did not reply.

Gertrude's Hand

Sonny at no time complained about being left out of Gertrude's will. Perhaps he never thought he would ever be remembered by her in any case. Still, everybody was a bit surprised Gertrude had left everything to her cook and companion, a dark-complexioned woman of thirty who appeared to cultivate the pronounced mustache growing above her hard, thin lips. Sonny had been just as devoted as Gertrude's cook, Alda, but whereas Alda had almost never left the house, Sonny had run his legs off for Gertrude on errands of all kinds, had assisted Gertrude in her atelier where she made the iron-wrought primitive sculptures that had given her at the end of her life a kind of local fame. Sonny had gone sometimes even thrice a day to the blacksmith's where Gertrude's sculptures were finally finished. He must have worn out fifty or so boots during his fifteen years' service with the sculptress.

Once Gertrude was gone and lying beneath a very simple headstone in Cypress Grove Cemetery, Alda sat in the same oak chair her former employer had always occupied, moved into the larger, more airy, and better lighted bedroom that was Gertrude's, and from then on cooked very little. Gertrude had been a hearty eater, and Alda, thin and pinched, though with the beginning of a pot belly owing to poor posture rather than overeating, was easily satisfied with an omelet and perhaps some pea or bean soup to eke out the rest of her diet. She occasionally invited Sonny now to these frugal repasts, although in the days of Gertrude he had never been asked to partake of anything at the table, but had once in a while "pieced" on something in the pantry.

Gertrude's distant great nieces and a nephew had attempted to break the will, but in the end, partly because the will had been drawn up so well, partly because Gertrude herself had written down dreadful criticisms of these far-away relatives, all of Gertrude's not inconsiderable fortune had passed to the bird-like, mustached Alda, whose eyes were never still. (Sonny had once remarked that he wondered if her eyes did not move all night rather than close motionless in sleep.)

Alda was a bit puzzled at Sonny's obvious signs of mourning over Gertrude's passing. He wore a large, almost purple armband immediately she was dead, while Alda made no change in her attire, for she had always preferred in any case black dresses and black hats.

Alda had planned to go to an island off the coast of Georgia shortly after the reading of the will, for the New England winters had come to be a trial to her, and wealthy as Gertrude was, she had insisted on their going on living together in the converted Maine farmhouse. But after Gertrude's death, Alda had had a serious fall and her dream of going to Georgia vanished. After her accident, Alda hobbled considerably, and her doctor had advised her to remain at home in Maine and rest, for she could hardly travel without assistance.

Of course Alda could have called in other people to aid her, but the fact that she had passed from being Gertrude's cook to Gertrude's heir had caused her to look on everybody with slightly different eyes. She distrusted Sonny, but she knew him. She was aware he had expected to be included in Gertrude's will, but he had never spoken of it, and, what is more, went on from time to time to shed tears when he thought of the sculptress's death. These tears were a source of wonder to Alda. She had never seen a grown man cry so much.

Though she was only in her thirties, Alda's fall reminded her that she too might need a lawyer, and improbable as it seemed for her, a woman who had been poor all her life, an heir. She had neither. Well, she could have Gertrude's lawyer, of course, Mr. Seavers, but she had never liked him. He had certainly never been kind to or considerate of her, and at the reading of the will in his spacious, blindingly bright law office he had pronounced the legal words in a kind of fury as if it were the warrant for her arrest.

"Do you understand everything in it?" he fairly thundered at her after he had read it all. "You are the only heir," he had added when she did not respond at once.

"She left Sonny McGuire nothing?" Alda had managed to say in the rather menacing silence as Seavers waited for her to say (obviously) something.

"I told you, Miss Bayliss, you were the only heir. It's a very well-written will," he smiled bitterly.

"I'm surprised," Alda had said. "I can't believe he is to have nothing." She looked though considerably satisfied on the whole and accepted a copy of the will from his broad hands which might have been more comfortable behind a tractor. "You are a very wealthy woman," the lawyer remarked before closing the door on her.

When Sonny did not come by for a week or so, Alda

fully realized her predicament. Though she could now walk with a cane, she felt considerable pain in her back and legs. But even had she not had the fall, she realized she would need to see somebody. She had not quite been aware during Gertrude's lifetime that she knew only her. Sonny had not counted then. He had been merely an errand boy. Now she had nobody to think of but him.

His grief over Gertrude's death seemed to have dried up. He never referred to her, and he acted more like a servant than ever under the changed circumstances. With Gertrude he had acted almost as an equal. Sonny was only about thirty-five years old at the time of her death. He looked even younger, perhaps because he spent most of the time in the open air, rode horses a good deal for exercise and did very little hard work of any kind. He lived down the road in a remodeled farmhouse which had been in his family for three generations.

"Would you like to take supper with me every evening?" Alda asked him one morning.

Sonny removed his stocking cap and thought over her statement. Alda fidgeted when there was no immediate response.

"I would prepare a genuine meal for you," she added, fearing perhaps that he thought she would serve only soup and corn muffins.

"If it would make your feet comfortable," Sonny finally said.

"The evenings are pretty long," she told him. He made no comment on this.

After a pause he asked, "Do you suppose I could have the little weather-vane she completed about a year ago? I am pretty fond of it and helped her to make it."

Alda stirred in her chair, and took hold of her cane and brought it in front of her dress. "The rooster?" she wondered. He nodded.

"I don't see any reason why not," she said uneasily. "In fact, I wonder she didn't leave it to you."

"Well, she didn't," Sonny said somewhat tartly.

"Then take it—it's upstairs in the storeroom." Alda gave out a long sigh.

Alda began to cook rather ambitious suppers then. She herself ate sparingly, and sometimes when her hip pained her she partook of almost nothing, while Sonny ate everything in sight, including, one supposed, her portion.

"Was the meal to your satisfaction?" she said one night when they had dined on venison, wild rabbit, scalloped potatoes, Indian pudding, and coffee with thick, farm-fresh cream. He had merely nodded.

"Do you think Gertrude would be surprised to see us mixing socially though?" Sonny inquired.

As there was no reply, Sonny turned around and looked at Alda. She was, he saw, considering the question.

"I don't think she looked down on you socially, Sonny, if that is what you mean," Alda responded. "But she thought of you as a boy. Almost a child."

"But they invite boys or children to supper," he said in a somewhat spiteful tone. Her face became even more impassive.

"I mean, you cook quite different grub for me than you did for her," he commented.

Alda grasped her cane as if she meant to rise, but she actually fell back further into her chair. "Gertrude was a picky eater," she observed. "It cost me a lot of worry and trouble to tempt her appetite. She liked dainty things mostly, and fattening ones too. Towards the end very little pleased her."

"I would enjoy having the same menu you prepared for her," Sonny spoke in a low toneless voice, yet it sounded like a command. "For instance, you would never have prepared venison and rabbit for her, would you?"

"Will Hawkins brought me the venison and the rabbit," Alda replied. "I wasn't of a mind to let it go to waste."

"Would you have prepared it for her, though?" Sonny inquired.

Alda fidgeted. "I would have made her some broth out of it, I guess," she conceded.

"I would be quite satisfied if you prepared the same menus for me as you did for her." He spoke neutrally now, and smiled a little. Her face looked discomposed at the sight of his smile. "Otherwise, I could just drop in on you once every week or every two weeks."

Alda now leaned forward with the cane. Her face had gone white, then flamed into a kind of hectic flush.

"Just tell me what you'd like to eat, Sonny. Then we'd both know where we're at."

"No, no." He raised his voice. "I ain't the cook. You are. And you cooked good for her all these years. I want the same grub you prepared for her. I can eat venison and rabbit with the hunters, but if I come here I want the quality grub or I don't come back."

She looked at his chapped, heavy hands. One of the thumbs was bandaged. As she stared at his hands he put on his mittens.

"I just never thought a man would care for her type of food." Alda spoke slowly, cautiously, and she stammered on: "I have been cooking you meals I thought a man would like."

"Well, go back then, why don't you, to the quality menu."

"I will, Sonny," she said in a sort of prayerful voice, "I'll oblige you," she added, and smiled weakly. He said good night then and went out.

Waiting until he was well out of earshot, Alda picked her cane up and beat it against the heavy timber of the floors. She beat several times, and then she broke into a fit of weeping.

Alda was cooking supper the next evening when she heard the scissors-grinder's bell outside. She hurried to open the door at once, for he had not come by for some months and all her kitchen knives, not to speak of the axe and hatchet, wanted sharpening.

Flinders, the grinder, was a tanned, wiry fellow of about forty, with lank yellow hair which fell from under his slouch hat, and he had already moved down the road with his wagon and horse when he heard Alda's imperious command.

He stopped the horse and walked back to the fence on which Alda leaned, having forgotten her cane. "You must have missed us last time," she was querulous.

He followed her on back to the kitchen, carrying his whetstone with him.

"You remember where I keep all the sharp-edged instruments," Alda said, and returned to her cooking.

"Where's the fat lady who was here before?" the grinder inquired after he had begun to sharpen her butcher knife on his grindstone.

"Gertrude, you mean," Alda said in a matter-of-fact tone.

"Yes, I guess that was her name." Flinders took up the

axe now and looked at it. "Why don't you take decent care of your tools?" he wondered. "You should always wipe these sharp-edged instruments after use; I'd put a little oil on them when you put them away—I told her that."

Alda said nothing. She was making dumplings.

"Well, where is Gertrude?" he inquired testing the edge of the axe.

"Gertrude passed away a few months ago," Alda informed him.

"Was it sudden?" he wondered, taking up the hatchet now and shaking his head over its wretched condition.

"Yes, it was fairly sudden," Alda replied.

He had finished sharpening all the tools and stood waiting to be paid.

"I've forgotten how much you charge," Alda told him, for Gertrude always took care of things like this.

He named a figure, and Alda hobbled over to a little china closet, opened one of its lower drawers and took out her purse.

"I'd appreciate it if you came more often," she had begun telling Flinders when the door opened and Sonny came in. The two men glanced at one another but did not speak.

"Why didn't you let me know your knives needed sharpening?" Sonny said when the scissors-grinder had gone, and he was tucking his napkin under his chin. "I could do that just as well."

"As long as he showed up, I figured he ought to do it."

"Remember I can do it just as good from now on—if not better," Sonny warned her.

" Look here," Alda said, dishing him out some veal stew and dumplings, "I don't like that tone of command in your voice." Her hands trembled as she gave him a portion of lima beans. "I'll do just what I think is right."

"Then do it alone!" He loosened his napkin and threw it down.

"Now, now, no need to get riled, Sonny," Alda spoke quietly. She went over into a far corner of the room and sat down in a cushiony chair whose bottom was beginning to fall apart.

"Ain't you going to eat nothing?" he inquired, staring at his plate.

"Put your napkin back around your neck, and eat, Sonny—I'm not hungry."

"Let me see how he done those knives." He walked into the little back room where all the tools were kept. He lifted up each of them, the axe, hatchet, butcher knives, and so on.

"Well, what is your verdict?" Alda inquired sourly when he did come on back into the room and sat down but with his chair pushed considerably away from the table.

"I can do everything for you," he told her. "We don't need no scissors-grinder."

"Good. Glad to hear you say so," she humored him. "Now eat your veal stew and dumplings."

"I don't like to eat alone," he told her. "Why don't you ever eat with me?" he cried.

"Very well, if it will make you have a better appetite. I will have some."

She laid a plate, knife, fork, and napkin quickly at her old place and sat down with difficulty. He helped her to stew and dumplings. "Ah, ah, that's too much," she protested over the amount of the serving.

"You eat it and shut up," he spoke in surly indifference.

"It is good," she admitted, chewing.

"How do I know you ain't poisonin' me when you don't eat from the same pot," he said at last. "From now on you eat what I eat," he told her, eyes flashing under his hair which had fallen down low. He pushed upward the black forelock.

"What's the matter with you?" Sonny almost shouted one evening after they had had supper together, and as usual Alda had only picked at her food. "I know you didn't care for her that much."

"I'd rather not talk about her," she sighed. "It's too painful. Too painful."

"It's painful also to deal with a silent woman like you. You make me tired."

He set his coffee cup down on the table with a bang.

"Go ahead and break the cup, why don't you," Alda told him.

"Do you feel guilty she left you so much money?" Sonny said in a more conciliatory voice after they had sat there glaring at one another in short little spiteful glances.

"The bequest does bother me, Sonny," Alda said.

"How?" he wondered.

"I came here from a farm, you know. Had no mother and father of my own. The Baylisses who brought me up was glad to be rid of me. Gertrude had come there one day looking for a hired girl, she said. She saw me and wanted me right away. What did I have to lose? She taught me everything I know about cooking, though I read cookbooks too, of course. I occasionally consulted Mrs. Bayliss. But mostly I taught myself. Gertrude was pleased with my cooking, and in a way with my company, though we never talked much."

"Why do you feel guilty?" Sonny wondered now.

"Did I say I did'?" Alda wondered. The color had come back to her face, and she looked more youthful. "I am puzzled."

"Why?"

"I don't know what to do with so much money. And another thing . . ." She hesitated a long time until his snort of impatience made her bring out: "I feel like there is nothing left for me to do! I feel my life is over."

"With all that money, over?" he shook his head.

"There's nobody needs me," she almost whined. "I worked for her twelve hours a day. Now what is there to do?"

"Mind?" he asked her, and took out his pipe.

"Smoke away, Sonny," Alda consented.

One evening when she had shown even poorer appetite than usual, he had all at once thrown down his napkin and said, "How do I know you did not poison Gertrude?"

Alda was so astonished she could say nothing. She remained dumbfounded for some time, and then she began to laugh hysterically. From laughing she soon turned to tears and wept loudly and had to use several handkerchiefs.

He sat gloomily watching her, cold and unyielding.

"I won't go to the police if that's why you're bawling," he said after a bit. He drank a little of the coffee, then spat it out in the saucer.

"That was the last thing in my mind. The very last," she said.

"Oh, I don't think you killed her," he said. Then he got up and reached for his overcoat, hat, and gloves.

"You cannot just up and leave after you have said such a

terrible thing," she told him. "Do you realize what you have done to me?"

"You didn't kill her?" he joked, tying his scarf tightly around his neck.

"No, no—I loved Gertrude," she cried, for she failed to note he was not serious. "We were real friends, life-long companions. Don't you see how miserably lonesome I am without her? And that you would even think such a thing, let alone say it. God in heaven! You are an evil, wicked man. Who put such ideas into your head? And why would I want to poison you? You are the only one I can depend on." She sat down in Gertrude's chair and began to weep even harder.

After a while he took off his scarf and unbuttoned his greatcoat and sat down at the table.

"If you put just a little poison in her food at the beginning she would gradually die from it all," he pointed out.

Alda cried harder. "I never expected to be her heir, and I don't really want all that money now," Alda said. "I never knew how to spend money. She handled all the business affairs. To think you would think such a thing of me—"oh, merciful Christ!"

"Yes, merciful Christ."

Mr. Seavers came out of his office when his secretary told him Alda Bayliss was waiting to see him. He looked at her coat and shoes in a critical fashion before he said good morning and then invited her into his office.

"I am very busy this morning, Miss Bayliss," he informed her, and he looked at the face of his pocket watch which he already had in the palm of his hand.

"It's very important," Alda began. "I have been accused of poisoning Gertrude," she brought out.

"By whom?" he said with glacial indifference, as if she had said she had been accused of having forgotten to stamp an envelope she had put in the mail.

"Sonny McGuire," she replied.

He snorted by way of reply.

"What am I to do, Mr. Seavers? If he should go around telling such a thing. . . ."

Mr. Seavers put his watch in his vest pocket and shook his head. "What did you tell him when he accused you?" he wondered.

"I denied it again and again."

"I will speak to him about it," he said. He looked at her very carefully then. "He could find himself in serious trouble spreading such a story," he went on, but with no indication he felt she was to be defended from such a charge.

As soon as Alda had left, he picked up the phone and asked his secretary to call Sonny McGuire and tell him to get over to his office as fast as his legs could carry him.

Every Saturday, much against her will, and only because Gertrude had insisted she do so, Alda would take her weekly bath. She invariably caught a chill after bathing, and felt miserable until Sunday afternoon.

She heard the front door open and then familiar footsteps. Sonny opened the door and stared down at her in the tub. She crossed her hands over her breast and mumbled something.

"Why did you have to tattle on me?" he wondered. He took off his greatcoat and sat down on the edge of the tub. He barely looked at her so that perhaps he was not aware of the consternation and confusion he was causing Alda.

Perhaps he hardly heard her cries of shame and alarm and suppressed rage.

"Of course I did not mean what I said. I was only angry. I knew you didn't want to poison Gertrude. And I know you do not care for money. I know all that. Alda," he cried, "look at me—Alda, look at me!" he touched one of her arms held over her breast.

She suddenly went into convulsions and writhed, and a kind of hoarfrost came over her mouth. He threw a huge bath towel over her, picked her up as if she were a doll and carried her into her room. He rubbed her thoroughly with the towel and then laid her down on the bed. "Where's your nightgown?" he wondered, then found it hanging in her closet. He put her in her nightgown and pulled back the sheets and put her between them. Her teeth chattered loudly.

"So I am sorry I accused you."

Alda said nothing. She had in fact become somewhat delirious and moaned a great deal. Occasionally she would look at him as much as to say, "Who are you?" or "Whose house am I in?"

All at once Sonny rose and hurried into the next room. A few moments later she heard the front door close.

Alda changed so markedly after he had looked at her in the bathtub that there were times, especially when he had been drinking, that Sonny wondered if some other woman had not slipped into the house and taken her place.

She no longer used her cane, and could walk without stiffness or discomfort. She spent all her time in the kitchen preparing him his "quality" evening meal.

And when they dined in the evening she did everything

possible to show her appetite had improved, and she was tasting every dish and morsel that he tasted. "If there is anybody who is being poisoned here," she seemed to say, "I am the first to be poison's victim."

One day when she felt strong enough, when her grief from Gertrude's death appeared to have dissipated, she dressed in her best tailored outfit, put on a large, almost-never-worn floppy hat, and went directly to lawyer Seaver's office.

His secretary, after having apprised the lawyer of who was waiting, had come out and said he could not see her. She walked past the secretary, opened the door and went directly up to the old man's desk; he, being partially deaf, was unaware for a moment she had entered.

"I want the will changed," Alda said.

"What on earth are you talking about?" he shouted at her.

"Will you lower your voice, Mr. Seavers?" She spoke as she thought Gertrude might have spoken, except of course Mr. Seavers would never have dared roar at her.

"No one can change the will of a deceased person," he cried "Have you lost what little wits you ever had?"

"I am aware that Gertrude cannot come back and change her will, Mr. Seavers. But I can certainly give away all she has left me. Except the house which I already owned with her and which was mine on her death."

Mr. Seavers put down his pencil and squared his shoulders. He took off his glasses, looked through them and put them back on, and went on scrutinizing Gertrude's cook.

"I want to give all the money to my church," Alda said in a magisterial voice. "And I don't want any discussion.

I've thought about it for weeks, and my mind is made up. So much money makes me very unhappy, Mr. Seavers. I won't have it."

He shook his head gravely.

"What is your church?" he inquired at length in a voice which if not kindly was civil.

"The Disciples of Christ, sir."

"But are you certain, Alda!"

"I am certain, or I would not be here. Now are you going to take care of it, or shall I go to another lawyer? Give me your decision."

Mr. Seavers rose then and cleared his throat. "You have changed, Alda. You have changed. I have known you since you were a mere girl. Yes, you have changed."

"It don't matter whether I have changed or not, Mr. Seavers. I hate that money. I will not be a rich woman. I can't stand it. I can't stand being wealthy and have people envy me. I want to be the way I was, and I will be it."

"Very well, if that is your positive last word. But why go to another lawyer? To someone who doesn't know you and never knew Gertrude. Besides, you'd have to go miles to find another. Old man McCready died last week, and he was the only other man practicing law here."

"Then you'll draw up the proper papers, Mr. Seavers?"

"You can count on it, Alda, of course you can."

She stood before him with composed features and almost a haughty angle to her chin. Her gray eyes were for the first time in his memory calm and unafraid.

Everyone in that small community soon learned of Alda Bayliss having given away her fortune to the Disciples of

Christ. Sonny was of course included among the number who learned of the event.

Alda had told him nothing, had not even hinted at such a decision, such a rash and precipitous turnaround.

"She don't even go to that church too often, and Gertrude used to have to scold her about her lax attendance," Sonny told himself.

He went to Alda's house early on the evening of the news, around five o'clock to be exact, and knocked rather than ringing Gertrude's old silver-throated chimes.

"Come in," said a composed and firm voice.

Sonny took off his hat and stood for a moment on the threshold.

"Close the door, if you please, and don't let in any more draught than already comes through the cracks and crannies of this old house."

"I don't imagine you will want me to come to supper anymore," he began, still standing.

"Why don't you sit down if you are going to say something," Alda spoke in her new, though comfortable tone of authority.

"Will you?" he inquired, sitting down as if the seat of his pants might touch something very hot or very cold.

"Supper always bored me," Alda said. "Cooking for her day after day, you know. Especially with me such a light eater."

"You'll go back to the dainty fare then?"

"I may skip supper altogether," she said. "Now I am free."

"Would you mind explaining that to me, Alda?" Sonny said. "I don't speak sarcastically. I just don't understand."

"The money she left me maybe wasn't enough after all," Alda spoke into her folded hands.

"Would you mind raising your voice?" Sonny said almost penitently.

"I said no bequest could be big enough to repay me for all those suppers I cooked for her. If I accepted the money, I would go on forever being her cook right over her grave. No, I am through with being a cook, through with being Gertrude's heir. I am going to Georgia."

"I'm sorry I walked in on you in the bathroom the other day," he said.

"Well, maybe that was what made me give up the bequest, I sometimes think. As long as I was her heir, as long as I lived under her bounty, people could do that to me. Walk in on me in my bath and have me cook their supper. No, thank you. No thank you, Gertrude."

Sonny stared at her dumbly. She saw the look of both wonder and admiration on his face and flushed under his scrutiny.

"I am happy, if not at ease, for the first time in my life. Not happy maybe, but relieved. That's as near happiness or freedom as I can get. I'm not Gertrude's cook any more. I'm not nobody's. And I will live on dainty fare from now on."

"Soups and salads?" he whispered.

"And an occasional sandwich . . . I'm through with victuals. Let the church worry about her money."

"Would you care for me to come by and do your odd jobs ever, though?" He had risen and was holding his hat by its stained frayed brim.

She picked up a shiny glossy travel folder.

She opened its many pages and maps.

"I'll tell you," she began. "I've been thinking of selling this place and going to one of these islands off the coast of Georgia."

He nodded.

"They say you can live on next to nothing, and the winters ain't fierce like here. . . . This house always reminds me too much of cooking," she added.

"I have to hand it to you," Sonny began again, but she stood up all at once. There was no trace in her movements of her recent stiffness.

About a month later, towards nightfall, Sonny was eating a warmed-over portion of hunter's stew composed of wild rabbit and squirrel and some not-too-choice pieces of venison, when he heard the tinkle of the doorbell. He started up because nobody had rung that doorbell in a number of years. His friends, and the hunters, walked right in.

"It's you!" he said staring at Alda through the glass partition of the door. "It's you," he repeated.

He did not think to undo the latch and let her in for some seconds. Her appearance was drastically changed, her hair had been cut or shampooed or something, at any rate it looked totally different, and she looked almost younger, certainly thinner, but her face was more wrinkled and drawn. Still, she looked better and more like a woman than he had ever seen her.

" 'There was nobody to go to," she began after he had motioned for her to be seated on the settee.

He went on eating his stew.

"Do you want some of my supper?" he inquired when she offered to say no more about the reason for her presence here tonight. "It's not your kind of grub," he cautioned her.

"I might take just about a half of what you have on your plate."

He walked out to the kitchen, took a plate off the pantry shelf and served her some hunter's stew.

He was surprised all over again to see her eat it, almost greedily. "They have turned down my gift," she told him.

"Who?" he wondered. Then without waiting for her to reply he said, "I thought you had gone to Georgia to live. You said . . ."

"I didn't like it there. But that's not why I'm back."

He looked down at his empty plate.

"Well," he said gruffly, turning his attention to her.

"They turned down my bequest. The Disciples of Christ," she announced.

He stared at her with that rather imbecilic expression on his face that had always annoyed both Gertrude and her.

"You remember I was going to give them . . ."

"Yeah, yeah, Gertrude's money," he finished for her biliously.

"Well, the preacher and the congregation all voted not to accept it. They felt it would not be appropriate considering the source."

"Considering the source!" He was nearly thunderstruck. He rose with his plate and took it out to the kitchen sink and deposited it there. "What source?" he said coming back into the room.

"Perhaps Gertrude, perhaps me. She was an unbeliever, you know. And they never liked her kind of sculpture, either. They also pointed out I seldom came to church and never worked with the other church members on committees or church business. They have turned down my gift!"

"So you're rich all over again," he said. He had lit his pipe and was engulfing his face and chest in thick smoke.

"Turning down good money like that," he mused.

She began to weep very hard.

"What was wrong with Georgia?" he asked after a while.

"I don't know," she said. "Probably nothing. I am too old to go to a new place but I would have stayed if the Disciples of Christ had kept my money. That was the last straw, their turning down my gift. I feel now like the money is mine."

He rose and went to the window and looked out. "That's some rainstorm coming down," he noted. "You got here just in time." He turned around and stared at her. "Like you planned it that way, didn't you?" He laughed rather hysterically then.

"I just had to talk to somebody. I had my phone shut off when I went to Georgia so I couldn't call you."

"Well, anyhow, Alda," Sonny began shyly now, "let me say, welcome home. It was lonesomer than usual with you in Georgia, let me tell you." He started to move closer to his guest, then stopped abruptly. "I wonder, Alda," he almost stuttered now, "do you think you could join me in a libation in honor of your homecoming?"

"And why ever not, Sonny, for goodness gracious sakes?"

"Well, Gertrude once drew me aside and told me to remember you was brought up never to taste, or allow others in your presence to taste, strong drink."

"Gertrude told you that, did she?" Alda mused, scowling deeply. "Well, look here now, Sonny. That maybe was then, understand, but today is a brand-new day so far as I'm concerned."

Sonny hurried to a little cabinet and pulled out a tall bottle of French brandy and in a trice took up two glasses and poured each of them one-third full of the deep amber drink. Handing her a glass, Sonny said almost in a whisper, "To long life and happiness . . . and let them church folks go . . . you know where."

"Oh, go ahead and swear, Sonny, see if I care." Alda grinned broadly and took a long taste of the brandy. "To your own good health and long life, Sonny, dear friend."

They both smiled comfortably at one another and went on tasting their drinks, and then in the silence that followed they listened with undivided attention to the fury of the storm outside and its pelting the windows in a barrage of sleet and icy rain.

Entre Dos Luces

I write this letter to all my friends in the states to let them know the whole truth about what really happened.

I have been told on reliable report that there is a warrant out in New York for the arrest of myself and my close friend Rico Alonso. You will remember we lived in the same string of rooms together on East Fourth Street, Manhattan, and our landlord was Felipe Parral.

We are innocent of murdering Felipe and of all the charges except burglarizing a pet shop. We did burglar it, but we did not kill Felipe. He was found with his throat cut days after we have run off from him on account of we feared he would kill us. The basis of our fear was that he had gone crazy over the death of his birds, and then the fact that when we replaced the dead birds with the new ones, he thought they had come back from the dead. He has many superstitious fears, or rather he had many. Even though we told him the new birds was stolen and brought to him by us, he would not believe us. He thought they had come back from the other world because of his many sins.

And now since Felipe is dead and gone himself, I will tell you that he once told Rico he had murdered several men in New York. Whether he told the truth or not, Rico don't have no way of knowing of course, but Felipe swore to him he had killed them. That is why the birds coming back as he thought from hell scared him so. He had many enemies.

To explain our situation, let me go back then to how it all happened.

In exchange for a tiny room I had on the top of his building I was to keep his apartment clean, and water and feed the birds (he was so crazy about his birds) and keep their cages clean, but never to let them out. It was a hard task to clean the cages and not let them out, but I was successful until the unlucky day I am now going to tell you about.

His pet birds were not pets. They were more like wild animals, and I don't think they were like any birds people in cities are familiar with. Again, they were like small mammals with a hateful even vicious streak. I was taking care of them while he was in Havana. Felipe why he kept such large birds in such a small space eludes me also.

Felipe eludes everybody, in any case. The room smelled bad no matter how many times one cleaned their cages and aired the room even on bitter December nights in Manhattan. A bad bad odor, what a fellow I knew called fetor.

The trouble began in earnest when Rico who rented the side room from Felipe left his transom open. The birds while I was cleaning the cage as if they seen their chance all rushed up and out through the transom. I called to them to come back as if they were human.

I heard weak but prolonged hoarse cries coming from Rico's room. The door was always locked, and I had been told never to bother the tenant who was said to be recovering from a severe attack of something contagious.

I stood before this firmly locked door and asked if I could come in. For answer only the hoarse cries like someone suffocating to death. I tried the door, it was solidly locked, bolted.

As the cries continued, there was nothing to do but follow the birds and climb through the transom also. I pulled myself through the transom with some difficulty although I weigh only around 140 pounds at that time.

When I picked myself up from the floor in Rico's room, I was a good deal shaken by what I saw. All the birds, they were by the way some kind of crow or ravens, but of a kind Felipe told me not native to the United States, were, it seemed, holding Rico down and pulling on his skin like it was a worm.

He had nothing on at all but he was holding his rosary in his right hand. It was the rosary I later learned which had attracted the birds, but the Rico man thinking they meant to attack him, had struck out at the birds with the rosary, which either alarmed or frightened them, so that they began to pick and claw at him, and as he struck them again they attacked him finally in earnest.

I picked up a broom, and as the birds then turned their anger against me, before I knew it I had killed both of them by striking hard against their heads.

I gazed at them as they lay with their wings spread, their eyes open, their beaks streaming with blood. A little moan came from my mouth. Then I turned my attention to Rico. I was frightened to see that the two birds had badly torn his flesh, and he was crying and near hysteria.

"Let me put something on your cuts, Rico."

"Cuts," he said, "do you call them heridas just cuts."

"Well, whatever." I went to the sink and got a small

basin and filled it with warm soap and water, and fetched a cloth from a drawer. I bathed his wounds.

"They have attacked me before," he said, looking down at himself. "Whenever I paid the rent and they were loose they would get at me."

"Let go of your beads," I advised him, "for your hand is badly wounded."

I begun cleaning out the different bleeding wounds on his hand. "Now let me put some disinfectant of some kind on them," I said. I found a bottle of the stuff and put them on all his wounds.

How can anyone describe our landlord Felipe's anger when he returned and found his pets dead.

We knew he had a vile disposition, but we had not seen anyone gnash his teeth the way he did. The electricity of anger went up into his coal black hair, and each hair raised, as if it was seated in its own electric chair. Froth soon formed on his lips, and his heavily muscled arms trembled like an old man who has suffered multiple strokes.

He could not speak for many minutes, so strong was his wrath.

"What's your excuse," he finally turned to Federico, whom everybody calls Rico, but today he said, "Federico!" Like it was some big curse word he had found written on a wall.

"I was asleep," Rico began, "for I had worked all night."

"That's your story," our landlord said. "Cuentos!" he said in shame "Cuentos!"

"Cuentos!" Rico shouted, "Shit, I worked all night and was dead beat lyin' here with a sore foot I got caught in the subway train the other night."

"I want your alibi, Rico," he said rolling his eyes. "And I want to hear it good."

"I am tellin' you what happened and that ain't an alibi or nothing else, I am giving you the facts of what occurred, so don't foam at the mouth at me like a mad dog, or I'll pack and go."

"You don't leave owin' me five months back rent."

Now Rico rolled his eyes.

"All right, what's your excuse," Felipe turned to me, leaving Rico thinking about all his back rent, I guess.

"I don't have none, boss."

"Skip that boss shit."

"I was lax."

"You was born lax, and all your ancestors was born lax back to Eve and Adam. So what else is recent?"

"I said I was careless and didn't notice the transom was open."

"What did I tell you about leavin' the cages open."

"I have seen you leave them cage doors open yourself."

"Yeah but me leavin' 'em open, since I'm in my right mind, and you leavin' them open is two different stories, chulo."

"All right, they're your birds and your birds' cage doors. I stand corrected."

"You bet your ass you are corrected. Do you know how much them birds was worth?"

"I suppose ten or twenty dollars not countin' their beaks and claws."

"You should be on the stage," he said coming up close to me. "Look," he said, to me, "I'll tell you what them birds is worth, or was worth. Five thousand a piece on account of they talk, do dances, and wink at you like clowns."

"I don't have that much money to give you for their death," I told him.

"You bet your black dirty soul, you don't. All right. All right. You killed the best friends I ever had." Turning to Rico, he said, "how many times have I told you to keep that Goddamn transom closed."

"I got to breathe, man. I got to have air."

"There's too much air in there, you claimed last winter, from ten thousand cracks in the wall. Now it's barely June, and you say there ain't air. I tell you, fellows, I am a ruined man. I'm through."

That night Rico and I burglared the pet shop. It was easy, because the owner must have forgot to lock his back door. We just walked in, took the covers off the cages and chose two ravens, I think they was. We wrapped them in a blanket and carried them against us, leavin' the cages behind, and went to Felipe's room.

He was so drunk he didn't hear us come in, didn't hear us put the new birds in the cage.

That night I slept in Rico's room.

There was a knock on our door as we was eating breakfast. It was him, Felipe. We both saw he had maybe lost his mind.

"They're back," he cried. I saw clearly now he had as I say lost his mind. "They're back," he kept sayin', "they're back. They've returned from the dead."

"No, no, Felipe, we replaced them for you."

"Don't lie, hijo de puta, don't lie. The birds come back from the dead. I buried them so good too in a fashionable cemetery in Brooklyn."

He began eating one of our breakfast rolls, famished like, and drank half of the coffee in my cup.

"They went to hell," he went on, "and then they told them down there I missed them so much they could return and take me back down below to be with them again." He began bawling.

Rico and I looked at one another. We're sorry we had burgled the shop and brought him this new trouble, that is by bringing back the dead birds to life we saw we had driven him over the edge. Felipe was crazy.

But as the days passed, he calmed down a bit. Both ravens spoke Spanish whereas the dead birds only said things like, "Sailors sail the seven seas," or "Put on the tea kettle, dear." But Felipe paid no mind.

One night late while Felipe was drunk, Rico and I packed our valises, and went to the Greyhound station. We thought for quite a while where to go. Then we bought tickets one way for Tulsa, Oklahoma. We felt he would never follow us there. We got stuck for a while in Laredo, then finally crossed the border and headed towards Parras de la Fuente.

But believe me Felipe's death cannot be laid at our door. Though we did wrong by robbing the pet shop we did not kill Felipe. He was found lying in a pool of blood and there was no trace of the birds. He must have somehow made the whole thing come down on himself. It was his way to always carry on and never let a thing rest. "He was crazier than the devil on Christmas," as Rico always says.

Isidro Crespo
Mexico

Geraldine

S ue and her mother Belle no longer met in person,
but Sue called her mother daily, in fact some times
she called her two or three times in a day. The
subject was always her worries over her thirteen year-old
son Elmo.

"Now what has he done this time," Belle would sigh or
more often yawn.

They had never been close, mother and daughter, and as
if to emphasize their lack of rapport through the years,
Belle had from his birth taken an almost inordinate delight
and interest in her grandson Elmo. She gave him lavish
birthday, Christmas and Easter gifts and of late had begun
taking him to the opera. Belle could not tell whether he
enjoyed the opera or not, but he paid it a strict, almost
hypnotic attention and applauded the singers with frenzy.
Then they would go off to some midnight cafe and have a
dinner of quail or venison.

Belle had heard of course about Geraldine. In fact
Geraldine herself came to be very real to the grandmother.
The girl, Elmo's girl in Sue's phrase, had the persistent
presence of a character in great fiction, though Belle had
never met her. At night, under the covers of her bed, Belle
would often whisper "Geraldine" and smile.

"They are idiotically in love, and she is at least two years
older than Elmo," Sue would report on the telephone.

"They are together constantly, constantly. And their kissing! Oh, Belle, Belle." Sue had ceased calling her mother mother for at least ten years. Although the grandmother pretended to like this familiarity, it piqued her nonetheless. But then she had never ever been close enough to Sue even to correct her.

"*Don't put your foot down,*" was almost the only advice Belle ever gave her daughter. "*Let what will be be.* Let him love Geraldine."

Geraldine and Elmo came to an evening Sunday supper one day in December when there was a light spitting snow outside. Belle was not prepared for Geraldine's extreme good looks and beautiful clothes. She felt she had opened the door on a painting from some little known Italian hand. Geraldine's eyelashes alone brought a flush to the grandmother's face and lips. The girl's hands free of rings and her arms without bracelets looked like they were made out of some wonderful cream. And then Belle looked round and saw her grandson, not as he had always been on his previous visits but now as a young man with the first show of a beard on his upper lip.

"At last, at last," Belle cried and held both of the young people in succession to her. Tonight she only kissed Geraldine however.

They began going to the opera as a threesome. They attended all of Donizetti's operas that season, and after the opera they went to Belle's special cafe and spent hours there laughing as though they were all of the same age.

The crisis came when Sue called Belle at six o'clock in the morning.

"He has had his right ear pierced!"

At first the grandmother thought this referred to an accident of some kind. Only when she was given the explanation that the boy had gone to a professional ear piercer, did she recover from her fright. She broke into laughter at that moment which drove Sue into a fit of weeping, weeping propelled by rage and the revival of the feeling her mother had never loved her.

"No, no, my dear, you must not feel it is a disgrace," Belle advised Sue. "It is the fashion for young boys."

"Fashion, my foot," Sue screamed over the wires. It is Geraldine!" Then Belle as if in spite began even at that early hour to praise the beauty of Geraldine.

A torrent of abuse then followed on the other end of the wire. Sue told of the girl's excesses.

"They do not show, my dear," Belle disagreed. She is unspotted, unsoiled in every lineament of face and body.

Belle waited with a queer smile on her face while her daughter wept and told of all the shortcomings of Geraldine.

Sue kept a kind of "black book" of Belle's "crimes" against her. She considered in the first place that Belle had usurped her place in Elmo's affections. She had taken Elmo away from her as surely as if she kidnapped him, Sue wrote in her black book. She listed other of Belle's crimes as 1) making Elmo fond of imported sweetmeats, such as chestnuts covered with whipped cream, 2) reading him stories beyond his age group, stories which had questionable morality or contained improper innuendoes, 3) late hours, 4) breakfast in bed after a night of attending the opera, 5) imported hairdressing creams which made Elmo smell more like a fast woman than a young boy, and so on and so on. Then Sue would burst into tears. "Belle never loved me," Sue would whisper to the covers of the black book. Never never so much as one hour did she squander on me the affection she showers on Elmo or that bitch Geraldine.

Elmo once called his mother to her face a boo-hooer. That epithet rankled in her heart for a long time. It drove her, as if imitating her mother's largesse, to go to the most expensive women's shop in Manhattan and purchase for herself imported hand-sewn handkerchiefs. Into these she wept openly and with uncontrolled wetness. I will boo-hoo both of them, she cried. She even thought of taking legal action against her mother. In fact she called a noted lawyer who dealt in unusual family problems. He discouraged her coldly, even warned her to proceed no further. Then he sent her a bill for $1000.00.

"I hate Belle," Sue would often say as she looked out into the garden of her townhouse. "She will outlive all of us, including Geraldine."

"Your mother says I act like your fairy godmother," Belle said one late afternoon just before she and Elmo were to go to the opera.

Elmo smiled his strange little smile and pressed Geraldine's hand.

"She doesn't mean it as a compliment," Belle told him. "Are you as happy with me, dear boy, as with Sue?" Belle inquired.

"Oh, a thousand times happier, Belle," Elmo replied. He too had fallen somehow naturally into calling her by her first name.

The old woman beamed. "I would keep you forever," she whispered. "And Geraldine too. Wouldn't we all be a threesome of happy ones," Belle cried. Elmo beamed and nodded, and Geraldine grinned.

"As happy as larks!" Belle almost shouted. She held Elmo in her arms and kissed him on his cowlick. Then she embraced Geraldine.

"You love Geraldine, don't you?" Belle whispered.

Elmo stiffened a little under her caresses, then in a smothered voice said, "A lot, Grandma, a lot."

Whether it was the coming of Geraldine or the desecration of Elmo's and Geraldine's earlobes by the ear-piercing practitioner, Belle was hurtled back in time—what other way could she describe it—to her own youth. She examined her own ear lobes and found that the tiny holes put there so long ago were still ready to bear the presence of her own many earrings. And how many earrings she had! Yes, Sue had criticized her on this score likewise. "You have enough earrings to bestow on a museum," Sue had spoken this judgment on Belle not too long ago. "And you never wear one pair of them."

"But I will, now I will," Belle said aloud today. In her older years she often spent whole afternoons and evenings talking to herself. "But what am I saying. They shall wear them also! Geraldine and Elmo. How I do love them, Lord!"

The next evening before the opera the three of them all laughing and giggling and even guffawing began putting on Belle's many earrings.

"Too bad, loves, only one of your ears is pierced," Belle cried, and she showed them herself in full panoply, wearing first a priceless jade set of earrings, then the ancient turquoise pair, after that the diamond, and then to the hush-hush of the young couple, her emerald pair.

"O, may I wear the emerald tonight?" Elmo cried.

"Why, Elmo," Geraldine whispered and kissed him wetly on his mouth and chin.

"Why ever not, dears, why ever not! And Geraldine must not be left out. By no means. Oh, God in Heaven," Belle cried, "how happy I am. I never would have dreamed two people could have brought me such happiness. Never, never." And she held them to her tightly. "And I don't care what Sue thinks, children," Belle cried.

All at once, as if from a cue somewhere, perhaps from the opera house itself at which they practically lived now, they began dancing all three of them as if in some queer minuet. With their new earrings sparkling they might indeed have been part of the ballet of some rarely performed opera.

"The only thing that makes sense is gaiety!" Belle cried, a bit out of breath. "If one were never gay, it would not be worth a candle. One must sparkle like our earrings, children! One must sparkle."

Sue's conversion came swiftly and without warning. She had got used to Elmo's always staying the night—and often the weekend—with his grandmother. In fact Sue began somehow to believe that Elmo now lived with Belle. True, it had always been Belle's wish of course that Elmo stay—really live with her. And since Elmo never went anywhere now without Geraldine, in Sue's troubled mind she assumed that like brother and sister both now resided with Sue's mother Belle.

Sue kept touching her earlobes. The piercing in both her ears which Belle in fact had supervised some twenty years earlier needed attention. The skin in the pierced holes was beginning to close. "I must have them tended to," Sue spoke to herself. Her tall Finnish butler served her course after course tonight, all of which she left untasted.

She had stared at Jan the same way at the beginning of every meal when he asked "Will Master Elmo be dining?" Sue would look only at his long blond sideburns and reply, "He is still at his grandmother's."

"I must have my earlobes pierced again. My earrings don't go in." She spoke aloud within the hearing of Jan.

But that evening came her realization. Unlike Belle, Sue did not hold a box at the opera. But she kept a seat very near the stage which cost more or nearly as much as Belle's royal box. Actually she retained two seats, but Elmo almost never attended the opera with her.

"For where would Geraldine sit, then?" She addressed this statement also to her Finnish servant.

He could hardly wait until he reached the safety of the kitchen to burst out laughing to the cook. Sue heard his laughter but construed it as coming from his asthmatic attacks. "He wheezes like an animal," she once remarked to Elmo. "If he weren't so tall and personable, I would ditch him."

She arrived late at the opera but tipped the usher to allow her to go in against regulations when the opera was in progress.

No sooner had she disturbed forty or fifty people gaining her seat than her eyes swept away from the stage to Belle in her box. "Ah, ah," she cried again disturbing the opera lovers. She had never seen anything so resplendent! There they were, Belle, Geraldine and Elmo, but with what a difference. Each wore earrings, each wore some kind of shining necklace attached to the beads of which was a resplendent kind of brooch. Sue wondered why every eye in the opera house was not watching Belle and her retinue.

Sue wept unashamedly. She never heard a note of the opera. But her weeping refreshed her more than a dive in a cool spring. The vision of her loved ones—for she now knew she too loved Geraldine almost as much as her own flesh and blood—that vision dissolved then and forever her jealousy and rancor. She suddenly accepted Belle, and with her acceptance of her mother she accepted her jurisdiction and sequestration of her son and her son's sweetheart Geraldine.

"Let them love one another," she cried, and falling back against the rich upholstery of her seat she went to sleep.

She was awakened by an usher shaking her. The opera had long been over, every seat but hers emptied. Looking up at Belle's box, she saw it too was deserted, extinct of resplendence.

She was helped out to the street by the usher who summoned her a cab. She gave him an ostentatiously grand tip and sped away in the cab.

"Tomorrow, I will have my earlobes re-pierced," she spoke loud enough for the cab driver to hear. He nodded gloomily.

I wanted to please her, yes, Sue reflected after it was all over, I saw I wanted only one thing, to be Belle's little girl.

The world-famous jeweler was not too surprised as he had

been Sue's jeweler for twenty years when he saw Sue enter his private consulting room in the jeweler's shop, a room reserved only for the phenomenally wealthy.

"My dear, you look tired." He helped her to a green French settee. "Shan't I get you something?"

Sue could only nod. He brought her out a dark liquid in a glass so thin it resembled mere paper but sparkled like diamonds. One would have thought he knew she was coming, had prepared for her visit days in advance.

"I saw the earrings in the window," Sue only moistened her lips with the brandy.

"I had hoped you'd come by and look at them," Mr. Henton-Coburn confided.

" I want to please Belle," she brought out. "My husband spoiled me so I wouldn't bother him. Every time he felt I was going to ask something of him I got a gift. They were mostly jewels as you know. He purchased however very few earrings. I will need all the earrings on display."

"But two are spoken for."

She put down her glass, and touched her lower lip.

"But if you insist of course."

"I said I wanted them. I mean I have to have them. I have to please Belle. . . .

"But, listen, dear friend," and she took a noisy swallow of the brandy. "I think" (she placed a finger on an earlobe) "they need piercing again. When I had my trouble, my sorrow with Belle, I all but quit wearing jewels."

"May I?" he inquired and bent over her left ear. Then her right ear.

"What is needed, dear lady, is," and he produced a kind of stiff thread. "I will pull this through with your say-so where the old piercing was, and you'll be perfect for the displays in the window. Oh, my dear, why haven't you been by." He bent down and kissed her.

Her decision to attend the opera then one snowy bitter night with the mercury near zero ushered in what resembled, as she later noted in her book of records, what resembled different ceremonies, a first communion, a wedding, perhaps even a funeral. But it was none of these. It was more—she blushed as she wrote it down—like going to paradise.

She had spent hours on her toilet. She had tried on at least fourteen pairs of earrings.

That night at the opera looking down with his opera glasses, Elmo caught sight of a woman who looked somehow familiar, yet the more he gazed at her the less sure he was it was anyone whom he knew. Yes! Looking again he saw that it was someone who resembled Sue, yet this Sue was wearing the most elegant and ornate earrings he had ever seen anybody wearing.

"Is that Sue?" he inquired of Geraldine.

Geraldine took the opera glasses and looked only a moment, then merely shrugged her shoulders. Elmo stared at Geraldine coldly, and Geraldine returned the stare with a frigid contemptuous expression in her eyes and on her lips.

Belle now took the opera glasses and looked down. But at that moment the house lights dimmed, and soon the overture to the third act began.

Geraldine and Elmo had quarreled. And Belle had become distant, as if her real center of affection now was Geraldine and not Elmo.

It was snowing harder when the three of them left the

opera house. Belle looked at Elmo inquiringly as he summoned for them a cab.

"I will not be coming with you, Grandma," Elmo spoke with devastating aplomb. Helping Belle into the cab, he almost pushed Geraldine in after her. Belle was too surprised to protest, or even say anything but "Good night then."

"I am going home," Elmo spoke aloud, his mouth opened wide and received the thick goosefeathery flakes of snow. "It was Sue, I know that with her ears pierced."

"Yes, so it was you."

Elmo had entered his mother's room on the top floor as he said this. He was so covered with snow, his eyebrows and the hair sticking out from his ski cap white as avalanches, even a few hairs in his nostrils white.

Sue had just in fact put on an even more resplendent pair of earrings as if she was waiting for him to see her so arrayed. When as a matter of fact she thought he would stay on indefinitely with Geraldine and Belle.

"Mother, good evening," he said. He sat down on the divan near her.

She was still too astounded to speak, and his calling her mother further stopped the speech in her throat.

"Take off your wet clothes and put them in the bathroom to dry."

"I can't get over it," he said obeying her and going into the bathroom, a room as large as many New York parlors.

He looked at himself in the mirror. To his astonishment—or was it astonishment really—anyhow he saw that his own earring had disappeared from his earlobe. He touched where it had been pierced.

Coming out of the bathroom, he gazed at Sue. She looked almost as young as Geraldine and yes, admit it, Elmo, he thought to himself, admit it, more lovely.

"Well, Mother," he said again.

"What has brought this about?" Sue wondered. "Shall I wake up Jan and have him prepare us something." Elmo shook his head.

"Geraldine is through with me," he began. He sniffled a bit, whether from the snow or his grief was not clear. "Finished, finito."

"Ah, well, that is what being young brings," Sue said.

"And Belle prefers her to me."

"Oh, Belle," Sue said. Then minding her speech she merely added. "Well, she's old."

"And fickle," he added. "The opera is her lifeblood."

"Certainly the costumes and the sets are. She's deaf as a nest of adders."

"Belle is deaf?"

"And nearly blind."

"How many earrings do you have?" he wondered.

"I'm afraid enough for everybody in the opera."

"Do you mind if I stay with you now, Mother?"

"Nothing you could suggest would make me more happy." Two huge tears descended from her eyes.

Elmo sat back astonished, some wet snow drops falling from his thick black hair. His eyelashes, too long for a boy's as Geraldine had pointed out, sparkled with wetness.

"And you won't send me away somewhere."

Sue shook her head and mumbled, "Never."

"May I kiss you then?" he wondered. He came over to where she sat limp and disheveled for all her jewels.

"Mother, I believe . . ."

"Don't say anymore."

But he finished his sentence. "I feel I'm home."

Bonnie

People begin always by asking me about my dove, but what they really want me to tell them about is Bonnie. I think they find it, if not amusing, a bit outside the ordinary run of story. They tell it to others and pass it around. I resent this, but people ask me to tell our story, and I oblige them. So I am to blame if people retell it and maybe laugh behind my back.

I have after all only one story, and it is Bonnie. At first maybe I was ashamed that this was so, but now I admit it, and I don't care anymore what people say or think or how much they laugh.

I married her when I was only eighteen. She was a bit older than me, everybody said. Actually I never thought about her having any age at all, she was so all-in-all to me. It was even more than love, though it was that too, all of it. And I guess I would have loved her if she had turned out to be twice my age, or maybe even not a human being at all.

Our troubles started in earnest (though we had trouble from the very first night together on our honeymoon) when Bonnie began putting on weight. At first I sort of liked it, you see. It didn't spoil her appearance, or her prettiness as far as I was concerned, and Bonnie was the prettiest girl in the world. All the old worn-out phrases described her to a T, "peaches and cream, snow and roses."

And her yellow hair everybody always called "spun gold," and so on. Her weight in fact didn't seem to show because of such precious good looks.

But in the end it was her strange hunger for sweets that caused the final breakup between us, not her getting fat. When, for example, we'd pass a bakery, we would have to stop and she would gaze through the glass at the spectacle of the cakes, pie, jelly rolls, cookies and tarts, till once I said more good-humored than angry, "Bonnie, you love sweets more than you do me!"

When it got so bad, and she had put on thirty extra pounds, I said one day as she stopped suddenly to look in a pastry shop, "Maybe, Bonnie, we should see a doctor."

"Maybe you should, Danny," and the way she said "Danny" went through me like a knife because it had the real sound of goodbye in it. I can't explain how one word, my name, as she pronounced it could tell me everything was at an end, but when I heard her say it, I knew.

I knew too she blamed me in her heart for her not having babies.

So it went on like this for some months. Whenever I would come home, whether unexpected or not, she would be sitting at the big dining room table eating something fattening, a piece of pie loaded with whipped cream or a slice of Sacher torte, caving in with chocolate.

"Bonnie," I said one time, seizing her hand with the fork in it so that I hurt her, "You don't want to put on any more pounds!"

"How do you know what I want or don't want," she retorted, tears in her eyes.

Finally I could hardly recognize her. She was getting on

to becoming "circus fat." I moved to the small room down the hall and left her to sleep by herself. I began missing supper in the evening, and there were days I didn't come home at all, but slept in my office in this big firm in the financial district. I didn't have another girl, which was what she thought. The truth is I was still in love with Bonnie, more so than ever in fact, but there was no Bonnie for me, you see. Just this fat woman growing toward "circus fat."

Then I moved out entirely. She didn't put up the least resistance. We weren't going to be divorced even, for how could I divorce a woman whom I no longer even recognized? The real Bonnie was gone. At work I sometimes daydreamed about her as if she had left on a round-the-world voyage.

After a year or so had passed like this the thought presented itself to me that at least a legal separation might be better for us both. I stopped by the old place and rang the bell furtively, almost shuddering to think how it would be. A young man, hardly more than a boy, answered the door. I faltered for a moment, then got out, "Bonnie here?"

He nodded, studying me cooly as if he recognized her description of me easily.

The long wait in the hall made me wonder if she had gotten so heavy maybe he was going to have to wheel her out.

Then I was aware of a presence, and I looked straight forward and saw her. I had to hold my right hand on the doorjamb to steady me. For there she was, Bonnie, but just the way she had looked when I had been eighteen and taken her to dances and drive-in movies. In fact she was a little thinner I believe than when I first began going with her.

"Gosh all get out," was all I could utter and finally, "Bonnie! Bonnie!"

But though she looked just like the old Bonnie I had gone with and had married, so slim and if anything prettier and even more luscious-looking, there was no real look of recognition in her face for me, no greeting, warmth, certainly no welcome home.

"I'm glad you stopped by, Dan," she began icily, while I just stood there, and why not admit it, worshipped her, and kept muttering her name again and again until she cut me short with: "We do want the divorce now after all.

"Since you've been out of a job, I've heard," she went on without letting me catch my breath, "we can pay for it ourselves, can't we, Earle?" She turned to the young man who had greeted me and who now stood directly beside her.

"Oh, I'm going to work again soon in the financial district," I said too unemphatically and soft for them perhaps to have heard.

"Just the same," she continued, "since you've missed so much work, we'd like to pay all the court costs."

"I don't want a divorce," I tried to put some body in my voice, but it came out about as substantial as a whisper. "I may not have any ground to stand on," I was continuing, "but Bonnie . . . Bonnie. . . ."

"I have a good lawyer," she was going right forward, and all the time like a simp I was uttering her name. I couldn't stop saying it, like a man with the hiccups.

Then I saw the stare she was giving me. The leave-taking came like winter sleet. I would hear from them, she said and she added that they had tried to contact me several times earlier.

"If I could only speak what is in my heart, Bonnie," I think I said or words to that effect between the space left by the door closing against me.

Then the divorce was granted without my contesting it or replying to the many legal communications which piled up on my desk. Two years passed, maybe more. I became deeply absorbed in my new work on Broad Street and Wall. For a man so at loose ends my rise was perhaps surprising and probably impressed all who knew me except myself.

I worked often fourteen hours a day, the outside world became thin and insubstantial and even when leaving the office I noticed very little around me. My whole life was work.

Yet in the late evening, when I would leave my office, I usually passed a woman on a park bench who held patiently on her outstretched hand a small, beautifully shaped bird which I was to learn later as if in a school lesson was no ordinary pet shop specimen.

Up until then I had never been interested in birds, but I looked at this bird attentively while barely glancing at the woman who held it. In truth I had quit looking close at anybody for some time after my matrimonial fiasco.

But once soon after the very cold days arrived, one day when I was about to pass the bird and its owner, I stopped, as if frozen in my tracks, gawked, stared, was unable to take my eyes off her. The woman holding the bird was Bonnie, but not a Bonnie I believe even her own mother would have recognized.

"What is it, Bonnie?" I began as if there had not been our separation and the distance of time. "Can I do anything?"

She was so thin one could see many little veins in her face and hands and the protuberance of bones. She had not an extra ounce of flesh on her.

"Where is Earle?" I said at a loss as to how to continue.

"Oh, Earle? Remarried." She spoke indifferently, almost sleepily.

"Can I come to see you, Bonnie?" I asked against my own better judgment.

"It wouldn't be a good idea," she replied after a careful silence.

"Remember," I began awkwardly, my voice almost unrecognizable to my own ears, "I'm . . . yours Bonnie, if you want me!" I blushed at those last improvident words.

She cut me down with a look.

Every day then for many weeks I would see her sitting on the same bench under a huge sycamore tree, the bird always with her, each day a different kind of tiny neckband on its throat. I dared not go near.

Then at the beginning of a break in the weather, when sitting out would have been more customary, I missed her. The next day also she was absent, and the day after that, and so on. Several weeks passed without her turning up.

One Saturday when I had to go to work to finish some pressing details of my job, I stopped short. There on the identical bench all alone was the white small bird. I looked frantically. I waited, I forgot about my job. I picked up the bird, and kept looking up and down the street. He was quite tame and made no effort to struggle out of my grasp. I walked over to an outdoor stand which sold bird seed, and bought some to feed him. He seemed in fact hungry and partook of all I could give him. I sat there half the day, waiting, never going near my office, certain she must return for the pet.

That evening I returned home with the bird. I had purchased him a small cage from a variety store around the corner from where I live.

Sunday I went back to work to finish the task I should have performed on Saturday. While looking over my ledger, William Weston, a well-known investigator, happened to drop past and asked me a few questions about some technicality in an area in which I am now becoming somewhat expert. After I had replied to his satisfaction, I hesitantly asked him if he knew of an investigator who could trace the whereabouts of a missing person.

William's face did not change expression and hesitating only a few moments he said he'd be more than pleased to take the assignment himself.

A year passed, and he had come up with nothing. I then hired, without telling him, another investigator. It was not cheap, let me tell you, hunting for Bonnie. At last, since not the most minuscule clue came to light, I gave up the search.

After the end of our hunting, I used to go and sit on the identical seat and hold her pet in my hand, as I am doing today. Nothing, however, came of that either, so far as attracting her to come back to me.

One day a gentleman carefully dressed and wearing only a single eyepiece stopped and asked me if he could examine the bird. He bent over me for what seemed an eternity.

"Would you sell him?" he finally inquired.

I declined frigidly.

"Your bird belongs to quite a rare species of dove," he informed me.

"It wouldn't surprise me it's rare," I mumbled. My present rudeness and lack of interest recalled to me Bonnie's treatment of me.

"Are you aware, sir, of its worth, then?" he persisted.

"I am aware of only one thing," I raised my voice now in the face of his insulting condescension. "This is a dove, as you call him, placed in safekeeping with me against the owner's return."

He stepped back on hearing this and studied me with a curious mixture of disbelief, puzzlement and slight contempt.

After he had gone I held the "dove" gently against my overcoat.

He has grown so comfortable with me of late that I have put away his cage in a back closet, leaving him to come and go as if he were in his own great outdoor home.

No Stranger To Luke

T he first Luke realized that people in town had heard someone was stealing from his mother's kitchen cabinet was when he was having a haircut.

Young Pete Snyder, the barber, holding the straight razor up high and about to shave his young customer's neck, pressed his mouth close to Luke's ear and confided: "I hear you have a thief at your house."

Luke gave a slight shudder not so much at the sight of the straight razor at so close an angle as Pete's pronouncing the word *thief*.

"You don't have any suspicion who it is?" Peter queried.

Luke shook his head, and Pete began moving the razor through the thick suds and around the back of Luke's neck. Finished shaving, Pete took off the voluminous cloth covering Luke and bowed as the boy handed him the fifty-cent piece.

"I hope you catch him, whoever he is," Pete remarked as he opened the door for Luke.

"I don't know how Peter Snyder got wind of it," Luke's mother remarked that night at supper.

She was what people in that small town call a grass widow, for Luke's dad had deserted the family some years ago. Mother was a good-looking woman, still in relative youth.

"Once you open your mouth in this town, Luke, some-body is sure to hear you, and that somebody talks," Mother went on.

Luke fingered the slight cut on the back of his neck caused by Pete's shaving him, and then he winked just then at his younger brother, Vance, who sat always next to him at meals, for both boys were amused at their mother's gift of gab.

"But, boys," she went on, "I have been worried all the same about losing money from the kitchen cabinet drawer. You know I keep all my change for the milkman and the grocery boy in that little cabinet."

Mother then recounted all over again that the thief had taken the money in such a hurry he had failed to close the drawer in the cabinet and had left it to remain open as if to show he didn't care if she knew someone had stolen her money or not.

"But it does begin to add up to quite an amount over time," Mother finished.

"I bet this little tattletale here told the barber," Luke now turned his gaze on his younger brother, Vance.

Vance colored under his summer tan and hung his head.

"Now don't start on Vance, Luke," his mother warned.

"That's right, always take the side of your little favorite," Luke sneered.

Over the dishpan that night, Luke helped his mother dry the silverware and plates with a tea towel.

"Sometimes I wonder about Dan Schofield," Mother said all at once.

"Dan Schofield," Luke showed real surprise.

"Yes, Luke, your best friend," she added in a kind of sudden indignation.

"Well, I know it sounds far-fetched. You're so fond of him too, I know," Mother continued, "of course Dan comes from a good family. His folks are very well-off," she backed down now a little.

Luke frowned and waited, "You call him my best friend, Mama. But he calls on you and Vance more often than I see him. In fact Pete Snyder once asked if you was going steady with Dan!"

"Pete Snyder," his mother scoffed. "He would say that. Going steady with a boy young enough to be my own son! I declare."

Luke's mother had always pooh-poohed any importance to her going out with some eligible gentleman or other. "A person does get lonesome for the company of someone her own age, and a little company with an older gentleman isn't anything serious. But Dan Schofield, for heaven's sake! What a thing to say!" She laughed uneasily now at her own remark.

Luke was also a little jealous of how his mother always was praising Dan. She pointed out how he could play the piano like a concert pianist, and she recalled he often gave her presents and flowers on St. Valentine's Day and Easter.

"Poor Dan would be heartbroken if he knew we suspected him," Luke spoke somewhat sarcastically.

His mother all at once became thoughtful. She looked critically at the tumbler she had just scalded.

"What is it, Mama?" Luke saw her change of mood.

"The truth is, Luke, the thefts do seem to occur only when Dan has been here."

Luke put down the tea towel and shook his head.

His mother, sensing how upset Luke was, thanked him for helping her dry the dishes and gave him a stealthy kiss.

"We mustn't let on about this, Luke, to outsiders. And after all we have no proof it is Dan."

Mother feared Luke's hot temper, and she recalled the quarrels Luke had always had with his dad. Once Luke struck his father with a monkey wrench during an argument. It had frightened the boy so much he hid all night in the cellar where she found him lying in an old hammock near the furnace room. She had smoothed his hair and let him cry.

Perhaps Luke thought his mother saw he was thinking back now on all the good times he used to have with Dan. Lately, however, Dan had been seeing his younger brother Vance more than he did Luke, and Luke was somewhat jealous of this change in Dan's feelings for him.

Tonight Luke sauntered out on the front porch where Vance was seated. Luke came to the point of what he wanted to say at once.

"What do you make of Mama's fear that maybe it's Dan who has been stealing from the cupboard drawer?"

Just to be contrary, Vance pretended not to have any opinion about it.

"But you see Dan now more than I do," Luke went on, and he sat down on the porch swing beside his brother.

When Vance was silent and pouted, Luke gave him a shove. Vance was afraid of Luke who often "socked" him when they had an argument. And the mention of Dan as a thief frightened him. Then, too, Vance had once dreamed that his brother had killed him, and he had told his mother one day when she was ironing the clothes about his dream. She had put the iron down on its holder and stared at him. "You mustn't put any store on dreams, dear. They often mean the opposite." But Vance could see she was frightened.

"Did you tell Pete Snyder about the thefts?" Luke wondered.

"No," Vance was more communicative now, "all I know is what Mama has already told you. That she found the cupboard drawer pulled open with some of the string hanging out. Her small change was gone. I never said boo to anybody about it."

"And the long and short of it is *your Dan* took the money!" Luke said *your Dan* because Vance and Dan were chums now and often went swimming together in the summer and in the winter patronized the pool parlors or the movies. "I think you know something you're not telling me," Luke went on, puffing on a cigarette. Luke was smoking one of his mother's cigarettes.

Vance could see that Luke did not really enjoy smoking. He coughed a lot while doing so and was constantly removing little bits of tobacco from his teeth. Luke was proud of his white teeth and feared smoking would turn them to be dingy, for his secret ambition was to be a movie star or a nightclub singer. But tonight Luke was nervous and smoked.

"Could it be you know something you're not telling me," Luke went on puffing on his smoke, and he all at once gave Vance a push. Vance could hear the anger coming out from his brother. Luke kept swallowing so hard then in his riled mood that Vance laughed. Vance loved to mock Luke whenever he dared, although he was afraid usually to do so.

"Tell you what," Luke now rose from the porch swing. "I think after all I should have a talk with Dan then," he said, the cigarette hanging out of his teeth in the manner of a movie star he copied after.

"A lot you'll get out of Dan, Luke."

"Is that so?" Luke responded, and at that moment he sounded exactly like their absent dad. And if Vance had told his brother he sounded like his father, he would have beat the tar out of him.

"And think how rich Dan's parents are," Luke spoke moodily.

Vance shrugged his shoulders which annoyed Luke. He felt his younger brother knew a lot more about the theft than he was letting on. His Adam's apple bobbed up and down when he was angry, but this time instead of punching Vance he merely said: "See you keep an eye then on Dan, why don't you."

Luke opened the screen door, then went on inside.

"What is it, Luke?" his mother looked up when he entered the little alcove that led to her bedroom. She had put her hair in curlers, and her face was covered with vanishing cream.

Luke had almost never come into her own private room at this hour, and she knew he must be troubled.

"You've been worrying about Dan Schofield, Luke." She wiped some of the vanishing cream off her face with a fancy white cloth.

"As I said, we can't be positive after all it's him," she spoke in a conciliating manner, but she kept her eyes averted from him.

"I thought you told Vance you knew it was him."

She straightened one of her sheer hose from above her high heels and hesitated. "I said it only does seem to happen when Dan comes to see us."

"Is that proof then that it's him?"

"If it is him, Luke, then *why* does he do it?"

"Yes, *why*! Why can't you at least admit for once and all then Mama he's the thief!"

There was a note of real irritation in Luke's voice, and his mother winced because, like his father, Luke had a fearful temper.

"I think maybe you've spoiled Dan," he grumbled.

"Not anymore than I've spoiled you and Vance maybe."

"It's true what some people say, for one thing you've always acted like Dan was one of your fellows. Yes, your beaux!"

His mother drew in her breath and was silent. She looked in a little hand mirror and touched quickly where some of the night cream remained.

"I can't understand if it's Dan who steals, *why* he steals, when his family is more than well off; and Dan for all practical purposes has the big house all to himself since his people are gone most of the year."

"I don't like Dan being so thick with Vance, either," Luke shut his eyes as he said this.

"But Dan is no stranger to you! You used to see more of him than little Vance ever does."

"Used to is right," Luke answered hotly. "I seldom see him anymore at all, except of course when he comes to see you!"

"Luke!" his mother spoke in an almost syrupy manner. "The good thing about Vance seeing Dan, Luke, is Dan has been teaching him to swim, and they sometimes go hiking together. Vance is not very popular with boys his own age as you know. Being able to go with Dan has been a good thing for the boy."

"But if he is a thief!"

His mother made a deprecating expression then.

"So then you don't think it matters if Dan steals," Luke sneered.

"Don't misquote me, Luke, and don't go," she asked him, for Luke began to move toward the door. She wiped nearly all the night cream from her face and stood up. "I don't suppose you would want to talk to Dan," she said. "At his house maybe."

When Luke said nothing in return, she went on: "It's a great pity if he steals." She spoke as if she was thinking aloud. "Dan is quite talented in his own right—not only plays the piano beautifully, but is a good dancer. He lost two years from high school when he was in the navy, so he's older than the boys in his class."

When Luke remained silent, his mother continued: "So I don't guess you would want to speak to Dan then."

"About his going steady with you," Luke joked now.

"Oh, Luke, please, that's not at all funny."

"I'll speak to him if you say so, Mama."

"I'll leave that up to you," she spoke icily.

"Oh, I suppose I could sound him out."

"Yes, maybe it would be a good thing if you did some-time." She smiled encouragingly.

Luke sighed on the word *sometime*.

"Maybe it will all stop of itself, Luke," his mother said, and she looked pleadingly at her older boy.

"I'm afraid if he is a thief, it won't."

His mother shook her head. "I suppose you may be right."

Luke bent down then and kissed her on her face, the residue of the vanishing cream and all. They both laughed then that he would kiss her with some of her night cream still on.

Luke had never been inside Dan's house. He had forgotten, if he ever knew, how much larger and more imposing it was than where he and Vance lived with their mother. He almost lost his courage as he stood before the heavy front door with the golden knocker. He rapped, but there was no answer. He was a bit surprised when, as he grasped the gleaming brass doorknob, the door opened easily under his touch.

Inside, Luke was about to leave, under the impression Dan was not at home. Then he thought of the thefts. A kind of uncontrollable wrath gave him the encouragement to remain. He heard some sound down the long, brightly-lit hall. His sense of outrage over the thefts allowed him to walk toward the room where he heard the sounds. He entered a large kind of sitting room which contained a number of upholstered chairs arranged as if for a meeting of some kind. Then he could hear someone singing in the room adjoining.

"Just a minute!" It was Dan's voice.

Again Luke had the wish to leave and forget the whole affair. In his discomfort he had come to the conclusion Dan could not have been the thief.

As he turned to leave, the door to the room, from which Dan's voice came, opened. At first Dan appeared thunderstruck at the sight of Luke.

"Why, Luke," Dan greeted him, "I can't believe my eyes. What a surprise!"

Dan was silent, then stared at Luke for a full minute.

Luke on the other hand couldn't get over Dan's appearance. He had on evening clothes!

Usually Dan dressed (in the words of Luke's mother) in a very casual manner, by which she meant he appeared slovenly. Tonight he resembled a young man out of a fashion magazine. His curly hair was carefully combed (his mother once laughingly called it marcelled). His cheeks were flushed to an extent they appeared almost touched with rouge.

"Take a chair, why don't you," Dan spoke unlike his usual self-assured manner.

Luke almost stumbled into one of the mammoth, cushiony affairs which might have just come from the upholsterer.

Dan walked around the room aimlessly, occasionally glancing at his guest.

"Tell me what I can do for you, Luke," he spoke as if he was addressing a stranger.

Luke shook his head. A sigh almost like a sob came out from him.

"See here, Luke, what is the matter? You look so confounded upset."

Then going directly up to Luke and observing him closely, he all but shouted, "Do you know how pale you are, Luke!"

Luke touched his face with his hand, as if paleness could be checked by touch.

"You're so dressed up tonight, Dan," Luke changed the subject. "Are you going to town?"

"I was going to the dance tonight," Dan mumbled.

Then Dan sat down in a chair rather at a distance from Luke and studied Luke's face. "But I needn't go now you're here!" he finished effusively.

Luke showed surprise at this remark. Then all at once, remembering Dan's comment that he looked pale, he felt all at once indisposed. A thin thread of spittle came out from his lips.

"Let me get you a drink," Dan jumped up and hurried out of the room.

He returned with a bottle of brandy and a glass, and pouring out a shot, he brought the glass directly to Luke's lips.

"Go ahead, drink it," Dan spoke with authority. Luke obeyed.

"Drink all of it," Dan insisted.

Even after Luke drank some more, there was some brandy left in the glass as Luke handed it back to Dan. Dan drank off the residue. Then grasping the bottle, he poured himself a full glass and downed that.

"You're very troubled, you know," he told Luke impatiently, and then all at once smiled a kind of smile Luke had never seen on Dan's face before.

"I'd best be going then," Luke proposed.

"Going! For cripes' sake!" Dan shouted now. "Before you've even told me why you came to see me, you're going!"

"But you're off to a dance!"

"I've already forgotten the dance," Dan replied and gave Luke so eloquent a look the younger boy let out another sigh; and removing a large blue handkerchief from his hip pocket, he wiped his lips assiduously.

"You must have come here for something, Luke. And do you realize you've never bothered to visit me before tonight."

"You never invited me," Luke complained.

"You didn't need an invitation, and you know that! You know you are welcome here more than anybody else!"

"Know! I don't know!" As he said this, Luke looked about the room as if the opulence surrounding him was the reason for his never having been here before.

"I want you to take a little more brandy," Dan spoke with a kind of lofty inflection.

"If you think so," Luke said in a monotone.

"Unless you mind drinking out of the same glass I drank from," Dan laughed as he poured Luke another drink from the bottle.

Luke stared at the edges of the glass; then closing his eyes, he drank it all at one gulp and handed the glass back to Dan.

"What is it now?" Dan wondered softly. "What do you want to tell me?"

"You don't know?" Luke raised his voice slightly.

Dan avoided looking at Luke now.

"Dan, see here," Luke lowered his voice, "Why don't you go to the dance, and I'll be going back home."

"Because I don't want to go to the dance now, smarty. Why should I leave you alone here. Especially since you won't tell me why you've showed up here out of the blue!"

"Are you scared I might steal something if you go away and leave me?"

"What in the hell do you mean by that remark?"

"All right then. Let me ask you. Why did you do it?" Luke had gone very pale again.

"Do what?" Dan muttered between his teeth.

"Took money from my mom! When you're rich as Croesus!"

"Money?" Dan spoke crazily. "What money!" He turned and picked up the bottle of brandy and drank thirstily from it.

"You don't know what money I am talking about?"

"Wait a minute, just wait," Dan said. He passed his hand over his eyes; then blinking, he mumbled something.

"You did take the money, why not say it, Dan. Say it, Goddamn it. Get it off your chest."

Dan kept shaking his head. He ran his fingers through his thick auburn hair and was silent.

"That's why I came here tonight, and you damned well knew it the minute you set eyes on me!"

"Supposin' I told you I don't know why I took the money; what would you say to that?" Dan searched Luke's face for an answer.

"You sure don't need the money, do you," Luke sneered, and he waved a hand at the fancy wallpaper and drapes.

"So go ahead, judge me then! When you've never been through the mill, never had to go through the gauntlet like me. Always safe at home with your mom and little Vance. A real mama's boy, aren't you. Never did anything wrong!"

Having said this, Dan rose and walked aimlessly about the room. Then seizing the bottle, he drank more of the brandy and wiped his mouth noisily with his free hand.

"So look down on me and go to hell!" Dan shouted. "What do you know about life. You spoiled little snot."

"But you did steal the money. Why not say it?"

"You call taking chicken feed stealing? All right. Sure I took it. But not to steal."

"What in hell did you take it for then?" And Luke all of a sudden took the brandy bottle up and, following Dan's example, drank direct from the bottle.

"Ask me the question again, why don't you," Dan growled. "Why did I steal? Ain't that your question."

Luke shrank now at the rage in Dan's eyes and mouth.

"*Why did I steal?* And do you know what the answer is?" And walking over to Luke, he took both the boy's hands in his. "The answer is: I don't know if I was to be shot why I took it." Going more closely up to Luke, he slapped him sharply across the face. "You good people!" he shouted. "You make me sick."

"What's being good have to do with you stealing, will you tell me that," Luke said as he touched the place where Dan had slapped him as if the blow had given him something he stood in need of. "You sure didn't need the money, did you? A rich boy like you," and Luke snorted with anger but kept touching the place where Dan slapped him.

"For your information I am the poorest son-of-a-bitch who ever lived. It's you and Vance and your mother are the rich ones, but you are too spoiled and pampered to know it! I am dying of my own poverty! Dying!" As he said this Dan approached Luke again so closely Luke covered his face as if he expected a new blow.

Dan pulled Luke's hands away from his face.

"You and Vance and your mother have everything, everything I don't have and never will have! You have one another for one thing. You live in a real love nest. Don't interrupt me, or I will slap you to sleep! You three lack nothing in my eyes."

"And you stand there and tell me you don't have a lot!" Luke rushed to the fray. "All this luxury," and he waved his hand at the chandeliers and the fine molding of the walls.

"What do I have? Less than nothing. My mother hasn't got ten minutes a year for me. I'm not even positive she's my mother. I don't think I ever heard her call me *son*. My dad, if he was my dad, was never home. Spent all his time, before he shot himself, at the races trying to rake in more money. They meant zero to me, and I never even meant a zero to them."

"But what's all that got to do with your thieving!" Luke cried out as if he saw another blow coming.

"Thieving!" Dan jumped up as if a hot iron had touched him.

"What do you call it, taking money from my mother's meager earnings!" Luke drew closer to him.

All at once Dan became quiet, thoughtful. "I always left a few quarters and fifty-cent pieces from what I took."

"And what good did that do you, then?"

"Now you're getting to it, ain't you. What good did it do, yes. Let me tell you something," Dan advanced again as close as possible to his visitor. "I don't have a clue as to why I took the money in the kitchen cabinet. All I know is you and Vance and your mom have everything. As I say, you live in a love nest! That's right, a love nest! You have each other. And I have nothing and never have had anything and won't never have anything in the future."

Luke stared speechless. His mouth was filled with half-swallowed brandy, and as it overflowed to his chin, he began to wipe his face with his handkerchief. Dan grabbed the handkerchief from him and began to wipe the boy's lips carefully and then silently handed him back the handkerchief.

"I always hoped I would have the three of you for my own friends," Dan said looking up at the ceiling. "I thought you would share some of the love you had from each other. But you didn't have none to spare, did you."

Luke now held the handkerchief awkwardly in his hands, staring at it as if it was something that had a pulse.

"You are the only family that I ever had," Dan spoke so

low his words were nearly inaudible. "But, as I say, I soon realized you didn't have nothing to spare for me. So it was, I guess, *then* I began to steal from you. I did so 'cause I wanted to have something from you, I guess. Something I could touch and feel."

Luke covered his eyes with his hands. Dan stared at him fixedly; then going over to Luke he pulled his hands away from his eyes.

"I want you to watch me as I testify against myself, do you hear." The sternness of his voice made Luke gaze at Dan in a kind of hushed desperation. "I have kept all the small change and some loose strings that happened to be in the drawer in a little hiding place of my own. I wish somebody loved me enough to steal them from me! But nobody loves me. Nor ever will."

"My head is swimming," Luke mumbled, but perhaps Dan did not hear him.

"Anyhow, I was planning on leaving town even before you came here tonight. So when you go home, Luke, you can tell your mother I will never come to your house again. You can all sleep peacefully from now on. I won't trouble your domestic bliss! Will you tell her?"

Luke had wanted to tell Dan that if he left town after what they had said tonight that he would not be able to bear it. He felt he could almost fall to his knees and beg Dan not to leave. He wanted to say he would feel somehow lost without him. He walked toward the door.

"I don't know what I'll say to her," Luke said, after the silence between them.

"Before you go, Luke may I ask one last favor of you."

"What is it?" Luke turned to stare at Dan.

"Will you grant me the favor?"

"Yes I will," Luke practically shouted.

"Let me kiss you."

Luke advanced toward Dan in the manner of a sleep-walker.

Dan waited quite a while before slowly, chastely, even icily kissing Luke quietly first on his mouth then over each of his eyes. Dan then broke away and rushed into the next room and closed the door.

Where were you so long?" His mother was waiting up for him.

"Where's Vance?" Luke wondered.

His mother went up to him just then, "Do I smell liquor on your breath?" she asked. When there was no answer she said, "Vance is asleep upstairs."

"I hear tell Dan is leaving town," Luke said, and sat down in mother's favorite chair. "Maybe for good."

"Did you have a talk with him?"

"No."

"Are you going to?"

"No, Mama, I'm not. I don't see what the point would be now if it's true we won't be seeing him for a good long time. It ain't likely he'd admit to anything now anyway."

She shook her head. It was the thought Luke was drinking which occupied her mind.

They both sat there then in complete silence.

"It's so very late, Luke, I will bid you goodnight. Don't stay up too much longer then. Do you hear, Luke."

Luke nodded.

His mother blew him a kiss and went toward the front stairs.

But then coming suddenly back into the room, she said

looking nowhere in particular, "If Dan didn't steal the money, who did then, Luke, I ask you?"

"The wind, Mama. The wind."

A Little Variety, Please

Alice Drummond feared the Green Dragon almost as much as she did being late to tea. (Her stepmother always whipped her for tardiness.)

The Green Dragon did not have it in for Alice, but his only pleasure, it is true, was to frighten small girls. He had been wintering in Mountain Gulch and was now rested up for hearty springtime activity.

Alice's stepmother warned her the Dragon was back and would be looking for her in particular, and to kindly practice her roller-skating.

"If you have on your skates, you'll be sure to outpace him," the stepmother assured her. "He's also, remember, out of condition from wintering."

"If I could be sure of that," Alice Drummond whispered to herself. Alice tired so of roller skating, and spring made her sleepy and careless.

Mildred Terry, a friend of Alice's stepmother, had a bad fright the day Alice was getting warned by her adopted parent. Mildred had come home unexpectedly from the store and found the Dragon going through her apple bin.

"If you'd written me a note, I'd have set out a bushel or so of apples beforehand," Mildred scolded him. "I don't like you coming in here like a harum-scarum."

She sat down on her best divan, folding and unfolding

her handkerchief. The Dragon threw one apple after another upon the floor.

"These are all Northern Spy and of a poor quality at that," he said finally. Then he ate a small apple at the bottom of the pile. "Just so-so," the Dragon remarked between chewing sounds.

"In all my years in Centerville I've never known so inconsiderate a creature as yourself," Mildred cried on. "You've frightened poor little Alice Drummond something awful. She feels you're after her. Are you?"

The Dragon wiped his paws clean of apple parings, and then began picking and cleaning his front teeth with the remains of a rolling pin.

"Why in Sam Hill did you come back here?" Mildred finally said, when she saw he was not going to answer. "Isn't there another place for you to go firecrackering about?" Suddenly the Dragon began to moan and whine almost like a small cat and held his left arm to his stomach. His eyes rolled in his head, and his scales lowered their lights.

"Oh, me and my," the Dragon cried. "I feel on fire. . . ."

Mildred got up and went to the medicine cabinet, and brought out a bottle of essence of peppermint. She poured a few drops in a tumbler and handed it to the Green Dragon, who swallowed it down.

"Mmm, better already," he mused. "Where now does Alice Drummond live . . ."

"You can't go there, Green Dragon," Mildred spoke, still holding the tumbler in her hand. "You must promise me to give up little girls. Think of all I've done for you. I want you to leave Centerville."

"I am going to cure Alice Drummond of being afraid of

tardiness," the Dragon said. "You know," he repressed a fiery belch, "that I have never harmed the hair of a living creature. However, even I, if pressed by aggressive fear on the part of my inferiors, will frighten. . . ."

"Little girls." Mildred sobbed

"Little girls!" he roared. "I hate the creatures. Only like old parcels like you." He fondled Mildred against his scales briefly.

"Oh, Draggie, why can't you be satisfied?" she cooed. "Why don't you stay out of sight and live with me then at night. You're so selfish."

"I'll see the Drummond Girl. . . ."

"You'll frighten the poor dear to death." The Dragon smiled. "Oh, Draggie, why can't you let well enough alone."

"Mildred has warned me that the Green Dragon is coming to teach Alice a lesson," Mrs. Drummond told her husband that evening. As Alice was only an adopted child of the Drummonds, they were not so frightened as they might have been. Alice had been left on their doorstep six years before, and though they had never wanted her, nobody else would take her, and so she had boarded and lived with them. They were all very unhappy with one another.

"He may be here any moment," Mrs. Drummond said.

"Who?" Mr. Drummond inquired, looking up from his cribbage board.

"I just told you, simpleton."

"Oh, the Dragon," Mr. Drummond replied. "Mae, perhaps it would be better for all if Draggie took her."

"Don't think I haven't entertained the idea," Mrs.

Drummond said. "But the principle of the thing is wrong, Corless, you know it is. We'd be criticized by the community."

"Well, warn the girl, and if he comes, I suppose he'll have to take her." At supper the two Drummonds and Alice discussed the contingencies of a visit from the Dragon. Alice cried right through dessert, and had to be taken into the front room and laid on a sofa. She continued to cry until Mrs. Drummond slapped her. Then Alice made little whimpering sounds, and Mr. Drummond cuffed her for making those, and then she didn't know what she might do, and she held her breath until she turned purple.

At that moment the Green Dragon came through the wall and shot his tongue out. He had not recovered from his colic from eating apples, and he sat down in the large fireplace chair and looked at Alice. When she saw the Dragon she began breathing again. The Drummonds tiptoed out into the kitchen.

"I have fallen in love with you on hearsay," Alice began, looking obliquely at the huge animal.

The Dragon's eyes opened wider than usual, and the room became noticeably warmer. "You . . . fallen for me?" he roared. "That isn't in my book." The Dragon loosened his scales and moved his tongue about in his parched mouth.

"I had no idea you would look the way you do. I am ready to go away with you," she went on.

The Dragon looked out the window at the lengthening spring evening. "I am only interested in *scaring* little. . . ."

"Why are you pictured so differently by the press?" Alice wanted to know. She paced up and down the room. She could see her stepmother's eyes through the kitchen door keyhole. Her anger against her adopted parents suddenly gave her the courage to go directly up to the Dragon. Her fear of course had left her, and she sat down on the big animal's lap. The heat from his body made her terribly uncomfortable, but then Alice Drummond had been uncomfortable all her life. She threw her arms about him while the great animal shifted on his seat.

"Do you think you could get up long enough to get me a frosty cold drink?" the Dragon inquired.

"Anything you ask for is already yours," the girl spoke like one who talks to herself in sleep. The room was getting absolutely torrid. Mrs. Drummond who had heard his request for a drink was already reaching out from the half-opened kitchen door a glass, which Alice took and gave to the great animal. He drank it off and required another. Then a series of exhausting tasks for the Drummonds began. They brought over 300 glasses to the Dragon, but both he and the house became hotter and hotter.

"You're bringing me the wrong kind of liquid," he shouted at last and threw the glass straight at Mrs. Drummond. "Now get out to that kitchen and prepare a frosty drink, as I told you." . . .

But the wallpaper was already in flames in the room where Alice was proposing to the Dragon. "Have no fear, Alice D.," the Dragon spoke to her. "If it looks like a fire, we'll exit. But I must have a frosty drink, my dear. You understand that, of course. You have been unhappy so long, dear Alice, and though I could never love you as you require because you are only a little girl still—"

"You will grow to love me," she quoted from a favorite novel.

"Love you? Let me finish," the Dragon said. "I will adopt you, if not love you. For one thing I am perfectly indifferent to tardiness of any kind. You will live in my palatial castle and do as you please. After all, you are as much legally mine as theirs. . . ."

"We've got to leave, Alice," Mrs. Drummond was wringing her hands. "The entire house is in flames . . . the attic's going now, see, look out there . . . it's already fallen on the front yard. We've notified the fire department. Good-bye, Alice, my dear . . . I'm afraid escape is out of the question for you." She had noticed the girl was being hugged tightly by the big animal.

"Good-bye, my dear," Mr. Drummond spoke to Alice. He had on his fireman's hat, as he was a member of the auxiliary fire department. "Good-bye, sir," he said to the Dragon.

"We have nothing to fear from flames," the Dragon told Alice, as she nestled against his scales.

"I've never felt cooler, Draggie, never felt so much at ease."

The house burned entirely down, and the water from the firemen's hoses quenched the thirst of the huge animal, who had sat on during the entire conflagration hugging Alice Drummond to his scales.

"They were twined together like two lilies," the local press described their position. The townspeople at first understood that Alice Drummond had been burnt to an unrecognizable cinder, and hence Mrs. Drummond had permitted the Dragon to take her off to Green Dragon Lodge with no more feeling than a shrug of the shoulder.

But when all learned that she had not so much as suffered a singeing of one of her curls, everybody began going to Dragon Lodge in hopes of catching a glimpse of the pair.

Whether the Dragon had finally fallen in love with Alice, after being disinterested in little girls except for his liking to frighten them, was not known. But Alice showed by her every movement and gesture that she was hopelessly attached to the Green Dragon. She radiated joy.

Mrs. Drummond, in an interview with the girl who stood between the front paws of the Dragon, threw up to her all that they had done for her. "You were a very expensive child, my dear," Mrs. Drummond said. "You ate your weight in food every other month. We are poor people as a result of having provided for you . . ."

Alice said nothing, and Mrs. Drummond, unable to bear silence when she was having a quarrel with anybody, shrieked in anger and came up as was her custom to slap the girl to sleep, but the Dragon at the moment she was about to strike the girl emitted a kind of steam which drove the stepmother back.

"You're too young to know happiness like this, Alice," she said, on leaving, "and you'll pay for every hour of joy you enjoy with that hideous animal . . . This is good-bye, Alice. I've done all I know I can for you. Good-bye, and may you be brought to a realization of your selfish ways and pay for it dearly." Mr. Drummond who had hidden behind his wife now came out and seconded his wife's statements. "Happiness is much too good for both of you," he said.

"Shall we go on with our lessons in being late for

everything, Alice, my dear," the Dragon inquired. "Or would you like a cup of hot turtle soup . . ."

"I am so happy since we ran off together, Draggie, it don't make much difference . . . I want to enjoy all of our happiness to the full while I have it."

She embraced the Dragon, and they went back into Dragon Lodge and had a delicious cup of hot turtle soup.

And now it was Mildred Terry's turn to come to Dragon Lodge, and complain: "I would be ashamed of myself if I were you," she addressed the Green Dragon. "Living with a spoiled little snipe who never did a thing for a soul. You'll never know the real kind of happiness, Dragon. Never."

The Dragon listened patiently to all Mildred said.

"I could have made a wonderful life for both of us," Mildred tried to go on, but was weeping too hard. "A lot you ever cared about me. I sacrificed my youth for you, and this is what I get. You'll wake up one day, both of you, and discover the kind of person you are living with, and no punishment can be greater than that, none in the world.

"Good-bye, and try to learn from your mistakes," Mildred finished, and disappeared into the leafy streets of Centerville.

The Dragon came out, green as cabbage. Their luggage was all neatly in a pile about them, and they were leaving now to go to the Everglades to live. There was one tiny place in it, the Dragon knew, which would be lonesome, private, and natural. There they would live out their lives together, never having to care about being late, or indeed early.

"Good-bye, Centerville," they both cried as the Dragon took off, his wings making a great din over the streets of Centerville . . . "Good-bye," Alice shouted, "I won't be back, I'm afraid, or rather am not afraid."

That was the last the Drummonds, Mildred Terry, or Centerville ever saw of them, and after a while nobody believed there had been an Alice Drummond, and certainly nobody believed there had been a Green Dragon. But of course there was, there were. . . .

The White Blackbird

E ven before I reached my one hundredth birthday, I had made several wills, and yet just before I put down my signature, Delia Mattlock, my hand refused to form the letters. My attorney was in despair. I had outlived everyone, and there was only one person to whom I could bequeath much, my young godson, and he was not yet twenty-one.

I am putting all this down more to explain the course of events to myself than leave this as a document to posterity, for as I say outside of my godson, Clyde Furness, even my life-long servants have departed this life.

The reason I could not sign my name then is simply this: piece by piece my family jewels have been disappearing over the last few years, and today as I near my one hundred years all of these precious heirlooms one by one have vanished into thin air.

I blamed myself at first, for even as a young girl I used to misplace articles to the great sorrow of my mother. My great grandmother's gold thimble is an example. "You would lose your head if it wasn't tied on," Mother would joke rather sourly. I lost my graduation watch, I lost my diamond engagement ring, and if I had not taken the vow never to remove it, my wedding ring to Will Mattlock would have also taken flight. I will never remove it and will go to my grave wearing it.

But, to return to the jewels. They go back in my family over two hundred years, and yes piece by piece, as I say, they have been disappearing. Take my emerald necklace—its loss nearly finished me. But what of my diamond earrings, the lavaliere over a century old, my ruby earrings—oh why mention them, for to mention them is like a stab in the heart.

I could tell no one for fear they would think I had lost my wits, and then they would blame the servants, who were I knew blameless—such perfect even holy caretakers of me and mine.

But there came the day when I felt I must at least hint to my godson, Clyde Furness, that my jewels were all by now unaccounted for. I hesitated weeks, months before telling him.

About Clyde now. His Uncle Enos told me many times that it was his heartbroken conviction Clyde was somewhat retarded. "Spends all his time in the forest," Enos went on, "failed every grade in school, couldn't add up a column of figures or do his multiplication tables."

"Utter rot and nonsense," I told Enos. "Clyde is bright as a silver dollar. I have taught him all he needs to know, and I never had to teach him twice because he has a splendid memory. In fact, Enos, he is becoming my memory."

Then of course Enos had to die. Only sixty, went off like a puff of smoke while reading the weekly racing news.

So then there was only Clyde and me. We played cards, chess, and then one day he caught sight of my old Ouija board.

I went over to where he was looking at it. That was when I knew I would tell him, of the jewels vanishing of course.

Who else was there. Yet Clyde is a boy I thought, forgetting he was now twenty, for he looked only fourteen to my eyes.

"Put the Ouija board down for a while," I asked him. "I have something to tell you, Clyde." He sat down and looked at me out of his handsome hazel eyes.

I think he already knew what I was to say. But I got out the words. "My heirloom jewels, Clyde, have been taken." My voice sounded far away and more like Uncle Enos's than mine.

"All, Delia?" Clyde whispered, staring still sideways at the Ouija board.

"All, all. One by one over the past three years they have been slipping away. I have almost wondered sometimes if there are spirits, Clyde."

He shook his head.

That was the beginning of even greater closeness between us.

I had given out, at last, my secret. He had accepted it; we were, I saw, like confederates, though we were innocent of course of wrongdoing ourselves. We shared secretly the wrongdoing of someone else.

Or was it *wrongdoing* I wondered. Perhaps the disappearance of the jewels could be understood as the work of some blind power.

But what kind?

My grandfather had a great wine cellar. I had never cared for wine, but in the long winter evenings I finally suggested to Clyde we might try one of the cellar wines.

He did not seem very taken with the idea, for which I was glad, but he obeyed docilely, went down the interminable steps of the cellar and brought back a dusty bottle.

It was a red wine.

We, neither of us, relished it, though I had had it chilled in a bucket of ice, but you see it was the ceremony we both liked. We had to be doing something as we shared the secret.

There were cards, dominoes, Parcheesi, and finally, alas, the Ouija board, but with which we had no luck at all. It sat wordless and morose under our touch.

Often as we sat at cards I would blurt out some thoughtless remark, like once I said, "If we only knew what was before us!"

Either Clyde did not hear, or he pretended I had not spoken.

There was only one subject between us. The missing jewels. And yet I always felt it was wrong to burden a young man with such a loss. But then I gradually saw that we were close, very close. I realized that he had something for me that could only be called love. Uncle Enos was gone, Clyde had never known either mother or father. I was his all, he was my all. The jewels in the end meant nothing to me. A topic for us—no more.

I had been the despair of my mother because as she said I cared little for real property, farmlands, mansions, not even dresses. Certainly not jewels.

"You will be a wealthy woman one day," mother said, "and yet look at you, you care evidently for nothing this world has to offer."

My two husbands must have felt this also. Pouring over their ledgers at night, they would often look up and say, "Delia, you don't care if the store keeps or not, do you?"

"You will be a wealthy woman in time, if only by reason of your jewels," my mother's words of long ago began to echo in my mind when I no longer had them.

My real wealth was in Clyde. At times when I would put my hand through his long chestnut hair a shiver would run through his entire body.

He suffered from a peculiar kind of headache followed by partial deafness and he told me the only thing which helped the pain was when I would pull tightly on his curls.

"Pull away, Delia," he would encourage me.

How it quickened the pulse when he called me by my first name.

Yes, we came to share everything after I told him without warning that bitter cold afternoon. "Clyde, listen patiently. I have only my wedding ring now to my name."

I loved the beautiful expression in his hazel eyes and in the large almost fierce black pupils as he stared at me.

"Do you miss Uncle Enos?" I wondered later that day when we were together.

"No," he said in a sharp, loud voice.

I was both glad and sad because of the remark. Why I felt both things I don't exactly know. I guess it was his honesty.

He was honest like a pane of the finest window glass. I loved his openness. Oh, how I trusted him. And that trust was never betrayed.

I saw at last there was someone I loved. And my love was as pure as his honesty was perfect.

My secret had given us a bond, one to the other.

In those long winter evenings on the edge of the Canadian wildlands, there was little to do but doze, then come awake and talk, sip our wine so sparingly (I would not allow him to have more than a half glass an evening), and there was our talk. We talked about the same things over and again, but we never wearied one another. We were always talking at length on every subject—except the main one. And I knew he was waiting to hear me on that very one.

"How long has it been now, Delia," his voice sounded as if it were coming from a room away.

At first I was tempted to reply, "How long has it been from what?" Instead I answered, "Three years more or less."

"And you told no one in all this time?"

"I could not tell anyone because for a while I thought maybe I had mislaid them, but even as I offered this excuse, Clyde, I knew I could not be mistaken. I knew something, yes let that word be the right one, something was taking my jewels. Oh why do I say my. They never belonged to me, dear boy. I never affected jewels. I did not like the feel of them against my skin or clothes. Perhaps they reminded me of the dead."

"So that is all you know then," he spoke after minutes of silence.

I had to laugh almost uproariously at his tone. "I am laughing, dear Clyde, because you spoke so like an old judge just then. Addressing me as a dubious witness! And dubious witness I am to myself! I accuse myself—of not knowing anything!"

"Could we go to the room where you kept them?" he wondered.

I hesitated.

"No?" he said in a forthright almost ill-humored way.

"It's a long way up the stairs, and I have never liked that big room where I kept them. Then there are the keys. Many many keys to bother and fumble with."

"Then we won't go," he muttered.

"No, we will, Clyde. We will go."

Ah, I had forgotten indeed what a long way up to the big room it was. Even Clyde got a bit tired. Four or five or more flights.

"Well, it's a real castle we live in, my dear," I encouraged him as we toiled upwards.

"You must have a good heart and strong lungs," he said, and he smiled and brought his face very close to mine.

Then I pulled out my flashlight, or as my grandfather would have called it, my torch.

"Now the next flight," I explained, "has poor illumination."

As we approached that terrible door, I brought out the heavy bunch of keys.

"Put this long key, Clyde, in the upper lock, and then this smaller key, when you've unlocked the top one, place it in the lower one here."

He did it well, and we went through the door where of course another bigger door awaited us.

"Now, Clyde, here is the second bunch of keys. Put the upper key to the large keyhole above, give the door a good shove, and we can go in."

He fumbled a little, and I believe I heard him swear for the first time. (Well, his Uncle Enos was a profane old cuss.)

We entered. There were fewer cobwebs now than when I had come in so many months before.

"See all these velvet cases spread out over the oak table there," I said. "In the red velvet large cases were the jewels. Their jewels."

He looked around, and I gave him my torch. But then I remembered there was an upper light, and I turned it on.

He shut off the torch. He seemed in charge of it all and

much older than his twenty years then. I felt safe, comfortable, almost sleepy from my trust in him.

"Look there, will you," he exclaimed.

I put on my long-distance glasses and looked where he pointed.

He bent down to touch something on the floor under the red velvet cases.

I took off my glasses and stared.

"What is it, Clyde?" I said.

"Don't you see," he replied in a hushed way. "It's a white feather. A white bird's feather. Very pretty, isn't it." He raised up the feather toward my trembling hand.

A strange calm descended on us both after Clyde found the white feather. At first I was afraid to touch it. Clyde coaxed me to take it in my hand, and only after repeated urgings on his part did I do so.

At that moment the calm descended on me as many years ago during one of my few serious illnesses old sharp-eyed Doctor Noddy had insisted I take a tincture of opium.

Why, I wondered, did the glimpse of a white bird's feather confer both upon me and Clyde this unusual calm. As if we had found the jewels, or at least had come to understand by what means the jewels had been taken. I say *us* advisedly, for by now Clyde and I were as close as mother and grandson, even husband and wife. We were so close that sometimes at night I would in my bed shudder and words (I was unaware of where they came from) filled my mouth.

Clyde more than the jewels then—let me repeat—was my all, but the jewels were important I realized dimly only because they were the bond holding us together.

That evening I allowed Clyde a little more than half a glass of red wine.

"The only pleasure, Clyde," I addressed him, "is in sipping. Gulping, swallowing spoil all the real delicate pleasure."

I saw his mind was on the white feather.

He had put it on the same table the Ouija board rested on.

"We should see it in a safe place," Clyde said gazing at the feather.

His statement filled me with puzzlement. I wanted to say why ever should we, but I was silent. I spilled some wine on my fresh, white dress. He rose at once and went to the back kitchen and came forward with a little basin filled with water. He carefully and painstakingly wiped away the red stain.

"There," Clyde said looking at where the stain had been.

When he had taken back the basin, he sat very quietly for a while, his eyes half-closed, and then:

"I say we should put it in a safe place."

"Is there any such, Clyde, now the jewels have been taken."

"Just the same I think we should keep the feather out where it is visible, don't you?"

"It is certainly a beautiful one," I remarked.

He nodded faintly and then raising his voice said, "It's a clue."

My calm all at once disappeared. I put the wineglass down for fear I might spill more.

"Had you never seen the feather before, Delia?" he inquired.

The way he said my name revealed to me that we were confederates, though I would never have used this word to his face. It might have pained him. But we were what the word really meant.

"I think it will lead us to find your jewels," he finished, and he drank, thank heavens, still so sparingly of the wine.

I dared not ask him what he meant.

"I think the place for the feather," I spoke rather loudly, "is in that large collection of cases over there where Cousin Berty kept her assortment of rare South American butterflies."

"I don't think so," Clyde said after a bit.

"Then where would you want it?" I said.

"On your music stand by your piano where it's in full view."

"Full view?" I spoke almost crossly.

"Yes, for it's the clue," he almost shouted. "The feather is our clue. Don't you see?"

He sounded almost angry, certainly jarring, if not unkind.

I dared not raise my wineglass, for I would have surely at that moment spilled nearly all of it, and I could not have stood for his cleaning my white dress again that evening. It was too great a ceremony for ruffled nerves.

"There it shall be put, Clyde," I said at last, and he smiled.

Have I forgotten to tell how else we whiled away the very long evenings? Near the music stand where we had placed the feather stood the unused, old grand piano, by some miracle still fairly in tune.

Clyde Furness had one of the most beautiful voices I have ever heard. In my youth I had attended the opera. In my day I heard all the great tenors, but it was Clyde's voice which moved me almost to a swoon. We played what is known as parlor songs, ancient, ageless songs. My hands surprised him when he saw how nimble and quick they still were on the keys. My hands surprised me as a matter of fact. When he sang, my fingers moved like a young woman's. When I played the piano alone, they were stiff and hit many wrong keys.

But I saw then what he meant. As I played the parlor songs my eyes rested not only on him but on the feather. What he called—the clue.

I had suggested one or two times that, now Uncle Enos had departed, Clyde should move in with me. "There's lots of room here; you can choose what part of the house you like and make yourself to home, godson."

Whenever I'd mentioned his moving in up till then, he had always pouted like a small boy. The day we found the feather I felt something had changed not only in me, in the house, in the very air we breathed—something had changed in him.

As I went up to kiss him goodnight that evening, I noticed over his upper lip there was beginning to grow ever so softly traces of his beard.

"What is it?" I inquired when he hesitated at the door. He touched the place on his cheek where I had kissed him.

"Are you sure as sure can be, you still want me to move my things here?" Clyde asked.

"I want you to, of course. You know that. Why should you walk two miles every day to Uncle Enos's and back when it's here the welcome mat is out."

"You certainly have the room don't you," he joked. "How many rooms have you got?" he grinned.

"Oh I've almost forgotten, Clyde."

"Forty?" he wondered.

I smiled. I kissed him again.

The feather had changed everything. I must have looked at it every time I went near the piano. I touched it occasionally. It seemed to move when I picked it up as if it had breath. It was both warm and cool and so soft except for its strong shaft. I once touched it to my lips, and some tears formed in my eyes.

"To think that Clyde is going to be under my roof," I spoke aloud and put the feather back on the music stand.

Dr. Noddy paid his monthly visit shortly after Clyde had come to stay with me.

Dr. Noddy was an extremely tall man, but as if apologetic for his height he stooped and was beginning to be terribly bent so that his head was never held high but always leaned over like he was everlastingly writing prescriptions. This visit was remarkable by the fact he acted unsurprised to see Clyde Furness in my company. One would have thought from the doctor's attitude Clyde had always lived with me.

He began his cursory examination of me—pulse, listening to my lungs and heart, rolling back my eyelids, having me stick out my tongue.

"The tongue and the whites of the eyes tell everything," he once said.

Then he gave me another box of the little purple pills to be taken on rising and on getting into bed.

"And shan't we examine the young man then," Dr. Noddy spoke as if to himself.

He had Clyde remove his shirt and undershirt much to the poor boy's embarrassment. I went into an adjoining closet and brought out one of my grandfather's imported dressing gowns and insisted Clyde put this on to avoid further humiliation.

Dr. Noddy examined Clyde's ears carefully, but his attention seemed to wander over to the music stand. After staring at it for some time and changing his eyeglasses, he then looked at Clyde's hair and scalp and finally took out a pocket comb of his own and combed the boy's hair meticulously.

"Delia, he has parted his hair wrong. Come over here and see for yourself."

I took my time coming to where the doctor was examining my godson, and my deliberateness annoyed him. But all the time nonetheless he kept looking over at the music stand.

"I want you to part his hair on his left side, not on his right. His hair is growing all wrong as a result. And another thing, look in his right ear. See all that wax."

Dr. Noddy now went over to his little doctor's bag and drew out a small silver instrument of some kind.

"I will give you this for his ear. Clean out the wax daily. Just as I am doing now." Clyde gave out a little cry more of surprise than pain as the doctor cleaned his ear of the wax.

"Now then, we should be fine." But Dr. Noddy was no longer paying any attention to us. He was staring at the music stand, and finally he went over to it. He straightened up as much as age and rheumatism would permit.

It was the feather of course he had been staring at so intently, so continuously!

He picked the feather up and came over to where I was studying the instrument he had recommended for Clyde's ear.

"Where did this come from?" he spoke in almost angry, certainly accusatory tones.

"Oh that," I said, and I stuttered for the first time since I was a girl.

"Where did it come from?" he now addressed Clyde in a kind of tone of rage.

"Well, sir," Clyde began but failed to continue.

"Clyde and I found it the other day when we went to the fourth story, Dr. Noddy."

"You climbed all the way up there, did you," the old man mumbled, but his attention was all on the feather. "May I keep this for the time being," he said turning brusquely to me.

"If you wish, doctor, of course," I told him when I saw his usual bad temper was asserting itself.

"Unless, Delia, you have some use for it."

Before I could think I said, "Only as a clue, Dr. Noddy."

"What?" Dr. Noddy almost roared.

Taking advantage of his deafness, I soothed him by saying, "We thought it rather queer, didn't we, Clyde, that there was a feather in the room where I used to keep my grandmother's jewels."

Whether Dr. Noddy heard this last statement or not, I do not know. He put the feather in his huge leather wallet and returned the wallet inside his outer coat with unusual and irritable vigor.

"I will be back then in a month. Have Clyde here drink more well water during the day." Staring at me then, he added, "He's good company I take for you, Delia Mattlock."

Before I could even say yes, he was gone, slamming the big front door behind him.

Dr. Noddy's visit had spoiled something. I do not know exactly how otherwise to describe it. A kind of gloom settled over everything.

Clyde kept holding his ear and touching his beautiful hair and his scalp.

"Does your ear pain you, Clyde?" I finally broke the silence.

"No," he said after a very long pause. "But funny thing is I hear now better."

"We always called earwax beeswax when I was a girl," I said. Clyde snickered a little but only I believe to be polite.

"He took the feather, didn't he," Clyde came out of his reverie.

"And I wonder why, Clyde. Of course, Dr. Noddy is among other things a kind of outdoorsman. A naturalist they call it. Studies animals and birds."

"Oh that could explain it then, maybe."

"Not quite," I disagreed. "Did you see how he kept staring at the feather on the music stand?"

"I did. That's about all he did while he was here."

I nodded. "I never take his pills. Oh, I did at the beginning, but they did nothing for me that I could appreciate. Probably they are made of sugar. I've heard doctors often give some of their patients sugar pills."

"He certainly changed the part in my hair. Excuse me while I look in the mirror over there now, Delia."

Clyde went over to the fifteen foot high mirror brought from England so many years gone by. He made little cries of surprise or perhaps dismay as he looked at himself in the glass.

"I don't look like me," he said gruffly and closed his eyes.

"If you don't like the new part in your hair, we can just comb it back the way it was."

"No, I think maybe I like the new way it's parted. Have to get used to it I suppose, that's all."

"Your hair would look fine with any kind of a part you chose. You have beautiful hair."

He mumbled a thank you and blushed.

"I had a close girl-chum at school, Irma Stairs. She had the most beautiful hair in the world. The color they call Titian. She let it grow until it fell clear to below her knees. When she would let it all down sometimes just to show me, I could not believe my eyes. It made me a little uneasy. I like your hair though, Clyde, even better."

"What do you think he wants to keep the white feather for?" Clyde wondered.

We walked toward the piano just then as if from a signal.

I opened the book of parlor songs, and we began our singing and playing hour.

He sang "Come Where My Love Lies Dreaming." It made the tears come. Then he sang a rollicking sailor's song.

But things were not right after the doctor's visit.

"It's time for our glass of wine," I said, rising from the piano. "We need it after old Dr. Noddy."

A great uneasiness, even sadness, now came over both of us.

I have for many years had the bad habit of talking to myself or, what was considered worse, talking out my own thoughts aloud even in front of company.

Dr. Noddy's having walked off with the feather Clyde and I had found in the jewel room was the source of our discontent.

Thinking Clyde was dozing after his sipping his wine, I

found myself speaking aloud of my discomfiture and even alarm.

"He is making us feel like the accused," I said, and then I added more similar thoughts.

To my surprise I heard Clyde answering me, which was very unlike himself.

I felt we were in some ancient Italian opera singing back to one another, echoing one another's thoughts.

"I didn't like the way he stared at us with his holding the feather like it was proof of something," Clyde started up.

"Exactly, godson. The very words I was trying to express when I thought you were dozing."

"What does he aim to do with it?" Clyde raised his voice.

"And what does he mean to do with it regarding us," I took up his point. "He acts more like a policeman or detective than a doctor where the feather is concerned."

"You take the words right out of my mouth," he spoke loudly.

"Oh Clyde, Clyde, whatever would I do without you."

"You'd do all right, Delia. You know you would." He picked up the empty wineglass, and to my considerable shock he spat into it. "It's me," he said, "who wouldn't know where to turn if I wasn't here with you. I would be the one didn't know up from down."

"With all your talents, dear boy," I cried almost angry he had spoken so against himself. "Never!"

"Never what, Delia. You know how I failed in school and disappointed Uncle Enos."

"Failed him, failed school! Poppycock! Then it was their fault if you did. Uncle Enos adored you. You could do no wrong in his eyes. Oh if he was only here to tell us about the feather. And about that wretched doctor. He would set us straight."

"Now, now," Clyde said rising, and he came over to my chair, and all at once he knelt down and looked up into my troubled face.

"Does old Dr. Noddy know your jewels have disappeared?"

"I think so."

"You think so?"

"I'm sure I told him when I was having an attack of the neuralgia that they had all vanished."

"And what did he say then?"

"It's not so much what he said, he never says much, it was the way he stared at me when I said, 'All my jewels are gone.' "

"Stared how?"

"As he stared at us today when he held the feather. Stared as if I had done something wrong. As if I had done away with my own jewels."

"Oh, he couldn't think that against you, Delia."

"He thinks against everybody. He feels anybody who needs him and his services has something to be held against them. If we are ailing, then we are to blame. That's what I gather from old Dr. Noddy."

"And now, Delia," he said rising and standing behind my chair so that I could feel his honey sweet breath against my hair. "And now," he went on, "we have to wait like the accused in a court of law."

"Exactly, exactly. And oh my stars, what on earth can he do with a feather anyhow? Make *it* confess?"

We both laughed.

"I can't go to bed on all of this we're facing now," I told Clyde. "I am going to the kitchen and make us some coffee."

"Let me make it, Delia."

"No no, I am the cook here and the coffee maker. You make it too weak. I must stay alert. And we must put Doc Noddy on trial here tonight before he can put us in the witness box and call us liars to our face."

With that I went into the kitchen and took down the jar of Arabian coffee, got out the old coffee grinder, and let Clyde (who had followed me without being asked), let *him* grind the beans.

"What a heavenly aroma," I said when our chores was finished. "And I made it with well water of course, for as old Doc Noddy says, you must drink well water religiously, dear lad."

We felt less threatened, less on trial at any rate, drinking the Arabian brew.

Then a great cloud of worry and fear descended upon me. I did all I could to conceal my feelings from my godson.

The source of my fear was, of course, who else, Doctor Noddy.

I recalled in the long, heavy burden of memory that Dr. Noddy was nearly as old as I, at least he must have been far into his eighties at this time. But it was not his age which weighed upon me. It was the memory of Dr. Noddy having been accused a half century or more ago of practicing hypnotism on his patients. And also being suspected of giving his older patients a good deal of opium. But the opium did not concern me now, has indeed never worried me. He only gave it in any case to those of us who were so advanced in age we could no longer endure the pain of, or the weight of, so many years, so much passed time.

No, what gave me pause was hypnotism if indeed he

ever had practiced it. His taking away the feather had brought back this old charge. But my godson sensed my sorrow. He watched me with his beautiful if almost pitiless hazel eyes.

At last he took a seat on a little hand-carved stool beside me. He took my right hand in his and kissed it.

"You are very troubled, Delia," he said at last. He seemed to be looking at the gnarled very blue veins on the hand he had just kissed.

"I am that," I said after a lengthy silence on my part.

"You don't need to say more, Delia. We understand one another."

"I know that, godson, but see here, I want to share with you all that is necessary for me to share. I want you to have everything you deserve."

"I don't deserve much."

"Never say that again. You don't know how precious you are, Clyde, and that is because you *are* perfection."

He turned a furious red and faced away from me.

"Let me think how I am to tell you, Clyde," I spoke so low he cupped his ear and then he again took my hand in his.

"I can see it's something you've got to share."

"Unwillingly, Clyde, so unwillingly. Perhaps though when I tell you, you won't think it's worth troubling about."

He nodded encouragement.

"Clyde, years ago before even your parents were born, before the days of Uncle Enos, Dr. Noddy was charged with having practiced hypnotism on his patients."

Clyde's mouth came open, and then he closed it tight. I thought his lips had formed a cuss word.

We sat in silence for a lengthy while.

"That is why his taking away the feather has worried me."

"And worries me now," he almost gasped.

"My worry over the white feather finally recalled the charge he had hypnotized some of his patients."

"But what is the connection," he wondered, "between a bird's feather and hypnotism."

"I don't know myself, Clyde. Only I feel the two have a connection we don't understand."

He smiled a strange smile.

"We must be calm and patient. Maybe nothing will happen at all, and we will resume our old, quiet evenings," I said.

He released my hand softly.

Looking into his face, yes I saw what I had feared. My trouble had fallen upon him. And so that long evening drew to its close.

For a whole month we could do nothing but wait in suspense for Dr. Noddy's return. Now that I come to think of it, how happy I would have been if there had been no Dr. Noddy! Yes, I do think and believe that had he never appeared out of the fog and the snow and the bitter winds, Clyde and I would have been happy and without real sorrow forever. Dr. Noddy having found the clue, the feather, began to dig and delve, uncover and discover, sift evidence, draw conclusions and then shatter all our peace and love along with our parlor song evenings and Clyde's solos on the Jew's harp. All was to be spoiled, shattered, brought to nothing.

But then as someone was to tell me much later (perhaps it was one of the Gypsy fortune-tellers who happen by in this part of the world), someone said to me, *"Had it not*

*been Dr. Noddy, there would have been someone else to have
brought sorrow and change into your lives."*

"Then call it destiny why don't you," I shouted to this
forgotten person, Gypsy or preacher or peddler or whoever
it was made the point. Oh, well then, just call it Dr. Noddy
and be done with it.

"In our part of the world nature sometimes is enabled to work
out phenomena not observed by ordinary people," Dr. Noddy
began on his next visit, sounding a little like a preacher.

Dr. Noddy had tasted the wine Clyde had brought him
from the cellar even more sparingly, if possible, than was
our own custom. (I had felt the physician needed wine to
judge by his haggard and weary appearance.)

To my embarrassment he fished out a piece of cork, tiny
but as I saw very distasteful to him.

"Fetch Doctor a clean glass," I suggested to Clyde.

Dr. Noddy meanwhile went on talking about Nature's
often indulging in her own schemes and experiments,
indifferent to man.

"She in the end can only baffle us. Our most indefatigable scholars and scientists finally admit defeat and throw
up their hands to acknowledge her inscrutable puissance."

I looked into my wineglass as if also searching for pieces
of cork. Clyde had meanwhile brought Dr. Noddy a
sparkling-clean glass. He had opened a new bottle and
poured out fresh wine.

"Dr. Noddy was saying, Clyde, whilst you were out of
earshot, that Nature is an inscrutable goddess," I summa-
rized the Doctor's speech.

"Yes," Clyde answered and gave me a look inviting
instruction. I could only manage a kind of sad, sour smile.

"The feather," Dr. Noddy began again pulling it out now from his huge wallet, "is one of her pranks."

Clyde and I exchanged quick glances.

"But we should let Clyde here expatiate on Dame Nature's hidden ways and purposes. Your godson was known from the time he came to live with Uncle Enos as a true son of the wilderness, a boon companion to wild creatures and the migratory fowl."

Clyde lowered his head down almost to the rim of his wineglass.

"Our young man therefore must have known that nearby there lived a perfect battalion of white crows, or perhaps they were white blackbirds!"

At that moment Clyde gave out a short, stifled gasp which may have chilled Dr. Noddy into silence. To my uneasiness I saw Dr. Noddy rise and go over to my godson. He took both Clyde's hands and held them tightly and then slowly allowed the hands to fall to his sides. Dr. Noddy then touched Clyde's eyes with both his hands. When the doctor removed his hands, Clyde's eyes were closed.

"Please tell us now," Dr. Noddy moved even closer to Clyde, "if you know of the birds I am speaking of."

"I am not positive," Clyde said in a stern, even grand tone, so unlike the way he usually spoke. He kept his eyes still closed.

"You must have known there were white crows or white blackbirds, what some who delve into their histories call a sport of nature."

"I often thought," Clyde spoke musingly and in an almost small-boy voice now, "often would have swore I saw white birds in the vicinity of the Bell Tower."

"The Bell Tower!" I could not help but gasp. The Bell

Tower was one of the many deserted large buildings which I had long ago sold to Uncle Enos at a very low price.

"You see," Dr. Noddy turned to me. "We have our witness!"

"But what can it all mean," I spoke with partial vexation. "It is so late, Dr. Noddy, in time I mean. Must we go round Robin Hood's barn before you tell us what you have found out."

"This feather," Dr. Noddy now held it again and almost shook it in my face, "let Clyde expand upon it." The old man turned now to my godson. "Open your eyes, Clyde!" He extended the feather to Clyde. "Tell us what you think now, my boy."

Clyde shrank back in alarm from the feather. "It could certainly be from a white crow if there is such a bird," my godson said.

"Or a white blackbird, Clyde?"

Clyde opened his eyes wide and stared at his questioner. "All I know, Delia," Clyde turned to me, "is yes I have seen white birds flying near the Bell Tower, and sometimes . . ."

"And sometimes," Dr. Noddy made as if to rise from his chair.

"Sometimes flying into the open or the broken windows of the Bell Tower."

"And did you ever see a white crow carrying anything in its beak when you saw it making its way to your Bell Tower?" Clyde's eyes closed again. "I may have, sir, yes I may have spied something there, but you see," and he again turned his eyes now opened to me, "you see, I was so startled to glimpse a large white bird against the high green trees and the dark sky, for near the Bell Tower the sky always looks dark. I was startled, and I was scared." Some quick small tears escaped from his right eye.

"And could those things the white bird carried, Clyde, could they have been jewels?"

At that very moment, the wineglass fell from Clyde's hand and he slipped from his chair and fell prone to the thick carpet below.

Dr. Noddy rushed to his side. I hurried also and bent over my prostrate godson.

"Oh, Doctor Noddy, for pity's sake, he is not dead is he!"

Dr. Noddy turned a deprecatory gaze in my direction. "Help me carry him to that big sofa yonder," he said in reply.

Oh, I was more than opposed by then to Dr. Noddy. Seeing my godson lying there as if in his coffin. I blamed it all on the old physician. "You frightened him, doctor," I shouted.

I was surprised at my own angry words leveled against him. I would look now to my godson lying there as if passed over and then return my gaze to Noddy. I must have actually sworn, for when I came out of my fit of anger I heard the old man say, as if he was also in a dream, "I never would have thought I would hear you use such language. And against someone who has only your good at heart, Delia. Only your good!"

Taking me gently by the hand he ushered me into a seldom used little sitting room. The word hypnotism seemed at that moment to be not a word but a being; perhaps *it* was a bird flying about the room.

"What I want to impart to you, Delia," the old physician began, "is simply this: I must now take action. I and I alone must pay a visit to the Bell Tower. For in its ruined masonry there lies the final explanation of the mystery."

The very mention of the Bell Tower had always filled me with a palsy-like terror; so when Dr. Noddy announced that he must go there I could not find a word to say to him.

"Did you hear me, Delia," he finally spoke in a querulous but soft tone.

"If you think you must, dear friend," I managed to reply. "If there is no other way."

"But now we must look in on Clyde," he said after a pause. At the same time he failed to make a motion to rise. A heavy long silence ensued on both our parts when unexpectedly my godson himself entered our private sitting room. We both stared without greeting him.

Clyde looked refreshed after his slumber. His face had resumed its high coloring, and he smiled at us as he took a seat next to Dr. Noddy.

"I have been telling Delia, Clyde, that I must make a special visit to the Bell Tower."

Clyde's face fell and a slight paleness again spread over his features.

"Unless you object, Clyde," the doctor added.

As I say, the very mention of the Bell Tower had always filled me with dread and loathing. But I had never told Clyde or Dr. Noddy the partial reason for my aversion. I did not tell them now what it was which troubled me. My great uncle had committed suicide in the Tower over a hundred years ago, and then later my cousin Keith had fallen from the top of the edifice to his death.

These deaths had been all but forgotten in our village, and perhaps even I no longer remembered them until Dr. Noddy announced he was about to pay a visit there.

While I was lost in these musings I suddenly came to

myself in time to see Noddy buttoning up his greatcoat preparatory to leaving.

"But you can't be paying your visit there now!" I cautioned him. "What with a bad storm coming on and with the freezing cold and snow what it is."

"This is one visit that should not be postponed, Delia! So stop once and for all your fussing."

He actually blew a kiss to me and raised his hand to Clyde in farewell.

I watched him go from the big front window. The wind had changed and was blowing from a northeast direction. The sycamore trees were bending almost to the ground in a fashion such as I could not ever recall.

I came back to my seat.

"Are you warm enough, Delia?" Clyde asked, smiling concern.

"Clyde, listen," I began, gazing at him intently.

"Yes, Delia, speak your mind," he said gaily, almost as if we were again partaking of the jollity of our evenings.

"We must be prepared, Clyde, for whatever our good doctor will discover in the Bell Tower," I said in a lackluster manner.

Clyde gazed down at the carpet under his feet.

I felt then that if I were not who I was I would be afraid to be alone that night with Clyde Furness. But I had gone beyond fear.

"Shan't we have our evening wine, Delia," he said, and as he spoke fresh disquietude began again.

"Please, dear boy, let's have our wine."

We drank if possible even more sparingly. I believe indeed we barely touched the wineglass to our lips. Time passed in a church-like silence as we sat waiting for the doctor's return. I more than Clyde could visualize the many steps the old man must climb before he reached the top floor of the Tower. And I wondered indeed if he would be able to summon the strength to make it. Perhaps the visit thither would be too much for his old bones.

It was the longest evening I can recall. And what made it even more painful was that as I studied my godson I realized he was no longer the Clyde Furness I had been so happy with. No, he had changed. I studied his face for a sign but there was no sign—his face was closed to me. Then began a current of words which will remain with me to the end of my days:

"It's hard for me to believe, Clyde, our good Doctor's theory that it is a bird which has taken my ancestors' jewels."

Clyde straightened up to gaze at me intently.

"Ah, but, Delia, do you understand how hard it has been for me over and again these many weeks to have to listen to your doubts and suspicions!"

"But doubts and suspicions, Clyde, have no claim upon you where I am concerned."

"No claim," he spoke in a bitterness which took me totally by surprise. "Perhaps, Delia, not in your mind, but what about mine?"

"But Clyde, for God in heaven's sake, you can't believe that I regard you as. . . ." But I could not finish the sentence. Clyde finished it for me.

"That I am the white blackbird, Delia? For that is what you think in your inmost being."

Then I cried out, "Never, never has such a thought crossed my mind."

"Perhaps not in your waking hours, Delia. But in your deepest being, in your troubled sleeping hours, Delia, I feel you think I am the white blackbird."

I could think of no response to make then to his dreadful avalanche of words launched against me. Nothing, I came to see, could dispel his thought that I considered him the thief, the white blackbird himself. My mouth was dry. My heart itself was stilled. My godson was lost to me I all at once realized. He would never again be the young and faithful evening companion who had given my life its greatest happiness. As he returned my gaze I saw that he understood what I felt, and he looked away not only in sadness but grief. I knew then he would leave me.

Yet we had to sit on like sentinels, our worry growing as the minutes and the hours slipped by.

It was long past midnight, and we sat on. We neither of us wanted more wine. But at last Clyde insisted he make some coffee, and I was too troubled and weak to offer to make it myself.

As we were sipping our second cup of the Arabian brew, we heard footsteps and then the banging on the door with a heavy walking stick.

Clyde and I both cried out with relief when Dr. Noddy, covered with wet snow and carrying three parcels stomped in, his white breath covering his face like a mask.

"Help me, my boy," Dr. Noddy scolded. He was handing Clyde three packages wrapped in cloth of old cramoisie velvet. "And be careful. Put them over there on that big oak table, why don't you, where they used to feed the threshers in summers gone by."

As Clyde was carrying the parcels to the oak table, I saw with surprise Dr. Noddy pick up Clyde's second cup of

Arabian coffee and gulp it all down at one swallow. He wiped his mustache on a stray napkin near the cup!

"Help me off with my greatcoat, Delia, for I'm frozen to the bone and my hands are cakes of ice."

As soon as I had helped him off with his coat and Clyde had hung it on a hall tree, Dr. Noddy collapsed on one of the larger settees. He took off his spectacles and wiped them and muttered something inaudible.

For a while, because he kept his eyes closed, I thought the doctor had fallen into one of those slumbers I had observed in him before. My own eyes felt heavy as lead.

Then I heard him speaking in louder than usual volume: "I have fetched back everything, Delia, that was missing or lost to you. And I have wrapped what I've found in scraps and shreds from the crimson hanging curtains of the Bell Tower."

His voice had an unaccustomed ring of jubilee to it.

"Bring out the first package, Clyde," he shouted the orders and as he spoke he waved both his arms like the conductor of a band.

Clyde carried the first bundle morosely and placed it on the coffee table before us.

"Now, Delia, let us begin!" Noddy snapped one of the cords with his bone pocketknife and began undoing the bundle of its coverings with a ferocious swiftness.

I felt weak as water as he exposed to view one after the other my diamond necklace, my emerald brooch, my ruby rings, my pearl necklace, and last of all my sapphire earrings!

"Tell me they are yours, Delia," Noddy roared as only a deaf man can.

I nodded.

"And don't weep," he cautioned me. "We'll have no

bawling here tonight after the trouble I've been to in the Tower!"

At a signal from the doctor, Clyde fetched to the table even more doggedly the second package, and this time my godson watched as the doctor undid the wrappings.

"Tell us what you see," Dr. Noddy scolded and glowered.

"My gold necklace," I answered, "and yes, my diamond choker, and those are my amethyst rings and that priceless lavaliere, and oh see, my long-forgotten gold bracelet."

I went on and on. But my eyes were swimming with the tears he had forbidden me to shed.

Then the third bundle was produced, unwrapped and displayed before us as if I were presiding at Judgment Day itself.

"They are all mine, doctor," I testified, avoiding his direful stare. I touched the gems softly and looked away.

"What treasures," Clyde kept mumbling and shaking his head.

My eyes were all on Clyde rather than the treasures, for I took note again that it was not so much perhaps Dr. Noddy who had taken him away from me, it was the power of the treasures themselves which had separated my godson and me forever.

And so the jewels, which I had never wanted in my possession from the beginning, were returned again to be mine. Their theft or disappearance had plagued me of course over the years as a puzzle will tease and torment one, but now seeing them again in my possession all I could think of was their restoration was the cause of Clyde's no longer being mine, no longer loving me! I was unable to explain this belief even to myself but I knew it was the truth.

The next day Clyde holding his few belongings in a kind of sailor's duffel bag, his eyes desperately looking away from my face, managed to get out the words: "Delia, my dear friend, now the weather is beginning to clear, I do feel I must be returning to Uncle Enos's so I can look after his property as I promised him in his last hours."

Had he stabbed me with one of my servants' hunting knives his words could not have struck me deeper. I could barely hold out my hand to him.

"I have, you know too, a bounden duty to see his property is kept as he wanted me to keep it," he could barely whisper. "But should you need me you have only to call, and I will respond."

I am sure a hundred things came to both our lips as we stood facing one another in our farewell. Instead all we could do was gaze for a last time into each other's eyes.

With Clyde's return "in bounden duty" to his Uncle Enos's, there went our evenings of wine sipping and parlor songs and all the other things that had made for me complete happiness.

I was left then with only the stolen jewels, stolen according to our Dr. Noddy by a breed of white blackbird known as far back as remote antiquity as creatures irresistibly attracted to steal anything which was shining bright and dazzling.

Shortly after Clyde had departed for his uncle's, I had called some world-famous jewel merchants for a final appraisal of the treasures. The appraisers came on the heels of my godson's departure. The men reminded me of London policemen or detectives, impeccable gentlemen, formal and with a stultifying politeness. As they appraised my jewels, however, even they would pause from time to time and briefly stare at me with something like incomprehension. They would break the silence then to say in their dry clear voices: "Is nothing missing, ma'am?"

"Nothing at all," I would reply to the same question put to me again and again.

I had by then taken such a horror to the jewels and to their beauty which everyone had always spoken of with bated breath that even to draw near them brought on me a kind of fit of shuddering.

After I had signed countless pages of documents, the appraisers hauled the whole collection off to a famous safety vault in Montreal.

Then for the first time in years I felt a kind of relief that would have been, if not happiness, a kind of benediction or thanksgiving, had I not been so aware I had lost forever my evenings with my godson.

Brawith

oira went for Brawith at the Vets Hospital despite the fact everybody told her it would not work out, and should he get worse, she would bear the blame for his death. There was no way for him to get well the same people claimed, and all her trouble would go for nothing. But Moira was his grandmother, she reminded everyone, and so she took him home to Flempton where she had a nice property near the copse. The river is close by, and there are lots of woodlands, and the town is only about a mile or so due west on a gravel road not too bad to walk on.

Brawith had been nearly made a sieve of from the war, as people in the hospital said, whether from bullets or an explosion or from both factors.

Brawith seldom spoke. When you asked him questions he blinked and looked at his nails.

Moira did not know how bad off he was until he had been home with her about a week or so, and then it was too late to be sorry. She was to have many a heartache over her decision to take him from the Vets Hospital, but if she sometimes was sorry, she never let on to anybody about what she felt.

Her cousin Keith came in occasionally and shook his head but said nothing and left after a short visit. Brawith's parents were dead and gone so long as to be nearly forgotten. They died long before the war. Moira was Brawith's grandmother on his mother's side. Moira had not known Brawith very well when he was a boy. And now she saw she hardly knew him once he had come to stay; she had certainly not known to begin with he had no control over his bowels and carried a roll of toilet paper wherever he went.

After he was back home with her awhile he seemed to get worse, but Moira would not hear of him going back to the hospital ward.

Most of the time Brawith sat quietly in a big chair remodeled from an antique rocker and looked out over the stretch of woods visible from the back door.

Strangely enough he had a fair appetite, and she spent most of her hours cooking.

"If I have made a mistake," Moira began a letter to her sister Lily who lived ten miles away, "I will not back down now. I will stand by my decision, let whoever say what they may." For some reason she found she could not finish the letter.

Brawith liked to walk to the post office and mail her letters, and so she would write something to her other relatives on a government postcard, and he would take it to the main post office, carrying the roll of toilet paper along with him. It was this habit of his more than what happened later on that drew attention to him. Moira did not have the heart to tell him not to take the roll of paper along, and besides she knew he needed it.

"If he did all that for his country, why can't people look the other way if they see him coming," she wrote Lily.

"Brawith, come in and rest. Take the weight off your poor feet," Moira said to him one hot August noon when he had been to the post office for her. "You're flushed from the walk in the sun!" She tried to take the roll of toilet paper away from him, but he held on tight and would not let her.

After that he always held on to it, whether at the dining table or sitting on the back porch watching the woods, or taking his walks to the post office.

Gradually it occurred even to her that he was slowly oozing from almost every pore in his body, and it was not that he did not think with words anymore, or not hear words, his attention was entirely occupied by the soft sounds like whispers arising from the wet parts of his insides, which shattered by wounds and hurts had begun gently coming out from within him or so it seemed, so that all his insides would one day peacefully come out; so his insides and his outer skin would merge finally into one complete wet mass. Moira began to understand this also, and she was never out of eyeshot of him except when he went on his walks. She did not ever relent then on having taken him from the Vets Hospital. She would not admit it was a mistake and agree to return him back there. No, he was her own, he was the only human being she felt who looked up to her, and she would keep him by her side therefore from this day forth.

Her reward, she always said, came when he would once or twice a week, no more, look up at her and say, *"Moira."* It meant thank you, she supposed, it meant, even love she felt. His soft glossy brown hair and beard, thick almost as the pelt of an animal, were bathed in constant streams of sweat. She would touch his hair at such moments, and her hand came away as wet as if she had wrung out a mop. His hair showed none of the affliction his body had undergone but was, one might almost say, blossoming. His hair and his beard had not been cut in the new fashion of nowadays.

After a few evenings she came to the understanding that Brawith did not sleep. She slept very little herself, but she did fall off toward morning for two to three hours of slumber. The realization he did not sleep at all harmed her peace of mind more than any other fact. She did not regret nonetheless her action. She had this home, and the wide expanse of land around it, and she was his own flesh and blood and there was nothing she would not do for him. Besides she had never wanted him in the Vets Hospital in the first place, but her cousin Keith had arranged that. She had countermanded his action—hence Keith's anger against her.

It had all begun the day when she was visiting Brawith in the hospital just as the sun was getting ready to go down. There was nobody in his ward at that moment but a colored man mopping the floor. She had taken Brawith's hand in her own, and not letting go her hold, she had spoken as if begging on her knees, "Brawith, do you choose Grandma's own house or this place? Tell me the truth." He had looked at her like a small child summoned in the middle of night by fire engines. He had despite his confusion tried to keep his mind on what it was she was saying, and at last after a long pause, he had said: "Grandmother's house," and nodded repeatedly.

Thereafter against all advice, instruction and pleas, against the opinion of the doctors and nurses who had talked and even shouted at her, she had taken him away with her. One nurse had handed her the roll of toilet paper as she was going out the door with him. Moira had been too astonished not to receive it, and as if he sensed her dilemma, Brawith took the roll from her, holding it in the manner of one who would receive a present, and so they went down the long flight of white clean-swept steps into Mr. Kwis's truck and thence to her property.

"I know of course I will be criticized," she finished the government postcard to Lily the same day she brought Brawith home, "but I feel as if I have had this call from the boy's mother and father from on high. And I want to do something for the boy before I go."

She had no more written these last words than she saw Brawith was, as if by means of telepathy, waiting to take the postcard to the post office.

Once in a blue moon Lily telephoned her from East Portage. During these phone calls Brawith was observed by his grandmother to sit down in the rocking chair, and letting the roll of toilet paper rest on his lap, he would rock and rock contentedly. She could see the damp emerging from his scalp and hair even from her position in the next room.

"He has given his all," Moira was heard again and again to retort on the phone to Lily, and as she said these words Brawith looked over at her, and something almost like a smile passed over his blurred lips, for there was never any real expression on his face—all there was of expression must have been kept now in the depths of his insides which nudged and urged more and more to come out, to be released themselves like a sheet which would cover his outside skin and hair.

Her cousin Keith visited her from time to time on the side porch and always insisted the same thing. "In the name of decency at least," Keith would say, "if not of proper care—which you cannot give him—send him back to the Vets Hospital."

"They were giving him nothing," Moira always contra-
dicted Keith.

She frequently looked anxiously within the house when
she and Keith talked on the side porch. She heard
Brawith's rocking chair going faster and faster.

"He has the right to die with his loved ones," Moira told
Keith firmly, and Keith got up and drove off in a fury after
these last words.

Coming back into the house, she took Brawith's hand in
hers, but he drew it away shortly to place it back on the roll
of toilet paper.

His hands were only quiet, actually, when they rested on
the roll of paper. The rolls were like a sleeping powder for
him she thought. He appeared to sleep with them over his
moving chest.

She kept a plentiful store of the rolls in her kitchen
closet. They were of varying colors, but Brawith paid no
attention to details of this kind.

"Nothing is too good for you, Brawith," she sometimes
would speak in a loud voice to him. And, she added in a
softer voice, "nothing is too good for my darling."

She felt he heard her, though she was beginning to
understand at last that all he heard, all he felt, all he knew
was the communications which the vast flowing wet of his
insides imparted to him, those rivulets of blood and
lymph, the outpouring of his arteries and veins, all of
which whispered and told him of irreparable damage and
disrepair, and of the awesome future that was to come.

Then one day when all was very still (Moira was somewhat deaf in one ear), when no automobile having gone past
for some time, as she was cleaning his feet in a basin, she
became perfectly aware herself, despite her own moderate

deafness, of the sounds inside himself. She paused for a moment, incredulous, fearful, yet at the same time with an anticipated relief that she could share his knowledge. She listened carefully and she heard enough of the many sounds that were coming from inside himself and which he listened to constantly. All this she was now aware of. Their eyes met briefly, and he gave her a kind of nod, meaning he knew she had heard the sounds and had understood. She held his feet in a tight clasp. That was the beginning of their even deeper closeness.

She moved her cot into his room, and now they were sleepless together in the darkness, as they both listened to his body and waited for the day or perhaps the night to come when the fearful event would take place.

He now never spoke, and she occasionally hummed tunes and songs to him rather than say anything in ordinary speech except an occasional, "That's good, that's very good. I want you to taste this mutton broth."

But the voices of his insides did something to her. She had known it all before, being mother, grandmother but hearing it in a young man's body, a young man who had not had a chance to live as yet, made her incapable to go about her work for a time.

Then gradually she resumed daily tasks, but nothing was the same.

Mr. Kwis, who had helped to bring Brawith home, now delivered the bread and other victuals for their meals, including a few fresh vegetables. He waited on the side porch always for Moira to come out and gather up the provisions.

Brawith tasted all the food she prepared, but spit most of it out in a container provided near the table for this purpose. But his appetite was unimpaired. Whilst he ate, Moira and he both listened casually to the sounds coming from inside his body.

After a time they ceased speaking to one another except when Moira issued commands for herself, as when she would say, "I must wash out all your underthings this evening. And I must think up a new dish to tempt you, Brawith, for my knowledge of cooking's gone from me."

Brawith would nod then and his nods were like a thousand smiles so far as she was concerned.

"It is better here than where you were," Moira often inquired in what was almost a shouting tone.

His eyes studied her mouth, or rather her chin. She repeated her question. Almost as if to answer her, the sounds in his body became louder in response.

They walked out now into the garden, and he stooped down and gathered some of the black nasturtium seeds and held them in his hands. He played with the seeds later that night when he tired of holding the toilet tissues.

As they lay near to one another at night, Moira began speaking aloud. She slept as little as Brawith did, that is, not at all. She said in a voice that was loud enough to carry into the yard by the window, "Brawith, I have been criticized for everything. I am only sorry, though, I didn't come for you sooner. Do you hear? It was the only thing to do, my dear, the only thing. . . ."

After a while his scalp and brow seemed to flow with a thick beady moisture. She often thought she spent most of the time wiping his brow free of the ever-gathering damp. It reminded her of driving in cars long ago before there were windshield wipers, and the snow, rain or sleet fell remorselessly against the car's panes of glass. They would have to stop the car, and clean off the windshield, but to no avail.

"I can't tell you what it means to me," Moira spoke as she wiped his brow often in the middle of night. "Having you here with me, I was doing nothing before you came," she went on. "Cousin Keith and my own daughter can hardly wait to leave now the minute they arrive here. I've told them all I know. They've heard my same old tale till they gag if I begin even to say what kind of weather we've been having. They've had all of me, but Brawith, you allow me to give you of the little I have for anybody."

Having spoken, she would then wipe his brow until it was almost dry, but then another sheet of the moisture came down, and he was as damp as before.

"My dear grandson, Brawith," she whispered too low for him to hear.

After a long pause she went on, "Mr. Kwis is more interested in what I say than my daughter or son. Certainly more than Cousin Keith."

As his brow became more and more sopping wet the voices inside his body grew more insistent, more authoritative. She felt they were crying out for something withheld from him, and now Brawith no longer swallowed what he chewed and tasted, but spat the whole thing out.

Moira and he sat listening to the dictatorial sounds issuing from inside him. Grandmother and grandson were pushed into a deeper silence as if they sat before a political orator or a preacher of the gospel.

One morning, coming out of a short nap-like sleep, she heard some new sounds arising from the fireplace. She called his name, but she realized now he could barely hear her because the sounds from his own swimming insides drowned out all other sound.

Walking into the next room, she found he had put his head up into the chimney of the huge fireplace. The fireplace was so high she could see his mouth and part of his nose, for he was not standing up very straight.

"Brawith, what is it?" She stooped low in order to look up at his eyes. "Are you more comfortable there, my dear boy."

After a long while he came out from the chimney. He looked happier, and this pleased Moira. They went out into the kitchen together, and she prepared him his breakfast.

She realized her danger then at last, that is that she had perhaps made a mistake in disobeying the trained nurses and the doctors, in ignoring the advice of her kinfolk. She remembered too, even in her good friend Mr. Kwis's face, the look sometimes of wonderment if not disapproval.

At the same time she could not go back on her decision in the first place. She felt even more strongly she could not give up Brawith. She studied her own heart, and she knew she had never loved anybody with such complete absorption as she did Brawith. She felt her own insides cried out along with his. Yet she made up her mind to ask him one last time.

Whilst she was mopping his forehead, she pressed his head toward her, and said, "Listen good now, Brawith, for Moira wants to do the right thing. Do you think maybe you should go back to the Vets? Say the word, and I will do what's right."

He did not say anything in reply, and in the silence she began combing his hair which was sopping wet.

"Just say the word, Brawith, and I will do as you see fit."

As he did not say anything, she sighed, for she knew his silence naturally meant he would not wish to return.

"You didn't think that I was indirectly asking you to leave now, did you?" she turned to him. "Heaven forbid you thinking that, Brawith. You're more welcome than sunshine. You've brought so much to me, precious."

After that she knew she would never need ask him about returning.

He would have certainly said something had he thought it was best for his condition to go back to the Vets.

Now for the most of the night, he began standing upright in the chimney of the fireplace, so that after a while she brought her cot there in the center of the big living room to be as near as possible to him. It was beginning to be more unbearable than ever for her, but she could no more have forbidden him standing in the fireplace than ordering him back to the hospital.

The odor from his sickness, however, now discouraged anybody from visiting them. Mr. Kwis himself came only as far as the side door, and having brought them the groceries, he deposited them on a small table and departed. Cousin Keith no longer came at all.

Moira often whispered with Mr. Kwis in the buttery.

"He gave his all, Mr. Kwis, and it's very little I can give him in return for all he has sacrificed, yes siree."

She felt now that he had come to her of his own free will, that she had not prevailed on him to join her here at the outskirts of Flempton, that he had in fact written her asking to join her in her home. She had never known such happiness, such calm, such useful tasks. Mr. Kwis, though he did not come so far into the house to see Brawith, was the soul of understanding. He listened. He understood, unlike Cousin Keith or her son and daughter. Mr. Kwis offered no word of contradiction, no bilious corrective or cold comment.

Brawith now refused to come out of the place he had chosen for himself in the chimney. He spent the entire day and night there. Moira saw that a terrible crisis was coming, yet she did not want to call the doctor or inform the Veterans Hospital. Brawith had promised her he would stay until the last.

Mr. Kwis came when the terrible thing was at its height. Owing to the stench he said he would remain as his custom was on the side porch, and if she thought it advisable he would go for help.

Brawith now began to scratch and claw the brick, but instead of dust coming down from the chimney, Moira saw a sheet of sweat was descending as if from a broken pipe, and this was followed by actual sheets of blood.

Moira begged him to come out of the chimney and lie down on his bed, but the sounds of his body all at once tripled in volume. Even Mr. Kwis heard them from outside.

Occasionally Moira would cry out his name, but the sound of his inside machinery as she thought of it drowned out her words.

At last he foamed at the mouth, and the foam fell down in thick cusps like what comes off cheap beer in the summer.

She felt she must hold him up into the body of the chimney since this was his wish.

Mr. Kwis kept calling from the side porch if there was anything at all which he might do, but she either did not hear him, or the few times she did hear him she was too distracted to reply.

The climax was coming or whatever it was, the end she supposed was a better word. His sufferings were culminating and here she was his only flesh and blood relation to help at this dire moment. No nurse or doctor could do what she was doing, and this thought strengthened and appeased her.

"Tell me, dear boy, if I should do anything different from what I am doing," Moira would cry out, but the sounds from his insides extinguished her voice.

All at once he lowered his head from inside the chimney and pointed with a kind of queer majesty with one hand toward a roll of toilet paper.

She unwound some of the roll and put it within reach of him. Then she saw that without her being aware of it he was naked, but looking again she decided that he still had his clothes on but they had become of the same color and wetness as his skin which breaking totally now exposed his insides. The clothes only resembled his broken skin and bleeding organs. He was not so much hemorrhaging as bursting from inside.

He managed to put the sheets of toilet paper over the worst of the bursting places on his body.

He soon used up the one roll of toilet paper, and Moira now called for Mr. Kwis to go into the buttery where she had put all the remaining rolls, and to toss her one from time to time for Brawith was quickly using them all up.

"You won't have to come much closer to us than you are now," she advised Mr. Kwis. "The crisis, dear friend, is near."

It seemed that Brawith exhausted one entire toilet paper roll almost immediately it was given to him. There were only four left. As he draped his body with the tissues they immediately became red from the wet stuff that was now breaking from within his entire body.

When the last roll was consumed, Moira wondered what would happen.

Then she thought she heard him scream, but she realized that the many noises and sounds which had been audible within his body were moving up now to his larynx and causing his vocal chords to vibrate as if he were speaking. Then she fancied he did speak the one word or part of an unfinished phrase: *"Deliver!"* repeated again and again: *"Deliver."*

Then like a flock of birds the terrible noise seemed to rush over her head deafening her. She fell, losing her hold on his legs, and as she did so an immense shower of blood and intestines covered her, and his body entirely wrapped in toilet paper from head to toe fell heavily on her.

Moira did not know how she was able to rise and finally make her toilsome way to the side porch where Mr. Kwis was waiting with anxious dread. She hardly needed to tell him her grandson was no more. In silence Mr. Kwis took her hands in his and pressed them to his lips. Then speaking in a faint whisper, he said he would go now to tell those who were concerned that the heavy burden of Brawith's life had been lifted at last.

Moe's Villa

T he presence of Frau Storeholder at the entrance of Vesta Hawley's sprawling forty-room mansion had always annoyed Dr. Sherman Cooke on his frequent visits to see Miss Hawley. Dr. Cooke was not paying a visit as a physician but, according to the town wiseacre, he came as her suitor of more than twenty years.

Even when Dr. Cooke finally remarried suddenly to wealthy Miss Mamie Resch, he continued his courtship of the only woman he had ever loved—Mistress Hawley, as people in Gilboa often called her.

Frau Storeholder who spoke German with more ease than English spent most of her time, Dr. Cooke was sure, reading the obituary notices in several local and out-of-town newspapers. She often would call attention to a recent death to Dr. Cooke who, however, pointedly ignored her.

"She is like an ill-tempered though usually silent watchdog," Dr. Cooke often remarked of Frau Storeholder to Miss Hawley. "Do you have to have her here, and if you do have to have her, why then can't she sit in her own room rather than station herself like a sentinel at your front door?"

Vesta Hawley would smile at the doctor's observations. "I find Frau Storeholder's presence most comforting," she would reply.

"And her reading aloud to all and sundry from the latest obituary notices?" the doctor complained.

Vesta chuckled at this remark.

"Why should hearing an obituary notice irk you, a doctor of medicine, dear Sherman?" Then Sherman Cooke would gaze at his only love with sheep's eyes.

Though no longer young, Vesta Hawley's hair was of a remarkable yellow color (one had to see it in the sunshine to appreciate it fully), and someone had once compared it to the hue of the Circassian walnut furniture scattered throughout her mansion.

There were different theories in Gilboa why Vesta Hawley had never married a suitor of such indefatigable faithfulness and ardour as Sherman Cooke. Of course her only previous marriage to Peter Driscoll had been a disaster, and Peter had decamped early on after only a few years of matrimony. And certainly Vesta could have been more comfortable with someone who could help support her mansion and herself. She was always in debt, owing many banks huge sums of mortgage money.

Not only had Peter Driscoll "decamped" but her only son, young Rory (whom she had foolishly thought might one day support her), had run away before he was even grown up.

Rory Hawley had taken his mother's name since there was some doubt Vesta had ever been legally married to Peter Driscoll in the first place.

Vesta Hawley had never bothered to send her son to school. True, the public schools of Gilboa were hardly equipped to teach their few pupils even the essentials of reading and arithmetic. It was believed, however, in any case that Rory had almost never attended classes from his earliest years. His mother pretended to believe he was at school when she must have known better.

Rather than attend school and learn at least to read and write, Rory often went from his mother's house in the morning to another mansion a mile or more away whose owner was a Shawnee Indian by the name of Moses Swearingen. Moses Swearingen's mansion, called the Villa, although it did serve admirable evening repasts, was more famous for its gambling salons behind the restaurant proper and the number of young men who waited on him hand and foot.

Moses Swearingen himself had taken an interest in Rory when he saw how neglected he was by his mother ("She lived in Cloud-Cuckoo-Land," Swearingen had often remarked after the different scandals which occurred around Rory and to a lesser degree himself).

Moses Swearingen had taught Rory to read, write and cipher, and finally how to play cards.

Rory soon surpassed his teacher in the art of card playing and finally gambling. It was both the boy's salvation and some said his eventual ruin.

Our story begins quite far back, or as we might say, in the era when there were still brawny men who delivered ice from the quarry to residents like those of Vesta and Moses Swearingen. For there was no refrigeration as we know it now in Gilboa, an unincorporated village of nearly 3,000 people. There were as a result icemen and also milkmen, and fruit and vegetable men, and knife and scissors sharpeners. All these came in vehicles drawn by dray horses.

Swearingen himself once said he could not have maintained his restaurant without the icemen and the rest of the horse-drawn vehicles.

Moses Swearingen did not look like an Indian. For one thing he had hair almost the color of Vesta Hawley's, except it was if anything more abundant and of a finer texture. His eyes changed, it was observed, like the tides. In the morning his eyes were almost robin's egg blue, but as the day progressed his orbs became darker, and as he sat overlooking the card players in the evening his eyes were of a fearful black.

A young man who had dabbled in anthropology and who visited Moe's Villa from time to time said that, despite Moses' fair hair, his pronounced high cheekbones were the telltale proof he had Shawnee blood.

Where Moses' great-grandfather came into his fortune and his mansion was never truthfully known. Indeed it has been an equal mystery where his family originally came from.

On the other hand Dr. Sherman Cooke did not resemble at all a family physician in his appearance. He had the chest of an athlete, almost a Samson, and even at an advanced age he gave the impression of a blacksmith or the wielder of a sledgehammer. He had a waist, some of his clients joked, not above twenty-eight inches in girth.

There were some blotches or scars on his weatherbeaten complexion. Rumour had it that Rory had attacked the doctor one evening when he saw the doctor emerging from Vesta's bedroom. Some claimed that the boy had thrown a pot of scalding water on the doctor's countenance. Others said Rory had stabbed him with a penknife.

Once, however, the doctor told one of his closest friends he had fallen as a child into a bonfire and was only tardily rescued at the last moment, else he would have perished.

Even more arresting to his appearance was his untamable

shock of very black hair, which appeared never to have been cut or indeed combed. And, until at a late age, it was all but untouched by gray. (He laid this fact to his eating foods rich in copper.) In short, Dr. Cooke (he also spelled his name indifferently now and again as Coke) resembled a Shawnee Indian more than Moses Swearingen. And townsfolk often jeered that the scars on the doctor's countenance were inherited from tomahawk wounds.

After the disappearance of Pete Driscoll, they came from far and near. At first perhaps the suitors were curious concerning Vesta's reputed wealth and the fact of course she owned one of the great showplaces of this remote rural area. For the general opinion was that whoever inherited her mansion was set for life. (What no one realized, perhaps not even Vesta Hawley, was that the house, in disrepair since the Civil War, was gradually turning to powder.)

But the indomitable untamable and indestructible suitor was of course Dr. Sherman Cooke of the blotched countenance and unruly uncut unbarbered hair.

It was also whispered that Moses Swearingen himself far back had often paid Vesta Hawley short mysterious calls. It was said he always left the premises with lowered brow and sagging shoulders.

Vesta herself frequently remarked that had she not had so intractable and unteachable a son as Rory, perhaps she would have married. Doubtful, in retrospect. For Vesta loved her own independence more than life itself. And she did not wish to marry for another reason: she wished one day to bequeath her mansion to Rory who she always called her fate and nemesis—as the only means she could make up for her failure as a mother and guide.

"Rory will never be satisfied," she once remarked to some of her gentlemen visitors, "until he sees me lying in a pinewood box on the way to Maple Grove Cemetery. Then and only then can he do exactly as he pleases!"

But Rory as soon as he could talk had done exactly as he pleased, and Vesta soon realized he was as intractable as a tiger cub.

So extensive was Vesta's mansion there were—she claimed—many rooms she had never set foot in.

But in all the rooms she was familiar with there were her clocks. Everyone in Gilboa had heard stories of them, and some lucky people had actually heard them tick and chime. Almost all the rooms on the main floor had at least one grandfather clock. In Vesta's huge bedroom (large enough to sleep a squadron) there were over sixteen clocks of varying size.

The irony of all this collection of timepieces was that most of them had long ago given out, and no matter how Vesta herself and her friends tinkered with them, they could not bring the clocks back to life.

But when none of the clocks kept time at all, and poor as she was or claimed to be, she was able to persuade a famous watchsmith from Toronto, Canada, to come to visit her.

Dr. Sherman Cooke had attempted to dissuade her from inviting an unknown man to her house. He scoffed at her assurance that the watchsmith was considered the finest in the hemisphere.

"Famous or not, you may be in actual peril," the doctor cautioned.

"The invitation stands, Sherman!" and she added, "If you really had been concerned over the years, you would have bought me a proper timepiece."

"*A* timepiece! You would only be satisfied with a hundred! And I am convinced, dear girl, that there is something in the temperature of your rooms which slows down and finally stops all your clocks."

They both laughed after he had made this little speech.

Vesta was more worried over how she would pay the famous visiting watchsmith than under any apprehension he might murder her.

"He was too young, much too young!" Dr. Sherman Cooke later recalled the watchsmith. "It cost me many a sleepless night while he was at her beck and call. And the scamp also fell for Vesta, wouldn't you know—the Canadian watchsmith! Head over heels he was!"

Dr. Sherman Cooke slowly began to understand why Rory had run away from home, if one could call such an establishment as Vesta's "home."

"Rory saw she was not his mother, but a Circe," Dr. Cooke confided to one of his oldest patients who was dying of an undiagnosed illness.

The young Canadian watchsmith had stayed a week and, to give the devil his due, he succeeded in making almost all the clocks run again except one ancient grandfather timepiece.

"It will have to be sent to my workshop in Canada," he told Vesta. "For we would have to repair almost all of its inner works."

Dr. Cooke saw the watchsmith's behaviour (he charged Vesta only five dollars for his extensive time and workmanship) as a kind of repeat performance of all the men, young and old, who had fallen for Vesta Hawley, including even her young son Rory. For the boy, constantly caressed and spoiled, then neglected and confused, had his own inner working ruined perhaps forever.

It was the schoolteacher Bess Byal who called on Vesta one blustering fall evening when all the countless clocks were by now ticking and chiming away.

Vesta insisted on giving the schoolmarm her best India tea together with fresh homemade Parker House rolls and gooseberry jam.

"Do you realize," Bess said after unwillingly enjoying the repast, "that Rory has not attended school since the first two days of the term."

Vesta's mind was a thousand miles away.

"He is either at the picture show, or when the picture show is not running, he spends the day and even most of the night at Moe's Villa."

"Moe's?" Vesta was evasive and toyed with her grand-mother's brooch.

"The very same," Bess confirmed and then swallowing some tea the wrong way, she burst into a seizure of coughing.

"And did the truant officer never talk to the boy?" Vesta inquired with the vagueness and indifference she might have shown had Bess told her of a child's kite which the wind had blown out of reach.

"I'm afraid we have no such officer, Vesta. Ben Wheatley, our truant officer, passed away last year, and the school board doesn't now have the funds to employ another."

"Yes, what is to become of Rory," Vesta said listlessly, and pinched the bridge of her nose.

Bess let the Parker House rolls tempt her again in the face of this absence of maternal responsibility.

Dr. Cooke was both fascinated and made uneasy by Vesta's many "fancies," as the doctor called her pet pleasures. There was of course her obsessive interest in—as an example—her countless clocks. But her unusual "fancies" extended to many other phenomena.

One evening when the doctor was seated beside her in the velvet settee of the parlour, holding her hand and hoping she would allow him to kiss her, he saw Vesta all at once leap up and go to the large front window, pull back the heavy curtains and bend her ear close to the pane.

"What on earth is it?" he wondered.

"Sh! Listen, only listen."

He heard from a distance a man's powerful whistle.

It was the sound of young men whistling, he learned finally, which created in Vesta Hawley an almost swooning pleasure such as she experienced when she heard the combined ticking of her many clocks.

Yes, she admitted, she found the sound of young men whistling from their powerful lungs as breathtakingly moving as a more sophisticated person might experience hearing a sax or fine piccolo solo.

"Oh, Vesta, Vesta, I will never understand you."

Then there came the day when it seemed clear that Rory had left his mother's house for good, that Vesta noticed Frau Storeholder grasping one of the out-of-town evening newspapers, standing worriedly and hoping to be allowed to tell her mistress something.

"No more obituaries, Frau Storeholder. I am not strong enough this evening to hear who has left us for the other shore! Please!"

"May I read from the marriage announcements of last month," Frau Storeholder was very firm and obstinate.

"But why on earth marriage," Vesta said, and then perhaps sensing at a severe look from Frau Storeholder what was to come, "All right," Vesta managed to say. "Read your news! But only if it is about the living."

Frau Storeholder in her heavy accent read then from a Chicago newspaper that Dr. Sherman Cooke of Gilboa had married Miss Mamie Resch also of Gilboa in a private ceremony.

Vesta made her way to the easy chair and slumped down against its freshly-laundered antimacassar.

"Shall I bring you the elixir doctor left you last week?" Frau Storeholder, having put away the newspaper suggested.

"That may be a good idea," Vesta answered in a voice at least two octaves lower than usual. "Kindly do so."

Sipping the elixir, Vesta muttered to her faithful friend, "I will weigh carefully what it is I must do next."

A bit afraid Vesta might mean an act of violence, Frau Storeholder spoke in her lullaby manner, urging Vesta to take no action until the shock had subsided.

Queerly enough, Dr. Cooke arrived at his usual hour of visiting the next evening, but Frau Storeholder informed him that Vesta was not at home to anyone this night.

"Not at home!" the doctor scoffed and then bore down his Herculean presence past the old obituary-reader and rudely opened the sliding doors which lead to the parlour. There he caught sight of his only love with a hot water bottle attached to her aching head, sprawled out on a fancy ottoman.

Dr. Cooke courageously removed the hot water bottle and took both her hands in his. She was too weak to rebuff him.

"Where is the pain?" he whispered, touching lightly his lips in her fragrant hair.

She tried to push him away, but in her weakness failed to achieve this action.

"Nothing will have changed, dear Vesta. You are my only one. You know that!"

She slapped him across the face, but he noticed this no more than had he felt a fly alight on his forehead.

"I have been in catastrophic financial straits," he began, and Vesta knew this was a sly reference to his having helped her modestly in days gone past.

"And you have moved in bag and baggage with her I am told. Have you departed your own place where you treated your patients for so many decades."

"My wife has given me her entire first floor for my professional duties," he spoke lamely.

More excuses now followed in a lachrymose delivery.

"The banks would not honor my last request for a loan," he finished, and without her permission he bestowed a kiss on her forehead.

Because she did not repulse him for this action he knew then she probably would continue to admit him to her presence, married or not! But then who could predict Vesta's changing moods?

That night Vesta had a strange dream. It had to do not so much with the doctor, though he flitted in and out of the dream, as it showed Miss Mamie Resch in the action of hiding a collection of gold pieces in what looked like an opening in the wallpaper.

Waking, Vesta could not get the dream out of her mind. She knew of course, as did everybody in Gilboa, that Mamie Resch was not only incredibly rich, but was even more famous as a miser who hid her money in all kinds of secret places.

The next morning Vesta Hawley was consumed with anger and outraged to such an extent she feared she might suffer palpitations for which Dr. Cooke had treated her in times past with tiny little red pills.

Under the pretext she had run out of medicine, she decided to pay a visit to Dr. Cooke.

Yes, Vesta Hawley who almost never left her own residence realized that was exactly what she must do. She summoned one of her "whistlers," a farmer's boy, Stu Hysted, who came at once in his rickety car with tires which appeared to be not so much punctured as shredded. He doffed his hat and bowed low when he saw Vesta come out of her front door and grinned showing his toothpaste ad beautiful teeth.

They rode then not to the Doctor's old lodging but to the imposing edifice of Dr. Cooke's new mistress—the heiress Mamie Resch who else!

Asking Stu Hysted to wait in his jalopy, Vesta strode up the twenty or so steep steps leading to Mamie's front living room. Out of breath more from anger than palpitations, Vesta flung open the door and then all but fell onto an ottoman.

She could hear the doctor's voice coming from the next room, advising a woman patient about remedies for the discomfort of the change of life.

Catching her breath slowly, Vesta surveyed the rather dingy furnishings in the room until her eye fell on the faded rose and gold wallpaper. It did and did not resemble the wallpaper she had seen in her dream. Rising, she walked about the room with its assortment of wandering jew plants and several vases of artificial flowers covered with dust.

Then her eye caught a metallic little something near the floor almost indistinguishable from the wallpaper.

Vesta was so disturbed by the metal's resemblance to her dream of the night before she had the sudden wish to leave the premises. She was afraid, afraid for herself, afraid for her dream.

The sound of the doctor's voice continuing and his patient's long-winded replies persuaded her to stay.

Almost before she knew what she was doing she had knelt down on the floor and touched the metallic protuberance from the wallpaper. Her hand had hardly done so than it came open like a loose door, and she saw inside a kind of passageway in which was located a thick envelope.

She pulled it out. Across the outside was written:

To be opened only in an emergency.

A kind of anger had almost blinded Vesta to such an extent she had trouble reading the message.

The envelope came open as she held it with trembling fingers. Inside she could make out several thousand-dollar bills.

"Is someone there?" the doctor's voice now reached her.

Like any ordinary burglar, Vesta, putting the envelope in the pocket of her outside coat, waited, breathless, then hearing no one approach, managed to tiptoe out of the room. Outside, she rushed toward her young chauffeur.

"Are you all right," he was saying to her as she sat in the backseat. She was unable to answer.

"Do you want me to call anybody?" he inquired worriedly.

"No, no, Stu," she wailed. "Let's go to my house as soon as you can drive me there."

Stu watched her carefully before he took the wheel and drove off at an almost reckless speed, which may have reminded Vesta of robberies she had heard of from Frau Storeholder reading from the evening news.

Dr. Cooke came a few evenings later.

"I'm sorry I missed you," he spoke lamely after she had served him with a hot bowl of his favorite soup. "I believe you paid me a visit, Vesta."

Vesta eyed him carefully.

Either Dr. Cooke was the greatest actor the nation had seen, she decided, or else the heavens be praised, he knew nothing of her theft, indeed now made no further mention of her having visited his new abode.

Taking his manner to mean he was ignorant of her deed or that he acquiesced in her crime, she allowed him to give her quick little kisses, with the satisfaction perhaps she was now not only a robber but guilty of adultery in the bargain.

Guilty people, according to popular works on the subject, often keep notes of their misdeeds, recounting in detail their crimes and their methods of performing them.

Vesta Hawley's method was not to write down what she had committed but to confide her misdeed to Frau Storeholder. It was like whispering, she felt, to a tomb.

One of the things about Frau Storeholder which puzzled Vesta Hawley was the fact the old lady's hair had not one strand of gray. Knowing her attendant so well over the years, Vesta was positive she did not dye her hair. And she often recalled, having read somewhere in a book on the occult, that persons who have second sight often keep the original color of their hair until death.

And then began Vesta's confession of her crime.

"My back was to the wall," she began her litany.

Frau Storeholder had never been to an eye doctor but made occasional visits to a drug store where the druggist supplied her with cheap reading glasses.

Frau Storeholder now took off her spectacles and gazed at Vesta without the aid of optics. She gazed as if she had to be sure it was Vesta herself who was confessing to her falling from the path of righteousness.

And when Frau Storeholder removed her spectacles, it meant Vesta could confide anything she wished to her "doorkeeper."

"My back was to the wall," she repeated these words now. "God pity me, Belinda! You know I cannot let the bank take my house away from me, now can you. For where would you go, dear Belinda (Belinda was Frau Storeholder's Christian name and known only to Vesta, though she was like everyone else more often than not to call the old woman Frau Storeholder. But for secret and even damaging information, she always said *Belinda*).

"As you know better than anyone else, I have fought for over a quarter of a century to keep a roof over our heads and in the bargain, my dearest friend, I have sometimes under such pressure stepped over the bounds of the straight and narrow."

Frau Storeholder now toyed with her store-bought spectacles but refrained from putting them on.

Vesta always took this gesture of Belinda's as encouragement to continue.

In any case, Belinda won't remember by morning, Vesta reflected, what I've told her at vespers!

And to whom could Frau Storeholder go if she wished to tattle? The old woman knew nobody now. All Frau Storeholder's friends, family, her near and distant relatives had joined the choir invisible.

And then would such a Christian person sully her lips with what Vesta told her.

"This is what occurred in Mamie Resch's living room," Vesta began in a voice more like that of an opera singer than her usual pedestrian, often mumbling, manner.

"I have as you know for some time been desperate to meet my mortgage payments on my house—our house, Belinda. You would probably say the Prince of Darkness himself showed me the way. I discovered an envelope hidden there. Don't ask me how I found it. I say I found an envelope. I opened it. I thought of my many years of worry and privation, my having lost Rory through my poverty and through my having sometimes overstepped the conventions with my men boarders. I say this woman had money to burn and I had nothing. I took the money. I have it now. Oh, have no fear, Dr. Cooke will see that I return it. You have noticed he continues to pay calls on me, him a married man. Has told me barefaced that he loves only me. So, Belinda, I have fallen from grace!"

Because of the long and dreadful silence on the part of Frau Storeholder after Vesta's confession, Vesta almost wondered if her good friend had fallen asleep, or, what is worse, had a stroke and had died owing to her revelation!

But no, now her Belinda stirred, smiled faintly and oddly enough nodded slowly several times.

The theft of the thousand-dollar bills, Vesta feared,

might be the one straw that would destroy their love and friendship. And unless Frau Storeholder actually did not hear her chronicle of dishonesty, at any rate she made no hint of disapproval or even judgement. And as Vesta studied the old woman's features, she saw something in the way her eyes closed and opened and the fact her pale lips became more crimson in the movement of a half-smile that gave her pause.

"My dear Vesta," Frau Storeholder began in a voice entirely unlike her own, a voice a little like that of the preacher speaking after communion or some other of the sacraments.

"We sometimes, Vesta," Frau Storeholder went on speaking in her new untypical voice, "yes, sometimes, dear lady, we must take the law in our own hands."

Astonished at such a statement from a student of Scripture, Vesta waited for Belinda to say more. There was no more!

But when Vesta gave Belinda an eloquent look, and this look took in that Frau Storeholder was smiling almost beatifically at Vesta, she assumed her normal behaviour and began talking rapidly.

"For what would you and I do after all, my dear Belinda, with no roof over our heads, no food on our plates."

As a matter of fact both ladies had often bewailed the fact that the village of Gilboa no longer could afford even a poorhouse for its indigent. The depression had destroyed charity itself! Many of the homeless lived now on the edge of Maple Grove Cemetery.

"She forgives me!" Vesta smothered the unspoken words into a linen handkerchief. "And people wonder, yes Dr. Cooke among them, why I put up with the poor dear. The real question I reckon is how come she puts up with me."

"I lost my boy from trying to keep a roof over his head," Vesta now recounted this episode of her life for the hundredth time.

Yes, Vesta mused, Frau Storeholder must have recalled from her incessant Bible reading that it was the Good Shepherd who forgave the harlots and sinners. It was the Good Shepherd indeed who forgave the thief on the cross and promised he would meet him in paradise. He would have understood also a woman like herself who erred on the side of the law in order to keep a shelter for her loved ones and for those lonely young men who shared the fare of her banquets.

Vesta Hawley had not recovered from her purloining a small fortune from Dr. Cooke's wife when Mr. Eli Jaqua, the principal of schools, telephoned to say he must meet with Miss Hawley immediately.

It was Frau Storeholder of course who took the message and who, disturbed by the urgency of tone of the principal, told Mr. Jaqua she was sure Miss Hawley would of course see him. Vesta Hawley was too ill with a sick headache to quarrel with her faithful friend's agreeing to this unwelcome visit from a man she loathed and despised—Eli Jaqua. (He had according to Vesta bad-mouthed her and her mansion for years.)

"I refuse to see him, dear Belinda," Vesta managed to say taking the hot water bottle away from her face.

When Vesta saw the look of anxiety and disapproval even on Frau Storeholder's face, she added: "Do you talk to the man, why don't you. For, dear friend, you know more about me and my affairs than perhaps I do. See him for me!"

Saying this, Vesta pulled a sheet over her face and head.

Frau Stockholder was majestic that day as she sat in the parlour with Principal Eli Jaqua. He noticed it and marveled as he had been marveling at the grand albeit decayed aspect of this once great showplace.

Principal Jaqua was not an old man, but the cares of his calling, the lack of funds for operating a public school in Gilboa and his wearing spectacles all added years to his otherwise rather handsome features and made him appear as a rule often old and tired. Such a face, such a man could hardly be asked as a dinner guest for Vesta Hawley's midnight banquets.

"I believe, dear Frau Storeholder, that you know the purpose of my visit, and I would not have come had the errand been anything but a grave one."

Looking around suspiciously, he coughed then inquired, "When may I see Miss Hawley?"

"She is very ill, Mr. Jaqua, and the doctor has told her she must see no one."

"That ill?" Mr. Jaqua said and looked at one of the many clocks ticking away.

He fidgeted, his mouth moved to say more, then was still, and as he fidgeted even more he colored almost violently.

"Frau Storeholder, let me say this: You know probably more about what the purpose of my errand is today than Miss Hawley herself does, racked in pain as I gather that she is."

Frau Storeholder nodded and agreed Miss Hawley was quite under the weather.

"Then I will say right out what it is. Rory Hawley, dear lady, can no longer be called just a truant. No, not at all."

Mr. Jaqua let this remark sink in before continuing, but regretfully saw no change of expression on Miss Hawley's beloved confidante. She was as cool indeed as Vesta Hawley always was when hearing bad news.

"Rory Hawley," Mr. Jaqua continued, "has gone from truant to deserter, and from deserter to a kind of, shall we say, turncoat to his own ancestry and upbringing. He is a resident along with many other young men who are out of work at Moe's Villa. Indeed he lives there!"

Even this last fierce and even dreadful statement failed to evoke any change in Frau Storeholder's countenance. Had Mr. Jaqua said only, "Rory Hawley is now fifteen years of age!" she would have been just as poker-faced and calm.

"There are worse places for Rory to be, I suppose," Frau Storeholder commented in the icy silence which had taken place.

"I beg your pardon," Mr. Jaqua spoke between his teeth and his eyes flashed under his ill-fitting glasses. "How, may I ask, could hell itself be worse than the Villa. Let me clarify my comment on the Villa."

"I have known Moses from the time he was a boy," she now explained her incendiary statement. "Rory will be provided for—if I know Mr. Swearingen at all!"

"But in a gambling hell, dear Frau Storeholder. A young boy in a gambling hell!"

"Every attempt, dear Mr. Jaqua, has been made to bring Rory back. Miss Hawley does not wish to do more. And time, Mr. Jaqua, if you will allow me to say so, is often the best arbiter of our dilemmas."

"Time—the arbiter!" He gave a kind of sound between a whimper and a groan and rose then, as did Frau Storeholder. "I see, I'm afraid," Mr. Jaqua raised his voice loud enough for perhaps Miss Hawley to hear, "I see and understand that my mission here has not borne fruit. But as a Christian gentleman, let me say I am glad I have put forth the effort."

In the awkwardness which now ensued, Mr. Jaqua, hands trembling, attempted to put on his long woolen gloves. But like his mission, they appeared to resist his best efforts. Finally, pulling off the one glove he had somehow managed to get on, he put both gloves in his outer coat and extended his hand to Frau Storeholder.

She took his very cold hand in her warm one and bowed slightly.

"You may tell our good Miss Hawley," he said at he outer door, "that she shall hear from the Superintendent of Schools with reference to the matter at hand, be assured!"

Fearing Mr. Jaqua might slam the door in the state he was in and perhaps break the rather delicate frosted glass of the ancient portal, Frau Storeholder now held the door wide open for him until her visitor had bowed himself out.

The next day Mr. Eli Jaqua, after his unsuccessful visit to the Hawley mansion, called an emergency meeting of the school board.

Although it was Superintendent Shingles's priority to arrange such a meeting, for some years he had allowed Mr. Jaqua to conduct almost all business without prior knowledge of the superintendent himself. After all Mr. Shingles was over ninety years old and was usually more than pleased to turn over most of his duties to the younger principal. In addition to Mr. Shingles, Bess Byal (the truant boy's teacher) and two other teachers were also in attendance.

Superintendent Shingles was more than a little deaf and inclined to doze off during the sessions which Mr. Jaqua chaired. And for some time the old gentleman was usually completely in the dark about any business at hand.

Today, however, Superintendent Shingles brightened at the mention of Vesta Hawley and then, to the annoyance of Mr. Jaqua, admitted he did not realize there was a son named Rory. He expressed surprise indeed that, in his words, so beautiful, young and attractive a woman as Vesta Hawley had ever had a child!

Superintendent Shingles furthermore annoyed Mr. Jaqua to no end today by reminiscing on Vesta Hawley's "showplace" of a mansion, and he recalled that some few years past he had often been invited as a special guest of Mistress Hawley to her soirees and banquets.

Finally interrupting Mr. Shingles's recollections, Mr. Jaqua with ill-concealed annoyance asked what measures should now be taken with reference to Rory Hawley, who, among his many wrongdoings, had not attended school for nearly two years and, what was more alarming to the school board, the young man had all but moved in with Moses Swearingen, without his mother's knowledge, in the residence known by the townspeople as Moe's Villa!

"Yes, Superintendent Shingles," Mr. Jaqua now raised his voice, "our young truant Rory is permanently quartered in a rather notorious domicile already referred to as Moe's Villa!"

"But see here," the Superintendent bridled, and he appeared all at once to be bright as a silver dollar, "I have known Moses Swearingen since he was a boy! He is actually a young man of remarkable resources, a former war hero, we must remember, and now the owner of a property called by Mr. Jaqua, Moe's Villa—rather despairingly I fear—a property nonetheless which rivals Vesta Hawley's own mansion but is, if I am correctly informed, worth a great deal more in value!"

Mr. Shingles now wiped his forehead of what was, one supposed, sweat at this unheard-of long speech from him, but noting Mr. Jaqua was about to interrupt him, the Superintendent continued: "So I believe if I may say so, gentlemen and Miss Byal, that Rory Hawley could be in a much worse place than the name Moe's Villa might imply." Wiping his forehead again carefully, he continued, "May I also indulge in a little local history by reminding everyone here today that Moses Swearingen has exerted every effort of muscle and brain to keep under his ownership the property of the Villa inherited from his great-grandfather, a hero in the Civil War; and in order not to lose this property from taxes and mortgages, Moses, it is true, began to operate a section of his house as a very stylish eating place and also a recreation room (billiards, card playing, I hear). He has hired many young men who have been, through no fault of their own, unemployed! He also defended himself against a bully who attacked him, leaving Moe seriously wounded. Yes, my dear friends, young Rory could be in a much worse situation."

"Yes, my dear Mr. Shingles, how right you are. Rory Hawley could be living in a den of thieves, I suppose."

Mr. Shingle smiled at the pointed remark only because he had not heard a word Mr. Jaqua had said.

The wind considerably taken out of his sails, Mr. Jaqua however managed to resume his role as chairman by saying: "What action then, gentlemen and Miss Byal, are we to take in view of the important information given us just now by Superintendent Shingles?"

Mr. Shingles then, to the astonishment of everyone present, had taken up Mr. Jaqua's gavel and with this gesture appeared to be now in actual fact the Superintendent.

"Let me say at this time, my dear friends and colleagues, that in my opinion we have no jurisdiction over the lives of the person we have been discussing. We are, let us remember, schoolmasters and teachers. What Mistress Hawley does in her private chambers, and Mr. Swearingen does in his, do not concern us. If the Hawley boy has gone to Mr. Swearingen of his own free will, as I understand he has, and if his mother, the excellent Vesta Hawley herself, has made no appeal to outside authority for his return, who are we, as I say, mere school teachers, to interfere in the freedom and privacy of these two leading citizens!"

No silence could have been more profound than the dead silence that now followed this speech (indeed had not only a pin dropped but a sledgehammer, no one would have heard it). Mr. Shingles, smiling a bit triumphantly and letting go his gavel, picked up his heavy felt hat and almost slammed it over his ears. And following this singular action, he took from his breast pocket a silver whistle and blew it forcefully.

His private chauffeur, Kurt Bandor, appeared immediately as if from nowhere on hearing the whistle blown and with a rather elaborate and possessive manner led the old man outside to his waiting limousine.

Mr. Jaqua, put in his place, and acting as if he had been slapped in the bargain, crimsoned to the roots of his hair and, for the first time in his tenure as principal, could find nothing to say until after a nervous question from Bess Byal, he managed to utter, "The meeting, Miss Byal and gentlemen, is indeed adjourned; thank you."

As everyone was filing out then, except for Mr. Jaqua, the members of the gathering were astonished to hear all of a sudden from the room just vacated Mr. Jaqua striking the table at which he still sat with Superintendent Shingles's gavel.

Bess Byal, at the sound of the gavel, turned back and stared questioningly at the principal.

"Good night, Miss Byal," he managed to say, still grasping the superintendent's gavel.

One frosty November evening as Vesta was entertaining some star customers over dessert and mulled wine, Frau Storeholder a bit ruffled entered and whispered in Vesta's ear: "Dr. Cooke says he would like a word with you."

"Tell the good doctor to join us in dessert."

Just then the clock struck twelve.

"Doctor asks a word alone with you," Frau Storeholder added solemnly.

"No, no, no!" Vesta cried. But she got up, dropping her napkin, and excused herself from her three dinner guests and faced the doctor.

"Why won't you come and have some dessert," Vesta scolded. "Don't tell me you won't."

Dr. Cooke knew enough from past experience not to vex her more at the moment. Doffing his heavy coat, he entered the dining hall. The guests were Dave Dysinger, a young man who worked at the greenhouse, Hal Bryer, a minister of the gospel, and Hayes Wishart, who lived off his family's income.

The three guests all rose and greeted Dr. Cooke, who unwillingly, then, and very grudgingly, consented to taste some plum pudding in a heavy sauce. But the pudding, against his will, actually revived him, and he broke gradually into a thin smile and then suddenly grinned and licked the spoon.

The three young men now left, using the excuse of allowing the doctor to be alone with Vesta, though they had been ready to depart an hour or so earlier.

In the parlour, Vesta now sat with the doctor as she yawned and occasionally sighed.

"We have had an unfortunate episode at our house," Dr. Cooke began.

Vesta looked at the folds of her evening gown and lifted the hem which had fallen on her high shoes.

"Episode?" she wondered indifferently. "And who do you mean by *we*?"

"My wife of course," he said deeply hurt, deeply offended.

"You mean Mamie Resch, I suppose," Vesta said as she looked up at the ceiling chandelier and yawned again.

"Oh, Vesta, try to be a little civil at least."

"Civil! After you have broken in on my evening supper and driven my guests out of the house. Civil! And you dare to mention that abandoned creature you now claim as your wife when you are in my house, and uninvited at that! And you barge in after midnight at that! Well, then, why are you here?"

"We have had a break-in, Vesta. A robbery."

"I hope you have informed the authorities."

He shook his head gravely. "That I will never do," he mumbled.

"Then the episode you speak of must be rather trifling."

"If ten thousand dollars is a trifle!" He bowed his head, and they both knew he was "licked."

Vesta rose grandly and touched a tiny silver bell. It brought one of the kitchen help almost immediately. A young man hardly more than sixteen, wearing a kitchen apron much too large for him, entered.

"Fetch the brandy bottle, Theo, and the little glasses, and be quick about it too."

"No, no, Vesta," Dr. Cooke implored.

"Yes, yes, doctor. God knows you need something to clear your brain."

Drinking first one glass of brandy and shortly thereafter another, Dr. Cooke all at once in a gravelly but loud voice exclaimed: "I forgive you, Vesta, and you will never hear me mention the affair again."

His statement only infuriated Vesta the more.

"You have been my suitor now for how long, doctor?"

"Oh, Vesta, please."

"Please, nothing! Answer my question."

"A good twenty years, I expect."

"And during all those difficult years when I wondered day in and day out how I was to meet my expenses, who lent me a helping hand? Who kept the sheriff from closing me down?"

He shook his head and stared into his drink.

"Shake your head a thousand times. The answer is Dr. Cooke certainly did not lend a hand. Yet he had free run of my house. Strolled at will through every one of my floors and my rooms like a baron!"

Here she raised her milk-white arms as if those arms held a rawhide about to fall.

"Yes, the good doctor, as he is known, enjoyed all this great house has to offer, including the upper chamber. Yet did he ever contribute more than one farthing to the upkeep of my regal outlays and expenditures? And then one fine day out of a blue sky without warning, or so much as a hint of what he was up to, he ups and marries a woman who had in twenty years never invited him to any of her skimpy soirees, was indeed barely on speaking acquaintance with him, a woman so desperate for conjugal closeness that it was she, old and unfrequented as the hills, who proposed to him, and he at the thought of Mamie's wealth, our good doctor, grasped her hand as if she had stretched it out to save him from drowning!"

Dr. Cooke, who had seen action, they say, in at least two wars and had won several citations for bravery, now flinched more than when he was under enemy fire. But Vesta, perhaps too disgusted to lay hands on her former suitor, merely groaned and moved her head vigorously until her star sapphire earrings threatened to come loose in her rage.

"If there is a thief anywhere in this blasted town I am looking at him now! And if money is missing, certainly over-the-hill Mamie Resch ought to know what become of it, and who took it."

"I know you took it." Dr. Cooke to his own astonishment was able to get these words out.

Vesta laughed shrilly and so loudly that hobbling old Frau Storeholder entered the room in alarm.

"Sit down, dear lady," Vesta smiled and made a cooing sound at her old doorkeeper.

"I will settle the score, then, Vesta, with my wife," Dr. Cooke said and looked longingly at the bottle of brandy.

"For all you have consumed here, doctor, over the decades and the rolling years," Vesta had begun again, "for all the grub, Canadian pheasant and venison, the roast suckling pig and fatted calf, the sweetmeats and pumpkin royals, and all the other bounty of my kitchen, and certainly the spirits which have flowed for you and only you like the waters of the lake in springtime, for all that, you could never repay me in a hundred years what you have over time usurped from me. For yes, God knows, you have bled me white. And you dare come here at this late hour to accuse me of robbery when I am looking right now at the greatest robber who ever entered any woman's life!"

Rising, or rather tottering to his feet, Dr. Cooke now shouted: "And I tell you I will make it all right with my wife."

"You have no wife," Vesta called out. "Do you mean to tell me you are capable of the marriage rite, you and that old bag of bones, wigs and paint that is Mamie Resch, a crone old enough to be your own mother. Yes, go home now, waken your legal spouse, tell her you *owe* the grass widow, owner of the finest showplace in the state, tell her, do you hear, you owe me at the very least twenty million dollars which no peephole in wallpaper is big enough to hide."

Dr. Cooke was already on his way out, bent almost double, and snivelling and choking from his own effluvia.

Vesta who had threateningly accompanied the doctor to the door and slammed it after him now returned to the parlour.

Had Frau Storeholder ever gone to the theatre, she might have thought Sarah Bernhardt had come back to the stage. And for a split second Frau Storeholder did not actually believe she had been hearing the Vesta she knew. She shivered a little. She shook.

Only when Vesta sat down in the best chair in the house and began laughing uproariously did Frau Storeholder return to reality.

"Oh, what a wonderful audience you make, what a divine onlooker, dear Belinda. Yes, you egged me on to one of my finest performances, I do believe. Dunning me for a few thousand dollars when he is in my debt for millions!"

Vesta picked up a half-empty glass of brandy left by her late-hour guest and downed it all in one swallow. She wiped her eyes of the tears which her laughter had brought forth and then sank back limp as a rag against the bolster of one of her antique overstuffed chairs.

For the zeal of thine house hath eaten me up.

Vesta found this verse underlined in an open copy of Frau Storeholder's well-worn Holy Bible.

The verse was from the Psalms, and whether owing to the fact the verse had been underlined with pencil or because of the words themselves, the text appeared to be blazing like hot coals.

Vesta felt the underlined verse was meant for her. She was not sure of its meaning, but she had been aware for some time that Frau Storeholder, if not downright critical of her, was not altogether comfortable with Vesta's behaviour of late.

"Yet what would the poor old thing do without me," Vesta muttered, still gazing at the passage in the Psalms. "Yes, I suppose I do have zeal for my house. It's all I have, and it was all my own people had before me. And, as I've told Frau Storeholder a thousand times, what would become of her if some day the sheriff came and closed the property. Where would she go? Where would I go?"

That evening, after an unusually sumptuous banquet and after every one of the guests had departed, Vesta came into the little parlour reserved primarily for Frau Storeholder. She was sitting in a wicker rocking chair, her eyes closed.

The Holy Bible was still open at the marked passage in the Psalms.

Vesta strode over to where the book lay and deliberately read aloud the underlined passage.

"You are quite a student of Scripture, Belinda," she remarked, turning to gaze at Frau Storeholder.

Frau Storeholder opened her eyes, roused as if out of sleep, brought on in part perhaps by the excellent dinner she had just enjoyed.

"I am afraid I am far from what anyone could call a student of Scripture," the old woman managed to say. She spoke as if she was talking in her sleep.

"Does the verse have some special meaning for you, Belinda, seeing you have underlined it."

"Let me look at it, Vesta." She rose now and came over to stare at the passage marked in the Psalms.

"I'm afraid I don't understand the verse myself," she confessed. "Perhaps that is why it's underlined."

"I was wondering if the verse had some reference to me," Vesta tried to make her voice kind and reasonable, but still it came out rather edgy.

Frau Storeholder now gazed lengthily at Vesta, then spoke up bravely, "I believe *house* here means the Temple of the Lord."

Vesta now took up the heavy tome in her hands and read the passage again aloud in her soaring contralto.

"Isn't the passage, dear Belinda, a pointed reference to someone who worships her *own* mansion?"

When Frau Storeholder did not respond, Vesta put down the heavy book on its stand.

"I'm afraid you think I worship my home more than I do anything else in creation."

Frau Storeholder moved about the room now as if she was looking for something which might explain the passage itself. Finishing her pacing, the old woman sat down in her favorite chair, and again closed her eyes.

"You believe, I feel, that I love my house more than I love Rory, my only child. For he has left me, think of it, just think of it. Zeal, zeal!" She almost shouted this word. "Yes, whatever you say, I am afraid the passage has more than a little to do with me. Say or think whatever you like."

"Vesta," Frau Storeholder's voice came now as distant as if from the banquet room, "we must do what we must do in this life."

"But *eaten me up*! That is a terrible way of putting it. For I do believe the verse has to do with me. With my life."

Vesta could not restrain a few short sobs.

"We should not try to understand Holy Writ, dear Vesta. Let me repeat, the word *house* here means the Lord's Temple, that and nothing more."

"Oh, how I wish I could believe you. I have heard there are many ways of interpreting Scripture of course."

"Don't fret, dear Vesta. It breaks my heart to see you fret."

"And you didn't leave the book open at this passage for my eyes?"

Frau Storeholder said nothing at this point.

"I wish you would admit you did. I think the passage does refer to my kind of worship. A house! It's all I have. My only son has deserted me. And his deserting me has been approved of by the Superintendent of Schools! Think of that. Rory has gone permanently to live with Moses Swearingen."

"Moe's Villa," Frau Storeholder clicked her tongue.

The mention of Moe's Villa drove out then from Vesta's mind the Bible and its verses. All she could think of then was they had taken her boy away from her. Of course she had neglected him, had not paid attention to his needs, to his truancy from school! She was not free of blame, but she had kept a roof over his precious head! Her *zeal* as the Good Book said, had been behind it. And the passage, no matter what Frau Storeholder might say, yes, it was about her!

Moses Swearingen belonged to one of the most respected families in Gilboa. His ancestors went back before the Revolution. And he had, like Vesta Hawley, inherited an antebellum sprawling piece of property which had possibly more rooms than the mansion of the grass widow herself.

Moses had studied to be a medical doctor, but having to work with cadavers had caused him to have such a horror of the profession, he had left school a few months before graduation.

He had returned to Gilboa and settled down. It was said he sometimes practiced medicine without a license, and even Dr. Cooke often remarked Moses knew more about the profession than many a licensed M.D.

But Moses Swearingen's real interest outside of cards,

gambling and strong drink, lay—unbeknownst to almost everyone—in the field of psychic phenomenona, which he had studied in the medical school, devouring every book he could lay his hands on.

He felt that he himself had some talent in the field, but he was afraid to go further into this science. It seemed to threaten something very deep in his nature.

Moses, being perhaps the wealthiest man in the county, could afford to hire the unemployed young men to do the hard work about his mansion and run his many errands. But he was always looking in them also for some hint that they might have psychic ability.

Moses Swearingen had noticed for some time the strange behaviour of young Rory Hawley, the neglected child of a ruined marriage.

Everyone in Gilboa knew Rory never attended school regularly, if at all, and was, as they said, a dyed-in-the-wool truant.

The word "truant" kept running though Moses' mind the first time some men in the pool parlor mentioned it in reference to Widow Hawley's son.

One cold winter day Moses spied young Rory wandering aimlessly about the town square. He wore no overcoat or gloves and was blowing his hands to keep them warm.

It did not take many words for Moses to invite him to his Villa, as his property was frequently, though sarcastically, called.

Moses rummaged about the garments in his clothes closet and came back with a thick sweater, two or three sizes too large for the boy, but which would give him the warmth he needed.

But the sweater, Moses soon saw, was not warm enough to keep Rory from a fit of shivering. His lips were almost blue. Moses felt the boy's forehead and took his pulse. Rory began shaking convulsively.

At Moe's Villa bottles of spirits were in evidence everywhere. He poured Rory a few jiggers of alcohol against the boy's resistance but got some of it anyhow down his throat. The remaining drops fell over the young boy's chin and chest.

Frightened at the boy's dangerous condition, Moses carried him up the long antique staircase to the front guest room where there were plenty of goose down comforters, quilts and pillows.

He didn't bother to remove the boy's clothing, but put him between the thick linen sheets and piled on the blankets and comforters.

A quaking fright took over him that the boy might expire in his care.

He called in one of his hired girls and told her to make some tea. The girl stared for a long time at the unfamiliar guest. Moses had to shout for her to get on with his request.

Moses sat up the rest of the night, unwilling to leave the boy for fear he might perish if left untended. Toward morning, however, Rory stirred and opened his eyes and half-smiled at Moses, then lay back and closed his eyes. A thin stream of blood came out of his nostrils. Moses wiped his nose and mouth delicately of the stains.

Sensing the boy might be conscious, he asked, "Do you know where you are, Rory?"

The boy's eyelids fluttered, his mouth twitched and then said, "General Yoxtheimer's."

Moses was unable to restrain a gasp, for General Yox-theimer was one of his remote ancestors who had fought the Revolutionary War and in several Indian uprisings. And it was furthermore the General's house where they were now present.

"And who was General Yoxtheimer?" Moses whispered.

The boy thrashed about now frantically, and then shaking his head, managed: "Died . . . the Indians."

"You mean they killed the General?" Moses was barely able to inquire.

No one, Moses reflected, could have known General Yoxtheimer had been killed in an Indian massacre. Even he had only lately learned this fact from a very old history of the Revolutionary period he had found in a library in Chicago.

"Do you hear me, Rory?"

There was no response.

"Do you, Rory?"

"I hear a man who is a card player and gambler."

Moses, to his own embarrassment and chagrin, let out a swear word, and now to his sudden anger he heard a strange laugh come from his visitor.

Moses sat on by the bedside of Rory Hawley, deep in thoughts he would never have thought himself capable of entertaining before.

Everyone of course in town knew that Moses Swearingen was fond of card playing and gambling and had initiated many young men into the practice. But the boy's mentioning the fact of his card playing and betting could hardly be proof of psychic ability, but could be mere repetition of what he had heard in his wandering about the streets when he should have been at school.

"Who let you in on the fact I am a gambler," Moses finally said after a long silence between them.

The silence was broken only after four or five minutes.

"You broke your mother's heart betting away your inheritance."

Having mumbled these words, Rory started up as if coming out of a deep slumber. Rising from the bed, he shouted something unintelligible or words in a foreign language.

Moses groaned and wondered what he was up against with such a boy.

"Who was it brought me here?" Rory now spoke in his ordinary wide-awake voice, and he came over to where Moses sat and seized him by the hand.

Moses was astonished at the strength of the boy's own hand in view of his otherwise rather delicate appearance.

"Who else brought you here but me," Moses snapped. "I brought you!"

Rory stood looking at Moses carefully. And it was then that Moses was convinced that maybe he did not have someone who had second sight on his hands, but a someone at any rate who was different from anyone he had ever known before.

For a while Swearingen wondered if the local authorities might not call on him and demand to know why young Rory Hawley was staying with him.

But as the days passed and there was no visit from "above," he reflected that the village of Gilboa was so bankrupt it could no longer even pay for a police force.

The condition of the boy showed every kind of neglect. His clothing was much too large for him, as were his shoes. And though a handsome fellow, everything about him indicated inveterate neglect. His teeth looked like they needed attention for they were almost black in places. His hair, a beautiful shade of the same color as his mother's (if, Moses mused, she was his mother), was long unaccustomed to tonsorial care, if indeed he had ever set foot in a barber shop. His fingernails were broken and some blackened. From wearing the wrong-size shoes his toenails were discoloured and broken. And under his paper-thin shirt (he wore no undershirt) one could count every one of his ribs.

Moses now ushered his visitor to the kitchen which was nearly as large as Vesta's banquet room.

The cook had left several dishes sitting atop the stove, all ready to be heated.

Moses took the lid off one or two of the pots to see what might tempt his guest, and he noticed with a kind of bitter amusement the boy's nose wrinkled and moved as he got a whiff of the victuals.

Without asking Rory's preference, Moses heated a soup of turkey, leeks, cabbage and potatoes.

He set the dish down before Rory and handed him an oversize silver spoon.

When Rory only stared at the steaming dish, Moses shouted, "Eat."

Rory dove in at this command. Moses grinned, noticing the boy did not bother to wipe his mouth and chin from his dribbling. He was too busy swallowing.

Moses picked up a stiff linen napkin and methodically wiped the boy's mouth.

For the first time then Rory gave Moses a searching look as if he had just now become aware of Moses' presence.

When Rory had eaten his fill, Moses ushered him into a lavatory which like the kitchen was the size of three or four ordinary rooms.

"Sit over here, why don't you," he used his drill-sergeant tone. Rory once again gave evidence that he was about to doze.

Moses opened a drawer and took out barber's scissors and comb.

"I want to untangle that head of hair of yours."

Before Moses had really begun his barbering, he took out from the boy's hair the remains of what looked like briars and petals of marigolds.

Moses clicked his tongue.

Rory, still sleepy, acted entirely indifferent to those ministrations, but occasionally sighed and let his head fall down to his chest.

When the cutting and combing was over, Moses pointed to the wastebasket now full of the yellow tresses.

Moses touched the down on the boy's cheeks.

"Quite a ways from a beard, ain't it," he remarked, perhaps to himself.

For the first time in his life Moses Swearingen felt, if not outright uneasiness, a kind of fearful awe of another person. This was the turbulence he experienced in the boy's presence.

He had taken the boy into his mansion because he saw how needful, even desperate, the young man was.

But instead of having ushered in a child in desperate trouble and need, he found he had taken in a kind of being who appeared barely of this world. And instead of Moses being the master, he was often to have the sinking feeling the boy held the real sway at the Villa.

He recalled then that years ago when Rory could have not been more than three or four-years old, he had seen the boy's grandmother taking him for drives in her horse-drawn buggy. The grandmother had always stopped when she saw Moses and would exchange a few cordial greetings.

The grandmother did not look like anyone remotely related to Rory or his mother. She was so dark-complexioned the townspeople often wondered if she did not have African blood. But older residents claimed she was, like Moses, part Shawnee.

One cold December afternoon long ago when the wind and snow had kept everybody within doors, Moses heard a—it could not be called a knocking at his front door—it was more like the sound of a blacksmith mistaking the door for an anvil. And Moses felt all over again now the same kind of sinking feeling he had experienced at hearing the knocking as when he looked into Rory's blazing countenance.

The late visitor with the fierce knocking was Rory's grandmother. Recovering from his astonishment, Moses greeted the old woman in a blithe manner foreign to his usual brusqueness.

"Sit over here, why don't you, by the fireplace where I've got a bit of kindling going to take the chill off," Moses urged his visitor.

The grandmother did not appear to be cold, but she chose a seat nearest the fire, and a tardy smile came over her lips.

Without being asked, Moses produced a glass with some kind of spirits.

His guest tasted the drink critically, and Moses for a

moment thought from her strange gesture she was about to toss the contents into the blazing logs of the fireplace.

Instead she finished her drink, and extending her glass, indicated she would care for another.

"I have had a presentiment," she began at last after they had both listened a while to the crackling sound coming from the burning logs.

When she said no more Moses asked, "And what was its nature?"

"Its nature—who knows, Moses. I will tell you my message through. *You are to look after Rory when I'm gone.*"

"I hope that will not be soon," he spoke under his breath so low perhaps she didn't hear him.

"My daughter isn't capable of caring for even a song sparrow. But you're a different story." She swallowed the last of her third drink and Moses offered her another.

"On that day, and I hope you're listening, Moe. On that day, which may be any day or the next day or never, you are to consider Rory your own flesh and blood."

As a matter of fact until this very moment when Rory took residence in his mansion, Moses had forgotten almost entirely the grandmother's December visit. In fact he had thought the night of her bequest she was perhaps crazy or, who knows, a bit drunk on his cheer.

But now it all came back. He could almost hear the wheels of the buggy and the snorting of the half-tamed horse she kept in her barn along with a half dozen or so other untamed horses.

Again Moses felt a chill come over him as if his visitor of so many years ago had also descended on him with bag and baggage.

He looked up just then and saw Rory staring at him.

Again the fireplace was going just as on the night the grandmother had delivered her bequest.

Rory now took the best seat in front of the fire, and then to Moses' astonishment he heard the boy spit into the flames and, as if in answer, the fire turned a queer greenish color and gave an echoing sound as it ascended the ancient chimney.

Vesta Hawley often found herself weeping against Frau Storeholder's comforting bosom. She sometimes even lay prone on the carpet in front of Frau Storeholder's chair. She was sobbing, imploring even, like a zealot before a number of votive candles.

So carried away in grief was she that an onlooker might have thought Vesta Hawley was drunk or indeed mad by reason of her finally embracing the old woman's feet in her sorrow.

But she was of course neither drunk nor mad. She was consumed with guilt and with homesickness for her son.

Whether Frau Storeholder ever listened attentively any more to this endless unburdening of Rory's mother is questionable. She had heard the story after all so many times. Countless innumerable times.

As if walking in his sleep young Rory often times entered his mother's bedroom and discovered her in the embrace of one of her banqueters or lodgers. The young man of the occasion holding his mother was probably drunk for he did not appear to notice that Vesta's son had entered the room and was staring at his embraces. For one thing Rory's eyes were so swollen with sleep the lover of the evening might have decided the boy was not actually seeing what was transpiring. Was dreaming in fact upright!

But Vesta knew Rory saw, even if he saw in deep slumber!

One morning after he had surprised her with a lover, Vesta was unusually affectionate and lavish to her son. She prepared his breakfast herself: a sumptuous plate of eggs laid by the hen within the hour, a mountain of brown steamed potatoes, cornbread, grits, and gooseberry jam.

Rory ate it all but without showing any appreciation or appetite for what he ate. At the conclusion of his meal, he took up the thick stiff hand-embroidered linen napkin and assiduously and repeatedly wiped his mouth and chin, even going on to wipe his open throat and chest, while muttering something. Tears followed slowly, painfully from his eyes as if those eyes, still flush from what he had seen the night before, were at last letting fall their water in sorrow for all the sins of the world.

As Rory, having gathered up his schoolbooks, began to walk toward the door, Vesta followed him meekly and said softly: "Aren't you going to kiss Mama good morning?"

Rory shook his head.

"Don't you know how much I want your kisses," she whispered.

Rory refused to look at her.

"Say something, or say anything even if it is a curse."

He only shook his head more slowly, more mournfully.

"Do you mean you will never kiss your Mama again then, Rory?"

He grinned unhumorously then, like a gargoyle or perhaps a frog.

"Never again?" she begged.

He only nodded and grinned more fiercely.

She had closed her eyes on getting no answers to her appeal.

Finally opening her eyes, she saw he had departed.

Weeping and between sobs, Vesta told Frau Storeholder the story all over again for the hundredth time.

"Didn't Rory know I yielded to the banqueters and the roomers only to keep a roof over his head, dear Belinda? Oh do say something. Don't be like Rory on that long ago, terrible morning. *Didn't he know I did it for him?*"

Frau Storeholder's own eyes were widening, the pupils a deep black.

"Tell me, Belinda," she began to try to rise but then only fell back on her knees, looking up at her confessor.

"Love is a very jealous god," Frau Storeholder managed to say. She removed her glasses and put them away in their satin case.

"I don't know what you mean, a jealous god. Are you referring to my boy when you speak so!"

The old woman nodded. "Love will not permit or allow for it to be shared. And you, poor child, have shared love with so many, so countless many."

"You are condemning me, unlike the Good Shepherd who forgave the Woman at the Well."

"I am not condemning you, my poor girl. I am telling you what love's commands are. He will never allow his love to be shared with others. In your case multitudes."

"Tell me this," Vesta coughed out the words as she rose from her, kneeling and exhausted, and fell into one of the antique lounge chairs.

"Tell me, Belinda, and do not lie to me. Will Rory then never come back to me, never forgive me, never, oh yes, let me say, never love me?"

Frau Storeholder weakly almost imperceptibly shook her head.

"You are shaking your head like he did! Oh wicked, wicked Belinda. You are pronouncing my doom with that idle movement of your head.

"He will never come back to me, then," Vesta muttered.

Even if Belinda Storeholder had replied then that Rory would return, Vesta would not have heard her.

The final realization came that Rory would not be returning home one cold clear December morning when a young messenger arrived, holding in his hands a stiff white envelope addressed to Miss Hawley in huge Roman letters.

Vesta for a few moments was unable to take the envelope in her hands.

The messenger kept saying, "It's for you, ma'am."

Vesta still hesitating then called Frau Storeholder to come to the door.

She received the message.

"Do you have any change for this young man?" Vesta inquired of Frau Storeholder. One thing about her friend which always amused Vesta was the old woman always managed to have money on her person. The change was hidden deep in a large beaded purse.

Frau Storeholder produced a shiny fifty-cent piece and hand-fed it to Vesta. But when Vesta offered the money to the messenger (he was, she supposed, one of the young gamblers who lived at Moe's Villa), he refused the emolument, uttering an excuse.

"May I leave the envelope now with you, ma'am? Please do take the envelope," the young man now quite flustered inquired.

As Vesta appeared at this moment incapable of taking the envelope, Frau Storeholder received it for her.

"I thank you," he told the old woman and touched his cap. Vesta returned to the front parlour then and threw herself into one of her favorite easy chairs.

Frau Storeholder was still holding the envelope.

"Shall I read you what the message is," Frau Storeholder's voice had a kind of tenderness in it, rare for her.

"I don't know if I can bear for you to read it. At the same time I've mislaid my glasses, so I suppose you'll have to oblige me. I'd just as soon throw it in the fireplace. A message from the kidnapper of my boy! What more can he want out of me!"

Frau Storeholder had opened the envelope with a letter opener and read the few lines contained in it silently to herself.

A very thin smile spread over her lips, and the sight of that smile, feeble though it was, heartened Vesta.

"Read the message, then, Belinda, I am ready!"

Frau Storeholder cleared her throat noisily, a bit like an elocution teacher, and read:

> *My dear Vesta Hawley,*
>   As cold weather has set in would you kindly send to us as soon as possible your son's heavy overcoat.
>   Yours most respectfully,
>   Moses Swearingen

"And is that all it says, Belinda?"

Frau Storeholder replied that it was all.

"I was afraid Moses Swearingen was going maybe to bring court action against me."

"He would never do that," Frau Storeholder assured her.

A heavy silence now intervened. At last Frau Store-holder gave out a great sigh, and Vesta, raising her voice, said: "I have no idea where his overcoat is. The last time I saw it the moths had been into one of the sleeves. The whole coat is probably in tatters. Oh, God in heaven, why am I plagued with such a child, will you tell me!"

"I know exactly where the overcoat is," Frau Storeholder spoke in her most soothing tones. "I once stumbled over a whole row of gold spittoons near the coat."

"Those spittoons belonged to Pete," Vesta reflected. "He chewed and was never without a plug of tobacco, let me tell you. Some time after he left me there came to see me a collector who was interested in one of my antique rockers, but when he saw the spittoons, he wanted to have them instead. I held off from selling them. Seems they are very valuable now."

Not wanting Vesta to begin on her reminiscences of Peter Driscoll, Frau Storeholder interrupted to say: "Let me go and see, Vesta, just what condition his overcoat is in then."

"Yes, go fetch it, Belinda, if there's anything left of it. But why can't that multi-millionaire of a Swearingen buy the boy a decent coat. He's smothering in money, he sweats money!" She took out one of her hand-embroidered handkerchiefs and gave a snort in it which caused Frau Storeholder to flinch, for she found the sound indelicate.

Vesta waited then for Belinda to return. Her long absence caused her frayed nerves to worsen.

"You was gone forever!" she greeted Frau Storeholder when she reappeared.

She was not carrying the boy's overcoat but instead was lugging an unwieldy package.

She almost dropped the cumbersome object on the floor but managed instead to deposit it on a long seldom-used end table.

"What on earth have you brought from upstairs," Vesta wondered, and her temper flared.

"The boy's overcoat, dear Vesta, is all rags and tatters from the moths."

"But where on earth did you lay hands on this package?"

"I found it near his coat. There's writing on the outside as you can see. It's from . . ."

"Yes, from Peter Driscoll," Vesta whined.

Peter Driscoll was Rory's father, though nobody was sure he was actually Vesta Hawley's legal husband. At least there was no record of their having been to the altar.

"But what do you suppose is in the package, Vesta?"

"Marbles, I think," she replied bitterly.

"Marbles!"

"It all comes back to me now. When this package arrived nearly ten years ago, and I haven't thought of it again until today, let me tell you, I only half opened it. And I have never looked into it since. But I thought then it must be marbles. When Rory was a little boy of five or so, he and his . . . Dad" (here Vesta choked on the last word), "they played marbles together on the big carpet. As I say, I peeked into the package when it was delivered, and as I was ill I barely saw Rory in the next few days that followed to inform him there was a package upstairs from his Dad. He had begun even then to keep himself away from me."

"You mean Rory never found out what his Dad had sent him for a present?"

"That's right," Vesta sighed.

Vesta's complete indifference may have given Frau

Storeholder the goad to undo the long-forgotten birthday present. Her old heavy-veined hands removed the heavy paper and excelsior which contained the father's gift. She felt a kind of fear nonetheless, exploring the package's interior. Perhaps, she wondered, maybe it was not something like marbles, but—who knows—explosives! But of course explosives was hardly a possibility.

Before uncovering the gift itself Frau Storeholder could not refrain from saying: "And you never looked all the way inside, Vesta, all these years."

"I told you, I peeked, Belinda. And I decided then it contained marbles. But I hated Pete Driscoll so much I didn't want to see what he had given my boy for his birthday. He ruined both of our lives, after all. And so I forgot in time there had ever been a birthday present for Rory! Go ahead, blame me.

"Open the confounded thing up then! What are you waiting for? Can't you see how the very mention of the name Peter Driscoll has brought on a sick headache. But wait a minute. I'm going out to the kitchen and take some of those drops Dr. Cooke prescribed."

Frau Storeholder went on attempting to extricate the birthday present from all the heavy wrapping paper and excelsior.

When the contents were finally exposed, Frau Storeholder at first drew back and gave a kind of stifled moan as if a nest of serpents had been uncovered.

Vesta had closed her eyes, waiting.

Frau Storeholder then drew out from the wrapping paper row after row of its shining contents.

The objects she displayed to a silent Vesta Hawley appeared to be a collection of gems, jewels, precious stones—whatever they were. Indeed their blazing red beauty caused her to gasp, and finally cry out.

"They're not marbles, Vesta," Frau Storeholder spoke in a lofty stern manner such as Vesta had never heard come from her before.

Vesta moved cautiously toward the shining red objects as if they might indeed be dangerous.

"Rubies?" she wondered.

"Rubies?" Frau Storeholder repeated wonderingly.

"Precious rubies, I do believe," Vesta gasped, and tears overflowed her eyes. "What else can look like that, I ask you!"

"But see how many there are of them, Vesta. Just come closer please. Row after row of the same stones or gems or whatever they are."

"I can't believe that's what they are, Frau Storeholder. Precious stones. Oh God in Heaven, what does this mean. *Rubies* all these years up there in that old attic. Let me sit down before I fall down. God in Heaven!"

"Rubies," Frau Storeholder muttered in awe.

Jeff Caldwell operated the local livery barn. His Dad had run the barn for many years, supplying carriage-drawn horses for the quality to travel short distances in.

Today, receiving a call from Vesta Hawley for a conveyance, Jeff decided to use his old Willys-Knight car. He cogitated long and deep however, wondering what on earth Vesta Hawley wanted a conveyance for, she who never set foot outside her mansion.

Arriving at the Hawley address, Jeff was met by Frau Storeholder at the entrance, holding a large package wrapped in pieces of old quilt.

"Let me give you a hand," Jeff took the package from her, and after eyeing it wonderingly, tipped his cap and asked: "Miss Hawley ain't going too?"

"I'm the passenger today, Jeff," Frau Storeholder had brightened a little at the sight of the young liveryman who had a face that betokened both health and kindness.

Still eyeing the package, Jeff wondered: "And where are we off to, Frau Storeholder?"

She hesitated only a moment.

"Moe's Villa."

Jeff almost lost his grasp of the package on hearing the name of the destination.

Frau Storeholder grinned at his surprise. Had she told him she was going to the disorderly house some five miles from the village limits, he could hardly have shown more shock.

They rode in silence, but after a while Frau Storeholder noticed Jeff was having trouble in not breaking out into, yes, a horselaugh.

Whether by reason of guilt or perhaps a usually hidden generosity, Vesta Hawley had provided Frau Storeholder with a tip of several silver dollars for Jeff Caldwell.

He jumped out after receiving the gratuity and, carrying the package, he proceeded with his fare up the twenty-eight steps leading to the front door of the Villa.

He had to ring a score of times before Moses Swearingen himself appeared in a kind of business suit and wearing a fedora hat.

"Jeff, I'll be damned!" he greeted the liveryman, and then he caught sight of Frau Storeholder.

Mumbling a good day to her, Moses grumbled and bowed in the direction of Frau Storeholder.

Inside they all sat down in the front parlour. Jeff had not bothered to remove his cap and was catching his breath perhaps at his horror that he had conveyed a respectable lady to the Villa.

"When do you want Jeff to call for you," Moses now inquired almost bashfully of Frau Storeholder.

Moses was as a matter of fact more bewildered and uneasy even than Jeff Caldwell over Frau Storeholder's visit, and he kept eyeing the bulky package weighted down in pieces of ragged quilt with increasing curiosity.

"Ah, but you mean I am to remain, Moses?" Frau Storeholder acted surprised that she had more to do here than merely deposit the package from Peter Driscoll.

"Of course you're to remain," Moses sounded almost hurt.

And Moses now to the astonishment of Jeff Caldwell smiled, a smile Jeff had never seen cross the face of the proprietor of the Villa.

"In about a half an hour then?" Jeff said rising.

"Make it an hour, Jeff," Moses told the liveryman, who touching his cap to Moses and again to Frau Storeholder made such a rapid retreat one had the feeling he had disappeared before their eyes until they heard the slamming of the outside doors.

Moses Swearingen now moved his lips awkwardly, but without being able to frame what he was thinking in words.

Finally, crossing and re-crossing his long legs, he got out: "Frau Storeholder, this is such a rare occasion, I can only wonder how I am privileged to have you for company."

Frau Storeholder's own lips now moved also without her being able to reply to his compliment, until the ensuing silence forced her to say, "The pleasure is all mine, Moses."

She smiled comfortably now, for after all she had known him since he was hardly more than a boy.

Moses went on staring fixedly now at the package. Seeing Moses' wonder, she exclaimed, "You see, Moses, Miss Hawley and I were looking for Rory's winter coat in answer to your message. The coat, well, is in tatters. But we came across this package meanwhile."

Both Moses and Frau Storeholder now stared in unison at the object in question.

"It seems," she continued, still gazing at the package as if it acted as a kind of prompter, "the package I've brought today was a gift sent ten years ago from Peter Driscoll for his son Rory."

Moses' features moved uncomfortably at the mention of Peter Driscoll.

"Miss Hawley, on first receiving the package sent as I say so long ago, told me she only peeked inside at the time. She thought it was marbles."

"Marbles," Moses raised his voice, and instead of crossing or uncrossing his legs now, he put both his feet down on the carpet with a thud.

"Because, you see, Moses, when Rory was a very small boy his Dad and he used to play marbles together on the big carpet in the living room."

Looking up from her recital, Frau Storeholder saw Moses wiping his face with a broad blue polka-dot hand-kerchief. He was sweating profusely.

"But what was our wonder," she went on doggedly, "when we opened the package up, and it was not marbles at all. It was something else."

"Something else," Moses repeated her last words in a kind of hoarse whisper.

"At any rate, I have brought the gift for the boy it was originally destined for."

She then drew out from her wraps a thick envelope.

"This letter," she pointed at it as if it might contradict her, "it is from Peter Driscoll to his son and was inside the package. I have glanced at the letter," she said guiltily. "I had to know if it might throw light on the package's contents."

Moses Swearingen nodded solemnly.

"My hands, Moses, are not quite up to opening the package. If you would be so kind. . . ."

He gave her an almost accusing look and then left the room to return presently, carrying some heavy shears and a hunting knife.

He grimly, almost angrily, tore open the package.

After nearly reducing the entire package to shreds, he halted just as Vesta and Frau Storeholder had halted the day they had looked inside.

Very slowly Moses began lifting one row after another of what appeared to be, if not precious jewels, certainly gems of some kind.

"And Miss Hawley called them marbles!" he shouted. He laughed. "Did you ever hear gems like these called marbles, Frau Storeholder? I am surprised indeed. These marbles are rubies, or I'll eat my hat!"

He held his right hand now to his eyes as if the sight of the gems had hurt his vision.

Having gazed at the jewels for as long as the sight of such a spectacle could be endured, Moses Swearingen rose unsteadily and began pacing around the room in an agitated manner.

Frau Storeholder looked after him concernedly. She felt

puzzled, even sorry for him somehow. It was obvious the sight of what is called rubies was highly disturbing to him—why, of course, she had no way of knowing.

"And then what about the letter Peter Driscoll wrote to his son," he now turned to face her. "Am I not to know the contents of it also?" he wondered, and he motioned with his hand to the gems now exposed to anybody's inspection after their long absence from the sun.

"Oh, the letter," Frau Storeholder exclaimed, and after a flurry she handed him the document.

Before beginning the reading, however, Moses Swearingen gave another long look at the gems as if they required some kind of say-so for him to proceed.

He read aloud, and as he did so Frau Storeholder closed her eyes.

My dear boy (Moses' voice boomed out), *I have had you on my heart and mind ever since I left you with your mother. I did not leave you willingly, always remember that. Not at all. There was no way your mother and I could see eye to eye. And there was no way I could earn a living in Gilboa, especially owing to the great expense of keeping up so large, so oversized a place as Vesta's. So I have been travelling not only through this country but in foreign lands to boot, hoping against hope I could mend my fortunes and come back to see you some day. In place of my coming home, I am sending this special gift for you. Be sure to keep good care of yourself. My own health is not of the best, and I do not know in fact when or if I will be better. Remember, dear boy, how much I care for you and miss you more than I have words to*

tell you. These little red gems are only a small token
of how much I care for you.
     Your loving father, ever
     Peter Driscoll

Moses Swearingen handed back the letter to Frau Storeholder with the alacrity of someone relinquishing an object aflame.

He sat down and, following Frau Storeholder's example, closed his eyes.

There was again a long silence during which one could catch the sound of a large green fly buzzing somewhere.

"He is dead, I take it." Moses inquired, his eyes still closed.

"Peter Driscoll? Oh, a long time ago, Moses. Years and years."

Moses nodded and a queer enigmatic smile broke over his mouth.

"I cannot say, Frau Storeholder, that I am happy to have such a possession as you have brought to me today. But I believe since Rory is the one who is entitled to be the owner, it belongs here for as long as he remains with me. Which I hope will be forever!"

He almost shouted these last words, and Frau Storeholder drew in her breath.

At that moment the front door bell rang, and Jeff Caldwell was seen staring at them through the frosted glass of the door.

"Must you go?" Moses wondered.

She nodded.

"There are a number of things I would like to ask you," he explained. He looked over at the gift again as if it were the cause of everything that faced or would face him.

"But I suppose we can arrange for you to come here again," he gave a faint smile.

"Just as you wish, Moses."

She was gone then without another word, but Jeff Caldwell shook Moses's hand and volunteered something about the change in the weather outside.

Moses sat down then. His eyes tried to avoid looking at the package of jewels. Finally he picked up the letter of Peter Driscoll and stared at the peculiar handwriting of its author.

Then his eye returned again to take in the gems.

A few hours after Frau Storeholder had taken her leave, Moses Swearingen was taken suddenly ill and retired to his bedroom without having spoken to Rory about the "rubies." Seeing he was going to be sick, Moses had instructed one of his hired men to apprise Rory of the arrival of the package and the letter from Peter Driscoll.

Moses Swearingen's illness was this: he had been in some kind of gunfight years ago when he was a fairly young man. The bullet of his assailant still lodged in his chest or, as Dr. Cooke said, near his breastbone. It was too dangerous to remove the bullet, yet every so often the pain was almost intolerable were it not for the morphine Dr. Cooke was always kind enough to supply.

Today, as if somehow the sight of the rubies had brought it on, Moses experienced the most fearful pain in his chest he could remember.

He was tossing and turning in his king-sized bed even after swallowing a heavy dose of morphine when Rory entered.

Rory had now been with Moses for some months—it seemed years—and the boy had changed. This was brought home to Moses when he thought he saw coming into his bedroom an unknown young man. He was about to cry out when he recognized Rory.

It was not impudence or ill-breeding, Moses recognized, but for some other reason that the boy came directly to his bedside and sat down on one of the heavy comforters. Moses' broad chest was bare, and Rory stared incredulous at the wound.

Then the morphine began to take effect or was it, Moses wondered bitterly, the presence of Rory that quieted his agony.

He was loath to admit that every time he saw Rory he felt a kind of calming effect. This was now especially true.

"Did you inspect your Dad's gift to you?" Moses managed to ask.

Rory gave an almost imperceptible nod.

"And you read his letter to you also?"

Rory mumbled a yes.

"You never told me you had a bullet lodged in your chest," Rory spoke now no longer like the boy Moses had brought home but like a young man.

"Well, now you know," Moses said, and attempted to rise, but the pain began again and he slumped down.

"May I have a look at where the bullet went in?" Rory inquired. He would never have dared say such a thing to the master of the Villa even a few days ago, but today the master was too much in pain to correct or even to notice his breach of behaviour.

Rory touched the place on his chest where the bullet had entered.

"What in the name of . . ." Moses began, then stopped. "I say, what did you do just then with your hand?"

"Just touched where the bullet is," Rory replied.

"The pain has all left me," Moses stared at his visitor. Then after a long pause: "Oh, it was Doc Cooke's dope, I guess."

Rory touched the sore place again, and more little threads of pain appeared to leave Moses' chest.

"What do you do when you touch the place?" Moses wondered. "You must do something."

Rory went then into one of what people called his absentminded "starts." He said no more and indeed acted as if he had forgotten where he was.

"Well, what do you think of your present?"

"Oh, the gems," Rory replied.

"And the letter too, don't forget."

Rory became silent.

Just then the pain in his chest began again. Moses tossed and turned and groaned. His face was dripping with sweat.

Then, as if it was his turn, Rory touched the hurt place and again all the pain left Moses.

"What is going on?" Moses wondered after the pain had left again, but he was still too out of breath to say more and was sweating profusely.

"I can see the bullet is trying to come out from your . . . hide," the boy remarked.

Moses tried to look down at his chest to see what Rory saw, but the effort tired him, and he lay back on the pillows under his head.

"So you're cool about the rubies from your Dad, ain't you," Moses managed to get out these words.

"Rubies? I guess I have to get used to them," Rory mumbled.

"The bullet will be working its way out, Moses," Dr. Sherman Cooke told his patient. The doctor had been summoned in the middle of the night to come at once for Moses Swearingen had taken a turn for the worse. Unlike many physicians, Dr. Cooke relished these midnight emergency house calls. He also relished, though he would be the last to admit it, that he got a great deal out of tending someone as unlike any of his other patients as Moses Swearingen.

"I'm surprised at you, Moses," Dr. Cooke was saying as he administered the hypodermic. "You boo-hoo and ki-yi more than any woman. Why, I bet Rory here could stand pain better than you."

Moses smiled a little at this last remark of the Doc.

"By the way, Moe, where are these gems I've been hearing about for the last week or so? For the jewels are in your possession, I gather."

Moses leaned up on one elbow and stared at the doctor.

"Do you know rubies, Doc?"

Rory had been sitting quietly and observing everything. He had found the news that the bullet was working its way out evidently of more interest than the gems.

"Rory," Moses barked, "go fetch the present from your Dad for the Doc to see, will you."

Rory took his own good time before rising and going out of the room.

"I wouldn't have recognized the chap," Dr. Cooke referred to the boy. "You've cleaned him up, got rid of his cowlick, and put some decent duds on him."

Rory entered with the package from his Dad and set it down on the counterpane beside Moses.

"Open up the box and show 'em to the Doc," Moses instructed the boy.

Again Rory hesitated, and then in his own good time took out one of the panels containing some of the rubies.

Dr. Cooke whistled at the sight of them, then chuckled and even slapped his thigh. Moses acted disgusted at the doctor's reaction.

"I almost wish my first wife was still alive," Dr. Cooke remarked, squinting one eye and examining one of the larger of the rubies. "Looks genuine enough. But it could be just glass!" he sighed.

"Glass, my eye," Moses almost roared, for he felt almost free of pain.

"You may scoff, Moe. But my first wife had costume jewels so splendid they fooled even the jewel experts."

The doctor held up another of the rubies to the light.

"And even the greatest experts can be fooled in the matter of precious gems," the Doc added.

"I wager these are the real McCoy, Doc," Moses muttered.

"And what does Rory say to all of this," Dr. Cooke gazed moodily at the boy. Rory looked brand-new to him now, and the gift of rubies somehow made him seem a complete stranger.

"Whatever did Pete Driscoll do to be able to lay his hands on these jewels, will you tell me, Moe," the doctor remarked.

Both men were then silent for they felt an awkward reticence in mentioning the character of Peter Driscoll in the presence of his son.

"Why don't they look like the real thing," Rory blurted out, an edge in his voice.

Dr. Cooke gave a start at the boy's remark for his voice was as new as his appearance, partly owing to the fact his voice was changing.

"Are you addressing this remark to me, young man," the doctor wondered. "Or to your benefactor here?"

Rory made a kind of snorting sound at the Doc's calling Moses his benefactor, then managed to say, "I guess I was asking both of you."

"They're too beautiful," Moses said, and he got up and took a seat in the rocking chair.

"Too beautiful for what?" Dr. Cooke asked.

"Why too beautiful to be anything but glass. I've read somewhere that fine glass imitations or what you called a moment ago costume jewelry can look niftier than the real thing."

Dr. Cooke now gave a snort.

"I must say, Moe," the doctor weighed his words now, "I have never seen anything to match them. But jewels, if they're real, pose a problem, and if they're not real, well, you have something else to worry about.

"But, Moe, I want to go back to the bullet in your chest. Let me look at your chest again."

Before he departed, Dr. Cooke issued instructions both to Moses and Rory.

"Now, boys, the bullet may come out sometime during the night," he told them. "I want Rory here to stay with you, Moe, at all times." The doctor hesitated, blinked, and then went on: "I recommend Rory sleep next to you so there will be no loss of time if the bullet begins to get dislodged. I am leaving a surgical instrument he can help retrieve the bullet with. It's good you have a king-size bed so Rory can have plenty of room as he looks after you. I've left some extra pills also," he pointed to a package on the big chiffonier.

"Rory talks in his sleep, Doc."

Dr. Cooke guffawed at this remark. "I said I want him as near to you as can be in case the bullet begins to come out. You can't dislodge the damned thing alone. Anyhow, hearing somebody talk in his sleep is better than having to sleep next to someone who snores. He don't snore, does he?"

"I haven't heard him, Doc."

"Then let him share the bed with you until the emergency is passed."

Dr. Cooke now rose in all his six feet four inches, and grabbing his little black bag, gave Moses a look which was akin perhaps to a benediction.

"Remember my instructions then," the doctor sternly spoke to Rory. "And don't leave my patient even for a minute. Do you hear? There is a chamber pot under the bed if you have to relieve yourself. Clear? Do not leave him for as much as a split second."

Rory's face was a perfect blank, just as it had also been when Bess Byal had tried to get him to understand long division and common fractions.

"Mind me now, Rory, or you will have to answer to me!"

Rory muttered somewhat grumpily to the effect he would obey the doctor.

The doctor had left one lamp burning near the bed, and Moses began to pile four or five pillows to rest his head on. He motioned to Rory to lie down half a bed's distance away from him.

"I hope you got by heart all the Doc told you," he said and motioned to his chest, which, at the doctor's instructions was left exposed.

Later Moses Swearingen would recall not so much the

moment the bullet had emerged as Rory's almost uninterrupted talking in his sleep.

The general subject of his whispering beside him seemed to enumerate Vesta Hawley's roster of lovers, whose names were repeated so often Moses could tick them off by heart:

Carl Gretzinger, soap salesman
Bud Hotchkiss, life guard
Elmo Larrabee, choir director
Joel Sausser, mail clerk
Hal Eoff, Railway Express delivery man

"Will you lay off," Moses would mutter piteously from time to time, begging for silence. He had forgotten if he ever knew that people who talk in their sleep, like sleepwalkers, can never hear what anyone awake and near them says.

"Will you give a guy a break, for Christ's sake?"

He had no more said this than Rory heard Moses let out a war whoop, which he later said would have been loud enough to wake the dead.

Twisting and turning, even frothing at the mouth, Moses tried to turn this way and that, but Rory took hold of him and pushed him down firmly so that he could keep his eye on the bullet hole.

Then as Moses cried out as if a torch had been set afire on his bare flesh, he felt those strong pitiless young hands moving as if to touch his beating heart, and he heard an echoing cry come from the "sleeptalker."

Moses stared openmouthed at the boy who was holding the bullet now in his hand and brandishing it at Moses.

"You mean it's out, Rory?" Moses said in a voice totally unlike his own.

Jumping up, Rory let Moses see the bullet close up as he held it in his right hand.

"Do you aim to keep it?" Moses moaned, and he somehow was able to rise and get out of bed.

"Can't I?" Rory wondered, still holding the bullet in plain view for the sufferer.

"What in hell do you want my bullet for?"

"Well, ain't I earned it by getting it out of you!"

"I say again, what in hell do you want to keep my bullet for."

When there was no answer from Rory, Moses sighed as he sat in his armchair. This time though he was not taking morphine pills, he was drinking right out of the bottle of bootleg whiskey.

"Keep the damned thing if you want to then. Guess you think you earned it, I reckon. Who knows, maybe you did."

"I was a fool ever to let those jewels leave my house," Vesta was speaking to Dr. Cooke the next evening after his visit to Moe's Villa.

Frau Storeholder, at Vesta's urging, was also in the same room with her and the doctor.

For one thing, Vesta had observed tonight that Dr. Cooke was if anything more beguiled by her than ever before. His dippy behaviour tonight both pleased and annoyed Vesta. The fact she had "stolen" the thousand-dollar bills somehow—evidently—made him more admiring of her.

He claimed he had come tonight only to report on his meeting with Moe.

The doctor was somewhat appalled Vesta did not ask about Rory.

"I believe Moe thinks the rubies are the real thing," Doctor Cooke was saying.

"A lot such a fellow as Moe Swearingen would know about gems," Vesta scoffed. "I fear they're no more genuine than Peter Driscoll was on the up-and-up. And do you think Peter would have sent his son anything worth even a half million if it had any market value. For you did know Peter Driscoll, didn't you, Sherman?" she shot at him.

Dr. Cooke winced at her tone.

"Of course I knew Peter. Treated him very often."

Amazed at this retort, Vesta wondered, "May I ask you what ailed him that he came to you?"

"His ears were full of wax," the doctor quipped.

Vesta made a sneering sound. Perhaps she hoped to hear her former husband had a more serious ailment.

"You are quite right, Vesta," the doctor sighed and looked at her with longing. "Pete Driscoll would never have sent anything through the mail as precious as rubies."

"But maybe he wanted a place to hide them in," Frau Storeholder spoke all at once out of her deep silence—in fact both the doctor and Vesta thought she had been dozing as usual.

"I never thought of that, Belinda," Vesta spoke almost in a whisper. "Do you think Peter Driscoll was seeking a hiding place, Sherman?"

Dr. Cooke dismissed the idea at first, but then Vesta noticed an expression of doubt, even uneasiness came over her suitor.

"I looked carefully at all the rubies," the doctor spoke now in his professional manner. "They are glass. Fine glass, but in my opinion, only glass. Very good workmanship. Worth something in their own right. But glass, Vesta dear."

The atmosphere had changed suddenly. Doubt was in all their minds, and that doubt had been created by the Doctor himself.

"The whole town is talking about my neglect of Rory," Vesta brought up this topic again. "Bess Byal was over the other day to say everybody is up in arms. But thank God the superintendent of schools will take no action. Yet people think Rory could hardly be in a place more unsuitable for a young boy than Moe's Villa."

"Moe Swearingen may not be a gentleman," the doctor said, "but he is far from being a bad sort. Not a bit of it."

The doctor as usual was annoyed that Frau Storeholder was present. He knew also that she was here because Vesta wished her to be and that she wished her to be here to punish him. And this thought made him more in love with Vesta than ever. Love forbidden is twice as powerful, he mused. And his for Vesta Hawley had never been so intense.

One snowy afternoon one of the young men who waited on Moses with such faithful attendance that he seemed to be everywhere at once entered the card room where Moses and Rory were playing a card game invented by Moses Swearingen himself.

"A lady is asking to see you," the attendant informed Moses.

"A lady?" Moses wondered sarcastically.

"Mrs. Hawley," the young man stuttered a bit.

Moses dropped his hand of cards and stared at Rory.

"Tell her to wait in the front parlour," Moses said after a pause in which he kept his eyes glued to his hand of cards.

In the parlour Vesta Hawley was seated on a rickety straight-backed chair. She wore a half-veil and large gold earrings. She had only one glove, this on her left hand.

"Yes," Moses said.

"Sit down, Mr. Swearingen." Vesta Hawley addressed him as if *he* was entering *her* parlour.

Moses hesitated a moment, grinned, then sat down on a faded settee.

"I want to speak with my son," she explained, and she fumbled in her purse and brought out a pack of cigarettes and stuck one in her mouth.

"May I smoke," she said although she had already lit her cigarette from a matchbox which she had found on the side table by her chair.

Moses shrugged.

"I supposed you wanted to discuss the gems," he said, and rising he brought her an immense cut glass ashtray.

Then he turned his back on her like a servant who, having given her the necessary attention, is about to leave.

"I do want to see the rubies again, I confess," she blew a ring of smoke toward him.

Turning to face her he said, "But you've already had a look at them, and besides you turned them over to your son."

He walked closer to her now and looked at the burning end of her smoke.

"At any rate, rubies or no rubies, you can't very well refuse me from seeing my own flesh and blood."

"Flesh and blood," he repeated as if he had never heard the phrase before.

"You have no idea how upset this has made me. I never dreamed . . ."

"Yes," he prompted her when she stopped speaking.

"How a man like Peter Driscoll. . . . Well, after all, you knew him, didn't you?"

Moses nodded in mock encouragement.

"I can't believe he could ever have acquired real gems," she spoke with the cigarette tightly between her lips.

"When I first set eyes on them, I had thought, you see, Moses, that . . ."

"That they were marbles!"

"All right. Marbles!" she snapped.

"And do you mean to take them from Rory now if you've decided they're maybe not marbles."

"No, no, no!" she raised her voice and got up and walked around the room, dropping cigarette ashes everywhere.

"The whole thing has really stricken me. Yes, that's the right word for it."

"You've always been very high-strung, Vesta."

"You say that as if it was my fault."

"I only speak from observing you."

"I wish we had never opened the box now. Actually as time passed I had forgotten Peter ever sent my boy a present. I was sure when it arrived it was of no consequence, considering where it came from."

"A present, though, from a boy's dad is usually not something to be put away and forgotten, its value aside."

"I broke out in a cold sweat when I saw his handwriting on the package," she confided, and put out her cigarette in the big ashtray. "After all Peter Driscoll had done to me, after all I had suffered at his hands. But no, I didn't mean to hide the gift from Rory. I was ill at the time, very ill, and by the time I recovered I had all but forgotten about it— until you asked for Rory's overcoat, and Frau Storeholder came across the forgotten gift package in the attic."

Moses consulted his large pocket watch.

"Let me see him, Mr. Swearingen." She was standing directly over him as she said this.

He pointed to the open door leading to the card room.

"Rory, my love," Vesta cried as she entered the card room. She took him in her arms and kissed him several times in rapid succession.

To Moe's disgust he saw a wave of happiness sweep over Rory's face.

"You have no idea how I've missed you," his mother went on. "I can see though that Mr. Swearingen has taken very good care of you. If I had his means, dear boy, I would see you wearing even better clothes than he has fitted you out with. Oh, I am grateful to him, no question about that. We have had hard times together, Moses," she turned now to Swearingen. "Very hard times. I suppose I should have sold the mansion and lived in some little flat somewhere with my boy. Holding on to an ancestral property with no husband to depend on, oh, well, you have heard it all a thousand times I expect."

She wiped her eyes of tears with a delicately scented handkerchief and sighed.

"I have been thinking, Rory, that if the gems are real, we might sell them, and if they are worth a fortune, we could buy back my mansion from the banks and the mortgage holders. Oh, I know some people say the rubies are not rubies," she almost sobbed now. "Tell me what you think, Rory."

"I don't know one jewel from another, Mama."

"Oh, my dear boy, when you say *Mama*, you have no idea how happy it makes me. Rory, your Dad never loved us. He deserted us. Do you think I neglected you on purpose? Think again. I love only you. You are my life, my all. The mansion is only something I have held on to so that one day I could leave it to you. But the mansion has been too heavy a burden for one woman to carry. Now, dear boy, let me see the rubies again, if you don't mind."

"Shall your Mother see your rubies?" Moe said, but there was now little trace in his voice of his usual biting manner and sarcasm.

At a nod from Rory, Moe went into an adjoining room and brought out the box of the jewels and placed it on a long table once used in his own banquets.

Vesta had to put on her glasses which she hated to wear as they made her look, she always said, like an old grandma.

"Oh, oh," she began as the jewels were uncovered. "But, Rory, they look so different from the time I first set eyes on them. Before the box was even opened of course—years ago, and I, merely peeping in, thought they were marbles, agates, maybe, but not worth the powder to blow them up with. Oh dear, now I don't know." She touched one of the gems cautiously. "They do look like jewels of some sort, I reckon. But they're sticky to the touch!"

Both Moe and Rory approached the box of gems and stared. The word "sticky" may have had something to do with their looking now at the gems with suspicion and puzzlement.

"We must call in an expert, Moe," Vesta spoke now familiarly. "You with all your worldly contacts must know of someone."

Moe could not help being pleased at Vesta calling him a man with worldly contacts. He half-smiled.

"There is a Russian, Alexander Oblonsky, or some such name. Met him once in France. Escaped from the Bolsheviks in the nick of time or they'd have beheaded him, he told me. Rich as Croesus and loves to show off his knowledge of diamonds, pearls and of course rubies. He claims to have been one of the most dependable and faithful retainers of the late Tsarina and that she gave him some of her own jewels for safekeeping.

"You don't say, Moe." Vesta was greatly intrigued. "And we can send for him?"

"We can, but will he come? A busy man, almost a celebrity."

"I suppose he would charge us a fortune then," Vesta complained.

"Not necessarily so. He owes me many favors. I helped him with all the paperwork when he became a Canadian citizen, and then there were other favors I won't go into."

"Oh, Moe, how can I thank you. And he will tell us if the rubies (or whatever they are) have value or not."

"A man who knew the Tsarina and her jewels!" Moe exclaimed. "I should think he would know their value right off the bat."

"And you will send for him?"

Moses thought for a moment and then nodded.

Vesta could not restrain herself from going over to Moses and kissing him on both his cheeks.

It was Rory's turn now to look displeased and disgruntled. But he said nothing. After all, when didn't he recall the time he had seen his mother kissing gentlemen in his presence.

"And, Moe," Vesta ran on, "you do think Alexander Oblonsky, if I have his name right, will come to a small village like ours?"

"If I ask him, I am sure he will. If he is still alive."

"Oh, dear. You think he might not be."

"No, I think he is alive. I heard from him by letter only six months ago."

"Thank fortune, then. Oh, if he will only come and tell us. I will be in your debt, dear Moe, forever."

Again Rory saw with deep dismay that Moe beamed at his mother.

"I first met Alexei when I was a young soldier in France," Moe now began his reminiscences. "I don't for a minute think that is his real name. But I believe he is Russian. The rest of his story, like his name, I don't know whether to believe or not. But he is a jewel expert, we can be sure of that."

"And why don't you believe *all* of his story?" Vesta Hawley inquired.

"For one thing," Moses replied, "though he claims he came into the possession of some jewels once owned by Alexandra Romanov, the Tsarina who died at the hands of the Bolsheviks, he may not have known her at all. Another version that circulated was that he got ownership of these jewels from a desperate Russian émigré in Paris who died shortly after he entrusted Alexei with the royal gems."

"And what become of those jewels," Vesta warmed to his narrative.

"Who knows, Mrs. Hawley, but he must have had some kind of fortune to fall back on in those dark days of exile in France. At any rate shortly after the Armistice, he emigrated to Canada. I have visited him there several times. He claims I have done him many favors, such as help him secure his citizenship. But even that is an exaggeration. I pleased him, I believe, by listening to his stories and believing them. He is very fond of me, and that I believe; but why he is fond of me, who knows? At any rate I have only to call him, and he will come here and inspect your gems. For his life work has been the study of jewels. And who knows, maybe he did possess gems from the Romanovs!"

"But isn't there any expert on jewels who lives closer to us?" Vesta wondered, for the thought of a Russian whose real name and origin was unknown and whose friendship for Moses Swearingen was also suspicious troubled her.

"There is no one any more, dear Vesta Hawley, who can give a better estimate of the worth of gems than Alexei. Trust me for knowing that."

"Oh, I will have to, I suppose. But let me also speak with Dr. Sherman Cooke about this matter."

Moses Swearingen, irritated, now stood and put his hands in his deep pockets.

"Speak to him all you like! Dr. Cooke knows no more about gems than the local blacksmith. Indeed I'd be more inclined to get the blacksmith's estimate of your gems than the Doc's."

"Oh, all right, Moe. You are always, like most men of course, right. Call your Russian then, even if maybe he is a Bolshevik himself."

Moe grimaced on this, and their "confab," as Vesta later called it, came to a close.

Later that evening, at home alone with Dr. Cooke, Vesta

was tearful and allowed the "good doctor," as she called him, to hold her hand and kiss, in her words, her careworn fingers.

"Oh I don't trust this Alexei Oblonsky or whatever his name is, and I certainly don't want him to be in touch with Rory. A Russian. God knows what he was up to during the Revolution. And he is said to have got hold of Alexandra the Tsarina's jewels! I don't believe a word of it. Oh Sherman, why can't someone from here evaluate these jewels of ours."

Between his furtive kisses, Dr. Cooke managed to say: "I went to our public library after speaking with you the last time. I located a book there on precious gems. A very learned work, also by a Russian, come to think of it. But evidently very rare gems have to be appraised only by an expert. And even experts can be deceived. Especially in the case of diamonds and rubies."

"And so we have called in a Bolshevik to let us in on the truth of this mystery!"

"Dear Vesta, he is not a Bolshevik, I think, or he would not have come to this side of the world."

Vesta smiled and to the doctor's astonishment she gave him a chaste and icy kiss on his cheek.

Alexei Oblonsky's arrival in Gilboa by coincidence took place when there was a great torchlight parade on Main Street in honor of the return of a state senator who had served the small town well in his day. The torchlight parade and the brass band which accompanied it had turned the entire community into a noisy resplendent gala.

Alexei Oblonsky himself arrived in a miserable state of health and, as he remarked, he was lucky to have gotten safely to Moe's Villa, for he explained he had had to change trains three times, owing to a snowstorm and the loss of one of the engines.

Moe Swearingen was taken aback when he laid eyes on his Russian friend, for Alexei had changed greatly in the two or three years since Moe had last set eyes on him. His hair was gone nearly white, and an eye disease of some kind afflicted him so painfully he was required to use at intervals several different pairs of glasses and in addition made use of an oversize magnifying glass.

The din of the brass band together with the fact that they all caught flashes of the passing torchlight procession was nonetheless much to Alexei Oblonsky's liking.

"How kind of you to arrange such a reception," he quipped, pretending the demonstration of the torches and the bands were in his honor.

His witticism broke the ice of those gathered in Moe's large front parlour and from then on there was an air of general relaxation and cordiality on the part of everyone assembled in honor of the Russian gem expert.

Alexei's eyesight was not so impaired that he failed to fully take in the invited guests. He was especially drawn to Rory. "What a handsome son you have, Moe," Alexei exclaimed after he had employed different spectacles to view the boy. "I had no idea you have a son."

Moe quickly disabused his visitor of his mistake and gave a brief introduction then to the presence of Vesta Hawley, the boy's actual parent.

Alexei Oblonsky appeared if possible, even more enchanted at meeting Rory's mother. He rose, hobbled over to her, and taking her hand covered for this occasion by countless rings, kissed hand and rings devotedly.

Dr. Cooke was next introduced to the visitor.

"My dear Doctor," Alexei cried with something like glee. "How grateful I am to see a man of medicine, for I have had a journey every bit as slow, dangerous and snow-bound as if I were in the vast wastes of my own mother-land once more!"

And he took the doctor's hand in a grip so strong Sherman Cooke winced with pain from the pressure.

Alexei Oblonsky then strolled over to the crackling fire blazing away in the chimney and extended his rather massive hands contentedly against the welcome heat of the logs.

"What a charming place you have, dear Moe," he now addressed the owner of the Villa. "I had no idea Fortune had smiled on you with such favor. And you deserve every one of her blessings."

Oblonsky now took a seat on a sprawling davenport (newly upholstered) and put on a new pair of spectacles and having looked about for a minute or so, removed these and replaced them with yet another pair of optics.

Several young servants now entered and served libations to all but Rory.

Oblonsky smacked his thin pale lips repeatedly as he tasted his drink. Then without warning he rose all at once to say: "May I propose a toast, ladies and gentlemen."

Almost losing his balance for a moment, he was assisted in standing on his two feet by one of the young servers, but this little awkwardness only added to the Russian's self-possession for he turned his momentary loss of balance to his own adroitness and somewhat theatrical poise, and as Moe gazed at his friend, he decided that Alexei must indeed have had some relationship however transitory with royalty.

At this moment, however, the brass band was passing close to the Villa, and Oblonsky was barely able to make his voice heard.

Perhaps he used the uproar of the band as an excuse for his cutting short his toast which nonetheless went something like this: "I am deeply moved and honored by the lavish and cordial welcome extended to a Russian in exile, and I extend my gratitude to the hospitable and distinguished gathering at this matchless Villa."

He put such an emphasis on his pronouncing Villa that everyone perhaps for the first time realized what a superb property their Moe was in possession of.

Everyone now stood and, after applauding, drank the toast.

It was possible in retrospect however that the banquet which now followed all but put in the shade the magnificence of the Villa itself and the background glitter of torchlights and brass bands.

Young servers dressed in gold-trimmed uniforms demonstrated furthermore that Rory was not the only handsome young man present, and Alexei Oblonsky found it necessary all during the eight-course banquet to put one pair of spectacles on after another in order to take in the resplendent magnificence he found everywhere his eyes wandered.

He later told Moe that not since his early days in St. Petersburg had he been regaled with such festivities. As to the banquet itself—with its venison, quail, guinea fowl, wild duck and, for dessert, its assortment of pies, including of course pumpkin, mince and rhubarb—Oblonsky humbly informed the guests he doubted that even in imperial Russia itself could there have been a feast to equal the one he was now enjoying.

Oblonsky had eyes however not only for the young Adonises who served the feast, but more and more for Vesta herself, who wearing her grandmother's opals, must have stirred the Russian's memories of the royal beauties of his own homeland.

Retiring after hours at the festive board, the guests were next treated to the outpouring of a young men's chorus discreetly distanced from the guests in the front parlour by handsome screens.

It was clear, however, at least to Moe Swearingen, if to no one else, that the guest of honor was a bit listless, even sleepy, after his long train journey through snowstorms, engine problems, and bitter cold and by his nearly regal reception and entertainment at the Villa.

Neither Moe himself nor any of the other guests dared breathe a word concerning the matter of the birthday gift of Peter Driscoll to his only son, the rubies themselves.

After an hour or so of talk and occasional listening to the young men's chorus, it was the Russian guest himself who ventured to say: "And now, my dear Moe, I believe you might wish to have my opinion concerning some gems you wrote me several times about. I must warn you and your distinguished guests, however (and here he turned his full gaze toward Vesta Hawley), that contrary to what my dear friend Moe Swearingen may have told you, I am not the world's leading expert on gems and jewels. I am in this matter only an amateur."

"Nonsense!" Moe raised his voice. "I have it on the word of a number of authorities (he now turned his gaze also on Vesta as he spoke) there is no one at all here or abroad who knows more about precious gems than my excellent friend, Alexei Oblonsky."

Moe rose, and going over to the Russian, embraced him in continental fashion.

In the strained silence which now followed, several young men entered with trays of after-dinner drinks, but Alexei Oblonsky, begging they excuse him, declined any alcoholic beverage.

Moe then rose again to strike a small silver gong.

Almost immediately one of the young "footmen" (as Alexei Oblonsky called the attendants) entered with the box of gems and put them on a long low oak table near the Russian jewel expert.

At that very moment, and as if on cue, the brass band blared forth—concomitant with a sudden reflection of the torches which spotlighted the parlour as if after all both the band and the torches were in direct correspondence with the presentation of the jewels!

And so the moment had arrived, the moment they had all been waiting for so long, the moment in which the value and the future reputation of the jewels were to be established and settled by the greatest appraiser of precious gems to be found anywhere in the world.

The lid of the box was now removed by Moe Swearingen.

A kind of low murmur arose from the onlookers.

Alexei Oblonsky smiled as he almost devoutly studied the gems before him. His smile was followed by a pleasing nodding of his head several times. He took off the pair of glasses he was wearing and substituted them for one of probably greater strength.

His smile had now disappeared and his nodding like-wise. He stared at the gems, picked them up cautiously one by one and to the surprise of everyone smelled them. He began to shake his head slowly. Then he would put down a single one of the gems and take up another in his hand.

Then he lay back in the throne-like chair provided for him, as if exhausted, and gave forth a series of short coughs, but his coughing sounded more like a person being strangled. It was a true paroxysm as Dr. Sherman Cooke would later describe it. It was certainly to the ears of those assembled the sound like that of a convulsion.

Dr. Cooke rose and rushed to the cloakroom where he had left his little black bag. He whispered something to Frau Storeholder who hurried out to the kitchen.

The doctor produced a small bottle and spoon, and Frau Storeholder hurried back from the kitchen with a tumbler of spring water.

"Do try to swallow this," Dr. Cooke was heard speaking to Alexei Oblonsky. The gem expert smiled and obeyed. He lay back against the chair's luxuriant backrest and closed his eyes. Then he opened them and smiled faintly to say, "Ladies and gentlemen, it is passing."

Dr. Cooke had ready another kind of medicine from a still smaller bottle, and the Russian tasted this docilely, smiled broadly and wiped his mouth.

"Let me retire to the kitchen with this kindest of kind ladies whom you call Frau Storeholder," Alexei Oblonsky spoke hoarsely but with authority. "I wish to examine one of the . . . jewels (he came near to not pronouncing the last word) where there may be running hot water."

He immediately left the room, carrying one or more of the jewels with Frau Storeholder in close attendance.

Everyone in the room was at that moment too bewildered and perhaps shocked to say anything. There was silence not unlike the silence of the conclusion of Thursday night prayer meeting.

Moe Swearingen thought for a moment of following Alexei Oblonsky out into the kitchen, but something ominous in the gem expert's manner forbade him to do so.

To the relief of all, the Russian returned in a few minutes and entered the room, solemnly chewing something. His hands were empty.

Instead of speaking however at once, Alexei Oblonsky roamed about the room, his fingers clasped behind his back, a patient almost-martyred expression on his old weathered and very careworn face. He resembled to some that evening a professor overseeing pupils taking their final examination.

Then he energetically strode forth to the center of the large room, cleared his throat and attempted to smile, but the smile changed into a somewhat disturbing thin line, and a deep frown arose between his inflamed eyes.

"I am at some loss how to report the results of my examination," he began, his eyes looking up toward the high ceiling. A few flurries of his cough persisted, but he waved away Dr. Cooke's offering of another taste of his medicines.

"If I may so say, ladies and gentlemen, I have tasted your rubies whilst in the kitchen with my dear Frau Storeholder. I say *tasted* with deliberate choice." He then pointed to his mouth as the receptacle which had partaken of the jewels.

"My dear and esteemed friends all, and my very special dear friend of many years past, the nonpareil distinguished host of tonight's beautiful reception, Moe Swearingen, I cannot tell him and you how anguished I am to give you the verdict, if I may use such a term, the conclusion then, let me say, yes, conclusion is a better word for my examination of the gems."

He raised both his hands then like a preacher who is about to invoke either a blessing or a request for their departing the premises.

"The jewels, dear Mistress Hawley, and dear, dear young Rory Hawley, are not jewels or gems or precious gems or precious stones."

He waited a moment then, half-lifting both his arms.

"They are candy! I repeat, *candy!*"

Alexei Oblonsky then waited, perhaps expecting someone of those who had heard his verdict to say something. There was only a silence as deep as the word eternity itself.

It was Vesta Hawley who broke the silence induced by the shock of the verdict by rising from her place of honor and advancing toward the Russian. But Moe Swearingen intervened and, whispering cautiously something to Vesta, persuaded her not to perpetrate whatever she intended to perpetrate, and which Moe, sensing danger, prevented.

She pushed Moe away from her but then merely stood staring open-mouthed at the Russian.

Hardly unaware of Vesta's having tried to reach him, the Russian now spoke more at length.

"They are very old, these candies. We have found similar confections in the tombs of Egypt. Time and chemistry and perhaps the eggs of wasps are in evidence—who can tell. I am only a jewel expert. Let us say then the vicissitudes of time have turned a box of birthday candies (here he bowed in the direction of Rory), turned them into a kind of sweet cement. Nonetheless some hot water in the kitchen allowed one of the gems to melt so that I could taste it and pronounce my verdict which is, alas, that the rubies are and were sweetmeats. Mummified of course, lost in time, and yet at first glance one is quite understandably pardoned in having thought them jewels of some sort, rubies, say. We have all been taken in, therefore. My first glance convinced me in fact we had before us rubies. We have been hoodwinked, you may feel, dear friends, but if hoodwinked, then by Father Time himself and by no human prankster."

Having spoken thus, Alexei Oblonsky sat or rather fell into the enormous chair he had sat in before, and he emitted queer little sounds that were either weeping, moaning, or perhaps again coughing, which resembled, in the mind of Dr. Cooke at least, almost the sound of a death rattle.

The news that the rubies were not genuine but were, in fact, candy, spread not so much like wildfire through the entire village of Gilboa, but more like the effect of a huge meteorite which, falling, had struck all the palatial mansions of the town.

There was especial sympathy and concern for Vesta Hawley; for everyone had assumed that the rubies would enable her to retain possession of her own mansion and perhaps allow her to welcome back her runaway son, Rory.

Even Moe Swearingen himself was, if not pitied, at least pardoned for his many past deviations from the norm. He had at least, by summoning a famous jewel expert, attempted to establish the authenticity of the gems, even though his attempt had revealed the jewels were bogus.

The scandal of the false rubies even broke into print across the nation, and reporters from New York City and Chicago visited Gilboa and made an attempt to interview Vesta Hawley, her son Rory, and Moe Swearingen. But in vain. These main dramatis personae indeed were as impossible to reach as if they were some kind of royalty and the rubies were genuine.

Though there was no reason for the brass band to play or the torchlights to parade about the town, somehow each evening for quite a while this was exactly what occurred. Young men carrying banners which were illuminated by the torches assembled in front of Moe's Villa and Vesta Hawley's mansion. On these banners one could make out messages such as:

WE LOVE YOU VESTA
COME WHAT WILL

and before Moe Swearingen's Villa another fluttering banner could be deciphered, to wit:

MOE, WE HONOR AND COMMEND
YOU AND YOR VILLA

If before Gilboa had some fame for the renowned splendour of some of its mansions, from this time forward the village became equally famous for the episode of the false rubies.

From then on Vesta Hawley was said to wear only black mourning attire and was seldom or never afterwards seen in public.

A rumour also spread that Moe Swearingen had taken

papers of adoption for Vesta's son Rory, but this was never proved, and no adoption evidently ever took place.

Stung as both mother and son were by this whim of Fortune, it was Rory who now began visiting his mother almost every evening for the duration of an hour or so. It is thought she obtained his pardon for never having given him on their arrival the box of candies from his scapegrace father, Peter Driscoll. For, as Vesta was reported having said, according to Frau Storeholder, "Had you and I eaten the candies on their arrival, as I suppose Pete meant us to, think of how different everything else would have turned out."

To meet the demand of the bank and Vesta Hawley's other creditors, Moe Swearingen, who was after all one of the most wealthy men in this part of the country, paid off all Vesta's debts so that she was the sole mistress at last of her mansion.

Did we say Vesta received no visitors except that of Rory? We hardly thought of mentioning Dr. Sherman Cooke in this regard, as he was now not so much a visitor as a permanent lodger at Vesta's by reason in part that his wife, having passed away shortly after the scandal of the rubies, he more or less took his place as a star boarder at Vesta's, chaperoned of course always by the ubiquitous everfaithful watchdog Frau Storeholder.

THE END